# Part II

Guy A Johnson

Guy A Johnson

*Note from author*

*There are four main narratives – but they start at different points in time.*

*Agnes' and Elinor's stories begin where **'Submersion'** ended. But Billy's story picks up where Augustus left off at the end of **'Enclosure, Part I'**. And Tristan carries on where Jessie left us – approaching the wall.*


*Main characters*

Elinor Taylor – a young girl

Agnes Taylor – her mother

Tristan Jones – Agnes' partner

Albert Jones – Tristan's father, missing and presumed deceased

Esther Morton – Agnes' sister

Billy Morton – Esther's son

Joe Morton – Esther's husband and Billy's father

Jessie Morton – Tristan's employer and friend, and Joe's twin

Augustus Riley – Elinor's secret grandfather

Xavier Riley – Augustus' son and Elinor's secret father

Monty Harrison – local gangster and Esther's employer

Tilly Harrison – Monty's niece

Ronan – Agnes and Esther's step-father

Papa Harold – family friend and hermit neighbour of Agnes

Jimmy and Penny – uncle and aunt to Agnes and Esther

Ethan – Jimmy and Penny's son, on the run with Elinor

Guy A Johnson

Joshua – Ethan's twin, taken and still missing

Nathaniel – Tristan and Jessie's guide, a senior member of the authorities

Solomon – one of Nathaniel's men

Marcie Coleman – Tilly's school friend

Otterley – a mysterious girl with a unique ability

Guy A Johnson

Prologue – Elinor

I'm in and out of consciousness for a long time.

*For days,* I was told later. The after-effects of whatever drugs Grandad Ronan had given me. *Made you groggy. So, you've missed most of what's been happening.*

I hadn't missed it all, though. There were flashes in my mind – pictures, glimpses between my fluttering eyelashes as I'd attempted to come round.

In the wooden boat with the man who'd called himself Ethan. My cousin, I soon learned.

Snatches of our town – houses, old shops – as we'd drifted along its river roads.

*'We're going south,'* Ethan had muttered.

Waking to find myself out of the boat, in a strange place I didn't recognise – with Ethan offering me food, some bread. The horror of seeing the blood on his shirt – Grandad Ronan's, I was certain.

Then we were back in his small boat again, the back and forth of the rowing and the small waves lulling me back to sleep. Back to seeing my life in short flashes.

Coming to open water, seeing nothing but endless sea and endless grey sky.

*'We're on the Black Sea,'* Ethan said at some point – confirming our direction south.

My eyes opening and closing again, the scene staying the same, while its colours altered – the sky darkening from grey to black, the sea from blue to darkest green then everything lightening again. We'd passed a night.

But it was the sound that changed things – the sound that broke my pattern of unconsciousness.

5

Guy A Johnson

A sound on the water, starting gently enough.

The sound of the rain.

A pitter-pattering that rippled the calm surface at first, gradually building up, till fists of water smacked into it, its violence conjuring a rage of waves – with our tiny boat caught up in its angry jaws.

The water and the horizon were blurred, a rising fog erasing their borderline.

*'It rained for ten days,'* Ethan would tell me later. *'Lucky we were rescued.'*

And we were rescued quickly – before the boat filled with rainfall, before the weather and waves used their might to toss us into the gut of the sea.

I saw the other boat cutting through the oblivion of mist, its engine silenced by the roar of the storm. Much bigger than the ones I'd seen before – bigger than Jessie's. A huge boat, heading in our direction, targeting us like a bullet from a gun.

And we were lifted onto it before I knew it – Ethan and me, our small boat left behind to be battered to driftwood. *Just in time,* our rescuer told us. *Seconds more and we'd have lost you.*


I slept again on that bigger boat – below deck in a small space, wrapped in coarse blankets and lying on a narrow bench that felt luxurious. People came and went, keeping an eye on me, bringing me a little food and drink.

Then the sounds changed – the rain stopped pouring and the sea stopped raging. And someone invited me up on deck – the man who seemed to own the boat.

'Come and see,' he said, holding out a hand.

I took it and followed him up to the deck.

Guy A Johnson

And I was somewhere I'd never seen or been before – surrounded by greenery I'd only ever dreamed of. The blurred, grey horizon of before had been replaced with a landscape of forest.

'Where are we?' I asked the man – in awe, but also frightened, as I was in the company of strangers and facing a strange land.

'We're at the place where two worlds meet,' he answered, turning from the view and looking directly at me.

'Two worlds meet?' I questioned and he sensed an attitude in my voice – a lack of conviction. I'd been lapping up Tristan's stories for years, so I knew a tall tale when I heard one.

The man smiled, ever so gently, as if he'd read my thoughts.

'This is the place where you, Elinor Taylor, will enter the stories yourself. You have arrived, if you like, at the point where your life will change – and many other lives alongside yours, if all goes to plan.'

I'm sure his words were meant to draw me in, to captivate me with their sense of hope and drama – but all I heard were fancy phrases with little substance.

'You don't trust me, do you?' he asked and I answered quickly.

'I don't know you, but I don't trust anyone, not anymore.'

'No, I don't suppose you do,' he conceded, but this response made me trust him even less. What did he know about me? How had he found me and Ethan, out here in the grey, misty void, seconds from our doom? And just why had he brought us to the edge of this forest, in the middle of wherever?

'Who are you?' I asked him, cold anger evident in my tone.

7

Guy A Johnson

'A fair question,' he said, looking back out to the tall wall of trees ahead. 'My name is Nathaniel and you're going to help me save the day, Elinor. You're going to help me put things right…'

Guy A Johnson

*Unfold*

*Dear Esther*

*I'm not sure whether you'll ever see this letter. I'm not entirely sure you should – not with what I've got to say. But I need to tell someone, and that someone really should be you.*

*See, I'm going to write down all that I know, in the hope it might reach you one day. If it does – maybe you'll be able to do something to change the course of things.*

*And if my words don't make their way to you in time, it might just be too late – for all of us.*

*You see, he's had a plan all along – a dark, deadly plan – and it's all finally coming together.*

*Unless we stop him.*

*Unless <u>you</u> stop him.*

*Fold*

Guy A Johnson

1.  Agnes

He came out of the water.

Like something in a dream.

Like something mythical.

As the ten days of ceaseless downpour began, and the water quickly rose up to the lip of the first floor in my house, he swam up through the surface.

I wondered – for an instant – whether this was another trick of Xavier's. Was this just another mind game and I wasn't really seeing this at all? But quickly I realised it was no trick, no fantasy.

And as I looked closer, I knew it was *him*.

Even though he was so changed – so altered by whatever had been done to him – I knew it was him.

I saw it in his eyes.

Saw the man I hadn't seen for so many years.

Only to call him a man was no longer quite correct.

'What have they done to you?' I asked, stepping towards him, an extreme mix of emotions stirring inside me.

Joy at seeing him alive.

Grief at what he must have suffered.

Fear of what he was now – what he might do to me.

And disgust too – disgust at the sight of this savaged, mutilated human.

Guy A Johnson

'Oh, Joe,' I cried, calling out my long-lost brother-in-law's name, as I got closer and wrapped my arms around his soaking frame – ignoring the fears and nausea that plagued me. 'Oh Joe, what has happened to you? And why are you here, now?'

But he couldn't speak, not really. Being in the water – how *long* had he been in the water? – had left him freezing cold and any words that left his mouth were chopped up in the chatter of his teeth, in the twitch of his jaw. So I stopped with the questions and simply brought him further into the house – stripped him of his wet clothes and wrapped him in a blanket that was hung over one end of the settee in my kitchen. Then I ran him a hot bath and watched him shake further as he lowered his cold, damaged body beneath its steaming surface.

'You'll have used all your ration,' were the first words I made out from him, once his body began to thaw and settle.

I'm not sure if he meant the hot water or the salts I'd sprinkled in it, but it didn't matter – he'd spoken. I'd heard Joe's voice clearly, for the first time in over five years – and it told me something. Told me it was really still him – and whatever had happened to him, whatever might have got lost along the way, there was still a bit of the original Joe in there.

Thinking he might need a little privacy – that the rest of my questions could wait until later – I turned to leave the bathroom.

'Don't call her,' he said to my back and I stalled. 'I didn't just come here because it's a safe place, Agnes. I came here because I hoped you'd be alone. I don't want her to know about this, not yet.'

Her.

11

Guy A Johnson

Esther.

'She's my sister, Joe – your wife. I can't just-.'

'Not yet. I'm not ready.'

'Joe-.'

'She's not ready, either. She can't be. Look at me, Agnes. Take a long look at me – is Esther really ready to see all of this?'

I turned back and, as I did, I heard the dispersing of water, as Joe's six-foot bulk unfolded from its seated position and I saw him fully exposed.

'Joe, please,' was all I managed, as I looked on.

I wasn't embarrassed by his naked body, but I was shocked by the state of it. By the map of angry tracks that mercilessly scarred it – a trail of red markings that crudely told the tale of his suffering. There were regular, circular marks all about his body – temples, neck, chest, forearms, calves and ankles – suggesting something had been inserted there at some point. A thick, dark pink artery of tissue plunged from the middle of his chest to just above his pelvis, as if he'd had major surgery – the line looked stretched, weak, as if a sudden move would see it tear, see his insides spill out. And where there weren't scars, there was thick, coarse hair – not like human hair, but like an animal's, in dense patches. And I knew instinctively which animal had such a coat.

But for all its horror, this wasn't the worst of his disfigurements – that was around his neck.

'My god,' I heard myself say, as my eyes traced the full circumference of the meaty, circular scar that was wrapped around him. A swollen necklace of mutilation I'd not really taken in until then. 'It's like they…'

12

Guy A Johnson

I couldn't complete the sentence or my thoughts, but Joe did – like he needed me to hear it out loud.

'It's like they took my head off,' he said and all I could do was put my hands to my mouth and sob.

Joe folded himself back under the water, covering up most of his damage – although that thick neck scar stayed above the surface.

'So please – don't call her. Just let me have a little time. And let me tell you what happened first, so I can get my head a little clearer before I have to face Esther.'

I nodded, then turned and left him again, returning a little while later with some of Tristan's clothes, which I put on the closed lid of the toilet.

'When you're ready,' was all I said, before pulling the door to and leaving him alone.


I'd left him for five or ten minutes when I heard his cry. Like the fur that sporadically covered him, his call was that of a creature – a creature in distress. And when I reached the bathroom and opened the door, I found him thrashing about in the water, his body in spasms, his face twisted in agony.

I reached out and used my body and my arms to hold him still, getting drenched in the process. But his strength was greater than mine and he instantly threw me off, knocking me across the room – and he let out a final of roar of pain, before the fit subsided, leaving him quickly, as if he'd been momentarily possessed.

He seemed to fall into a short sleep of recovery. And, while I waited for him to come round, I stayed where I was – on the floor, my back against the rusted radiator that no longer worked, thinking.

13

Guy A Johnson

Thinking about everything that had happened over the last few days, feeling its weight on my shoulders, feeling its searing pain in my heart.

Billy's truancy and subsequent exposure in the water.

Learning the truth about my cousin Ethan – and his escape from my aunt and uncle's old shop.

Tristan and Jessie's departure.

Finding out that Old Man Merlin was really called Augustus Riley – Xavier's father and Elinor's grandfather.

Discovering where my beloved Elinor had been all those months – *oh, Ronan, how could you betray us like that?* – only to find she'd disappeared again. Only to find a scene soaked in blood, with no trace of her in it.

And then there was Xavier. Xavier and his mind games. Xavier fooling me that he was Reuben – the ghost of my twin. Xavier appearing and then disappearing into thin air – the most inexplicable of all the things I'd encountered.

'Was all that not enough?' I said aloud, looking over at Joe, watching his soaking body twitch as he slept.

It made me shudder – that twitch.

What had they done to him? What evil had been inflicted on his body – and to what end? All these years I'd been cursing him for walking out on Esther and young Billy. All these years I'd been thinking him a coward. And now I knew, in all that time, he'd been someone's victim.

'Someone's experiment,' I mouthed, my words barely audible.

14

Guy A Johnson

His body twitched again, this time the tic was followed by the sudden opening of his eyes and he looked over at me. At my slumped body, in soaking wet clothes.

'What happened?' he asked, but before I could speak, he answered his own question. 'I had a fit, didn't I? Knocked you back. Sorry, Agnes. I can't…' Then his words faltered, dropped away and he began weeping. Gentle to start with, it quickly built to heavy, raw sobbing that shook his whole body with grief.

Despite what had happened the last time I'd touched him, I got up and put my arms around him – letting my clothes get wetter, holding on tight to the body that was partly his and partly something else altogether. Held on until the sobbing subsided and his body and mind were still again.

'How about you get out of the water and dressed?' I suggested, when I eventually let him go. 'I'll put on some dry clothes too. And then maybe you can tell me all about this.'

Joe took a moment to take it all in, as if he was catching up with himself – with where he'd ended up. And then he conceded with a nod.

'Good, I'll be in the kitchen when you're ready.'


Outside, the rain continued to pour down. Just before Joe's arrival, it had briefly stopped – and I'd come out of my room, hopeful it was at an end. But it had simply been a brief pause.

As I walked along the upper hall, I saw the water lapping over the top of the stairs, spilling onto the floorboards and wondered if the level would rise any higher. Wondered if this deluge would ever stop. Outside, the sky was the darkest grey and foreboding, and I

Guy A Johnson

had a dramatic sense that the world was coming to an end. That the rain would keep falling and the river road keep rising until everything and everyone was swallowed up – and there would be nothing but water for miles and no one to see it.

In the kitchen area, I put the kettle on and made some tea and by the time this was done, Joe was out of the bath, dried and dressed and I heard his feet slapping along the hallway. He sat on the settee and I took the place next to him, handing over the hot drink. As he took it from me, I looked at his hands – scarred, the skin interspersed with areas of thick hair, just like the rest of him. He caught my gaze as it stayed too long and I felt guilty, as his eyes burned into mine.

'I don't know what Esther told you,' he began, getting straight into his story – no lead up or announcement. 'Don't know how much of the truth she shared with her sister – or whether she simply stuck to the cover story we agreed. Either way, she won't have been able to tell you what really happened to me, as she doesn't know. But none of it will be quite what you thought.'

'She told me you left and I saw her heartache. Still see it,' I answered and a dry, sad smile creased up his face, his scars making it twice as puckered.

'I did leave, and I've no doubt it made her very sad, but I left on her instruction.'

He paused to acknowledge my surprise.

'I did something rash, Agnes. Took something I shouldn't have taken from the man I worked for.'

'From Monty?' I asked, but Joe simply continued without confirmation – even after all these years, he still couldn't admit outright who he'd worked for, what he'd been part of.

Guy A Johnson

'I took a puppy, Agnes,' he continued, not stopping this time when I gasped in shock. 'Brought it into our house. You can guess where I found it, who was responsible for its existence in our devastated city.'

'Monty,' I said and this time the smallest of nods recognised this fact.

'He had a small litter, Agnes. I didn't see the bitch who gave birth, but he had the litter – five little yelpers. God knows where he got them. Kept them on the ground floor of that club of his. *Breakers* – you know of it? Kept them down below, locked away in a cage, which was inside the sound-proofed ground floor space. Once the floods came, there was a rumour that the club's lower floor was filled with water and Monty took his enemies there for a swim, if you understand me.'

I tipped my head to indicate that I did.

'But it was bone dry down there – not a spot of damp or drop of water. He showed the little creatures just to me. I remember him saying: *there's our future, Joe. Right there before you – our future.* And then left me there, with the keys to lock up, while he went about other business. A sign of his trust – a test he set me, Agnes. A test that I instantly failed, without even trying and then paid for dearly. I took one home, Agnes – took it to Esther, to Billy, who squealed with delight at the sight of the small, furry, innocent thing. But Esther was livid, with an anger that brought me to my senses, but it was too late by then. I'd taken the puppy and couldn't simply return it. So we killed it.'

He paused again, as if in anticipation of my reaction, but I was already numb with shock and my disturbed mind was racing with thoughts of possible connections – the corpse Billy had found in the river road, the rumours of similar sightings, the mass grave Tristan

Guy A Johnson

and Jessie had unearthed. Did this all go back to Monty and the small litter he'd acquired all those years ago?

'Blood everywhere, and boy, didn't the little fella scream. Horrible noise. Dropped its remains in the river road. And then Esther hid me in the cellar – for days, weeks, waiting for the right moment for me to slip away. Esther told Monty that she'd killed me in an accident – a row that turned violent. Even showed him the bloodstains the dog's body had created – told Monty they were mine. Told everyone else, including Billy, that I'd walked out. Abandoned them both. And I had, of course – my recklessness meant I *did* have to walk out, eventually.

'She thought I was safe too. Esther thought I was somewhere safe. See, I managed to keep in touch with her.'

Another surprise.

'Esther didn't tell you this, either?'

I shook my head.

'I wrote to her, Agnes. At least, I was allowed to write to her.'

'What do you mean, *allowed to*?'

Joe paused here and, in this brief quiet, I heard the rattling in his breath – telling me another part of him was damaged. And I wondered if the next segment of his tale would tell me how this had happened – what horror had brought him to the state he was in, physically and mentally.

It did.

'They were waiting all along, Agnes. Not fooled for a minute by Esther's tale of domestic murder, Monty had his men keep watch. The night I finally slipped away from

18

Billy and Esther, I didn't get very far. I headed east, towards the forests that remained standing, but I only got as far as a few streets in our little wooden boat, before they caught up with me in one of Monty's speedboats. Took me to his headquarters.'

'*Breakers*?'

'Yes. Kept me with the dogs on the ground floor. Kept me in a cage of my own, would you believe it. *You'll have to replace what you took,* the man himself told me and he kept to his word. Caged me like a dog, fed me like one and in all aspects treated me like one. Did to me exactly what he intended to do to them.'

He shrugged and held out his arms to the side, as if to showcase the end of that treatment.

'Experimented on me too, just like he did those creatures. It was worse-.' He began his sentence, but faltered. Tears caught him, as did a fit of coughing that lasted so long I feared he might slip into another set of convulsions. But he eventually steadied himself.

I got up and quickly filled a glass with water, but Joe refused it – as if he were determined to endure his afflictions, to show he could defeat them.

'It was worse than when I was detained as a child, Agnes. I was experimented on back then too. I don't know if Jessie ever told you, but I was put through hell. Not just tests and injections, like many of those detained by the authorities.'

*Detained* – not *taken,* like it was prison, not abduction.

'He didn't tell me, no. Doesn't really talk,' I said, realising as it left my mouth that the sentence finished with the unspoken words *about you.* It felt cruel, as if my words were the final knife in his back. But Joe didn't react.

Guy A Johnson

'Well, the authorities I encountered took things much further than they've ever been willing to admit. Not torture for torture's sake, I'll give them that. But I wasn't exactly experimented on in the name of progress. What they did to me – the things they subjected me to in the name of science. Well, let's just say it wasn't human and have done with it.'

'What about when you were taken by Monty's men?'

Joe looked up at me and held out his arms, displaying himself in answer again. For a few moments we said nothing more and in that silence I imagined the gravity of what this wretched man had gone through. And yet – he was still there and he was still able to talk this through. That said something about him – something I couldn't capture in mere words.

He continued.

'At the authorities' camps, they played around with everything. All sorts of operations, experiments and injections. And they had the scientific know-how to mess about with your DNA – even post-natal. Did you know that, Agnes?'

I shook my head – no, I didn't.

'I know they can mess with your head. Mess with what you think you're seeing,' I said, thinking of Reuben, thinking of Xavier's trick.

'Yes. The serum. Once injected into your eyes, you have an overwhelming power to manipulate others.'

'Is that how they do it?' I asked, wondering just what cruel torture Xavier had been through, just to get that deceptive talent.

'It is, but the authorities' science program wasn't limited to mind tricks and injections. Years of secret experiments on unborn babies had seen them manipulate DNA and play god at the earliest stage. Created a decade of twins and took all of us for testing

20

once we reached puberty. Sent some of us home and kept some of us longer – to help solve the problems of the future and save the world, or simply to experiment a little more on us. As if they hadn't done enough.'

'Is this true?' The words left my mouth before I could stop them – it seemed such an outrageous claim. Yet, as that question hung in the air, unanswered, the evidence confirming its validity began to stack up.

Ethan and Joshua.

Jessie and Joe.

Me and my stillborn brother.

'Esther – there was no twin for her.'

'They'd stopped by then,' Joe confirmed.

'And Xavier.'

I said the name without thinking. Joe wouldn't know him, though – wouldn't know the significance.

'Xavier?'

'An old friend.'

'Our age?'

'Our age,' I echoed and Joe nodded.

'He'll have a twin – dead or alive, who knows? But he'll have been one of a twin. Monty has had years of filling me in on what went on. On what he knew. Years of sharing knowledge and replicating what the authorities claimed to have stamped out. Only worse.'

'How worse?'

'Look at me, Agnes. Look at my terrible scars. Look at the damage to my body. Look at what you see between those scars. The hair – the fur.'

He stopped there, holding my gaze with his own – letting the significance of that word sink in.

*Fur.*

Convinced of my understanding, he started up again.

'I told you the authorities messed with our DNA, but what Monty did was much worse. Remember what I said he told me when he showed me those baby dogs? *There's our future, Joe.* Monty didn't just have my DNA messed with, he had it mixed. Had certain things enhanced over others.'

'No, Joe, no…'

'Yes, Agnes. That's what he did. That's what he intended all along.'

'But why, Joe – what was he hoping to achieve? You look–.'

I stopped, faltered by tears and faltered by words I didn't want to say.

'I look like a beast, Agnes. I look like a beast from the worst of nightmares. But I got out and I got here, and we're going to help each other.'

'How?'

'I'm going to help you uncover the truth and bring down Monty. And then.' He stopped, pausing as he reflected on his next statement. 'And then you're going to help me. Just me.'

There was gravity in those two words – *just me* – that left me in no doubt as to what he intended.

Guy A Johnson

'Would you help me in that way, Agnes? It'd make it worthwhile – exposing Monty and then bringing his cruelty to an end. Imagine if someone else got hold of me. Imagine what they'd do. Imagine what the cruel authorities would do with an achievement like me. Would you help me prevent that, Agnes? Would you-.'

'Yes,' I answered, though tears burned through my eyes. 'I'll do that, Joe. I'll do it.'

'Thank you,' he countered, and his body appeared to sigh with relief. 'Thank you.'

The ringing of the telephone surprised me – something every-day, normal interrupting the surreal world I found myself in. A world enclosed by the wall of water that streamed from the sky.

I let the ringing continue.

'Answer it,' Joe said, as if giving me permission.

So, I left him momentarily and took myself into the hall, relieved to notice that – against the odds – the water level hadn't risen any further. I picked up the receiver.

'Hello?'

It was Augustus – checking in on me, making sure I was coping. And, when I told him that *yes, I was,* I realised how true it was. I had no choice really. With everything I'd seen and learned, if I hadn't coped, I wouldn't have made it through at all.

Augustus didn't keep me long and promised to check in regularly – a promise he kept.

After just a minute or so away, I returned to Joe. He was asleep, his chest heaving powerfully, suggesting he was deep under. So, I took a blanket, covered him over and left him. Caught up on some sleep myself – sleep that came much easier once I was in my bed, falling on me like a heavy weight.

23

Guy A Johnson

It was the telephone ringing again that brought me to – Augustus again, one of his regular welfare checks.

'I'm fine, Augustus, but you woke me,' I explained, getting to him after ten or so rings.

He offered no apology, but simply carried on with the agenda he'd planned. Typical Augustus, I was beginning to realise. But what he proposed shocked me a little.

'You hear me, Agnes?' he said, after a short silence fell between us. 'Agnes?'

'You want me to go back to Ronan's flat?' I asked, disgust evident in my tone.

'Yes,' he answered, softening and lowering his own voice, recognising my alarm. 'Despite everything, Agnes, I think it's the right thing to do. And I think it'll help you.'

Another pause.

'Agnes?'

'Let me think, Augustus.'

'Okay. Can't do anything while it's still raining like this.'

'No. No, we can't,' I answered, before letting him go.


It was a week or so later before the downpour relented to a gentle shower. And in that time, Joe and I spoke more – interrupted only by his need to sleep and Augustus' short calls. *I can pop round,* he insisted a number of times and I knew he sensed something was up. But each time I batted back the offer: *no need to worry, you'll catch a cold in the wet, I'll see you when it dries up.*

Guy A Johnson

When Augustus asked if there was anything he could do, I realised there was one favour I needed – someone had to let Esther (and Billy) know about Ronan.

'You want them to know everything?' Augustus checked, and I wondered if we should spare them some of the details. But I knew everything would come out in the end, and Esther would be sure to scold me for keeping her in the dark.

'Everything, Augustus, but go in gently,' I answered, and another thought came to me. 'Maybe you can enlist her help for this crazy plan of yours?'

'And which crazy plan would that be?' he asked and I welcomed his humour – welcomed its small light in the darkness that engulfed me. 'I'll call her, Agnes. I'll let her know it all.'


In the days that built up to our returning to Ronan's flat – one time my mother's home – Joe continued to unfold the story of his absence.

We talked less of the torture he'd endured, of the physical changes Monty and his men had inflicted on his body – *he had his own small team of brutal surgeons, Agnes* – and more of other things. Of the letters he'd written Esther, of the replies he got in return.

'They were altered, though,' he told me, from the settee in my kitchen – a place he kept to, night and day, finding some comfort as the old thing moulded itself around his maltreated frame.

'What do you mean?'

'They'd have parts blacked-out, as if they were afraid of what Esther might reveal about the outside world. And I had to be careful too – had to watch what I wrote. Couldn't give the game away. They'd never have sent them on.'

25

Guy A Johnson

Something puzzled me in all this.

'There's something I don't understand, Joe,' I said, and he looked at me quizzically. 'If Esther didn't know where you were, what had happened to you, how did her letters get back to you?'

'Through Ronan.'

'Ronan?'

Just saying his name out loud left a sourness in my mouth.

'Yes, Ronan. Sorry, Agnes, but he's not the man you think he is.'

'No?'

'No, I'm sorry,' Joe answered, not picking up on the sarcasm in my single word. 'Ronan was involved with Monty. Knew Monty had hold of me. He'd visit me, quite often. And he wasn't cruel, Agnes – I can't pretend he was. He made sure my letters got to Agnes and vice versa. I don't know what he told her, how he explained it all. And I really don't know how involved he was in Monty's plans, but he did do one good thing for me in the end, Agnes.'

'He did?' I questioned, hardly able to believe it. What other surprises would be revealed before the day was done?

'Yes, just the one.'

'Okay, but what?'

'He let me out. He's the reason I'm here.'

'What do you mean?'

Guy A Johnson

'He let me out, Agnes. Got into *Breakers,* got to me, had the keys and let me out. Helped me get here too – in his boat. But wouldn't come in – seemed to think he wouldn't be welcome.'

While I'd told Joe about Elinor, I hadn't explained everything – hadn't given him all the details of Ronan's involvement or his demise.

'So, he left me at your door.'

But there were gaping holes in this tale – alarm bells immediately ringing in my ears.

'When did he bring you here?' I asked, coming out sharper than I'd intended.

'What do you mean?'

'Exactly that: *when* did Ronan bring you to my house?'

Joe looked at me strangely, as if the question still didn't quite make sense. 'The same day – the same time I turned up. Just before you saw me, Agnes.'

But I shook my head at this. It couldn't be true.

'What is it?' Joe asked, anxiety creasing his already puckered face.

'Ronan's dead, Joe. And I know exactly the type of man he was – knew it before you told me. Old authority, through and through. Wormed his way into our family and betrayed us in the most unthinkable way. Ways,' I annexed.

Then I gave Joe the final details of what had happened to my dearest Elinor, right up to Ronan's death.

'So, there's no way he brought you here, Joe,' I said, keeping my tone level, keeping accusation out of it. 'He was dead at least a day before you turned up here. We found him at his flat. Covered in blood.'

27

Guy A Johnson

'You can't have, Agnes. You really can't. I swear, I'm not lying, or going crazy, or anything like that,' he said, as I shook my head at his every word.

*No, it couldn't be true – I'd seen him. I'd seen the body.*

'The day I came to you, it was Ronan who brought me. Left me at your door and sailed away. But one thing you've said I can confirm.'

'What?' I said, barely able to think straight, or know exactly what to believe.

Joe's answer got me closer to a truth I didn't want to consider, though.

'He was covered in blood, Agnes,' he said, his eyes looking straight into mine, clear, convincing. 'It was him, and his clothes were soaked in it.'

### Unfold

*Esther, my dear – where should I start with this twisted tale?*

*A tale of great deception and evil, there's no denying that. Dressed up as necessity and progress by everyone involved.*

*There's no easy way to start – so I'll just get straight into it.*

*Everything you knew about me – everything you've been led to believe over the years has been a complete lie. And by the time you read this – if it ever gets to you, that is – you'll probably have uncovered some of the truth.*

*But I want you to know it all.*

*I want you to know every word.*

*So I'll start with the very basics, Esther. I'll start with you – but it'll shock you. There's no way round that.*

*You see, Esther – you aren't who you think you are.*

*You aren't who you think you are at all.*

### Fold

Guy A Johnson

2. Tristan

I'd never been sure what we'd find when we set out on our journey east. We'd travelled further than we had before in the hope we'd find the answers to some of our questions.

I'd gone in search of my father – to discover his true fate.

And if, along the way, we found that other lost soul – our missing girl, our treasured Elinor – that would be more than we could ever have hoped for.

But the revelations on that journey were bountiful – a treasure chest of dark and dreadful plunder. Starting with Jessie – his suspicions about the legitimacy of his parenthood, his mother and father's escape from the Great Drowning that he'd assumed had swallowed them up. The breadcrumb trail that led us to Nathaniel – and his subsequent string of revelations: his link to *the Circle,* the truth about the dogs, his incredulous story about the manipulation of twin births and its link to the takings.

'What's *the Circle?*' Jessie asked one evening, quietly, while Nathaniel was sleeping.

We were heading for the wall he'd spoken of – an endless thing that kept us all enclosed in the flooded land, like lab rats.

'*The Circle* is the highest order in the authorities – the government elite, but its members are secret.'

'So he took a risk telling us, broke an oath?'

I'd nodded.

Guy A Johnson

'And how come you know about all this and I don't?' Jessie asked with a little suspicion in his voice.

I paused, wondering just how much I should tell him.

'Tris?' my friend questioned, growing ever more wary, the longer I took to answer.

'I told you that I came to the city looking for someone.'

'The terrorist you think Father Joe helped, the man you think killed your father?'

'Well, I didn't just come off my own back – I had a bit of help finding where he might be. And some additional encouragement.'

I rubbed my thumb against my fingers on my left hand to demonstrate exactly what I meant.

'You were paid?'

I nodded. 'By the authorities, Jessie.'

'Shit,' my friend expelled, shocked by this latest revelation. He shook his head, a curt smile of disbelief curving his lips a little. 'All your talk and you're a man on the inside, on the payroll after all?'

It was my turn to shake my head.

'No, no – it's not like that, Jessie. I'm not one of them. I'm not *him*.' I dropped my head in Nathaniel's direction. 'I don't know how they found out about me. How they knew I was looking for Xavier and what I intended to do once I found him. But they confirmed that he'd been involved in my father's disappearance, funded my trip to the city and that allowed me to hang around after the flooding, help put the place back together.'

'They still paying you?' Jessie asked, a foulness on his tongue.

Guy A Johnson

'No, Jessie – it was one payment. Enough to get me to the city and keep me afloat for a bit. They just wanted him dead as much as I did.'

'So how d'you know about this *Circle*?'

'The person who approached me said he was doing so on behalf of *the Circle*. Explained who they were, what they wanted, what they'd pay me and that they'd deny any involvement if I got into any trouble myself. Not that I could've traced them. I didn't even get a name.'

'Do you think that's how Nathaniel found us, how he knew so much about us, the likelihood that we'd listen to him, follow him?'

'Yes, I do. And I believe him too, Jessie. I believe he's one of them, but he's also one of us.'

'One of the good guys?'

'Yes.'

'Just like you?'

I walked into that, but I didn't walk away, just stared it out.

'Just like me, Jessie,' I eventually answered, letting him have that one.

But the biggest revelation for me – the most personal – slipped out almost incidentally, days later, as that soaring wall came into view, towering high into the dull sky.

About my father.

'I thought you'd already found him,' our new companion had revealed, as our horizon was filled with that man-made wonder.

Guy A Johnson

'What do you mean?' I'd asked, made anxious by this unexpected comment. I hadn't seen Albert since he'd disappeared – since he'd been reported drowned by the authorities. 'What do you mean?!'

But I didn't get my answer, not immediately.

Jessie wasn't listening – too in awe of the view before him. And Nathaniel hushed me, instructing me to kill the engine of his speedboat too.

'We'll need to be careful from here. We don't want to be spotted.'

'Nathaniel, I want to-.'

'I'll answer your question, Tristan. But I need you to listen and stay focussed for now.'

'What is it?' Jessie asked. He hadn't picked up a word of our exchange, but he read the vexation in my face.

I shook my head, dismissively – it would have to wait. Much as it irked me, Nathaniel was right – we were in foreign territory, government territory we weren't supposed to know about. And we could quite easily, quite quickly find ourselves in danger.

'So,' Jessie continued, turning his attentions to the man we assumed knew his way around – Nathaniel, 'how do we get beyond that thing?'

He'd pointed at the impenetrable brick formation ahead of us.

'Ah yes, that thing,' Nathaniel answered almost casually, like it didn't matter as much as it did.

Like he hadn't, only seconds earlier, said something that might change the course of things for me.

'Well?' There was impatience in Jessie's voice by then.

Guy A Johnson

'Hope,' was Nathaniel's reply.

'Hope?'

'Yes, hope that they've remembered,' he expanded, looking out onto the horizon, as if searching for someone.

'They've remembered?' Jessie continued to echo him, encouraging Nathaniel to uncover more.

'Yes,' Nathaniel confirmed, turning back to look at us both, seeing our exasperation – and my controlled, inner anxiety – for the first time. 'I hope they've remembered we were coming – and how much I'd promised to reward them for their help...'

Despite his light, almost flippant tone, I knew Nathaniel had a plan – we'd been discussing its detail ever since he told us about the great wall.

*'What's behind it?'* I'd asked him.

*'All the luxury you can imagine,'* he'd answered – and I could imagine a lot.

*'And why do you want to take us there?'*

*'Luxury isn't reason enough?'* There'd been a tease in his voice. But he'd nodded, conceding I needed a better answer. *'People want change, they want the truth, the inequality exposed – but they aren't brave enough to do it themselves. They'll join in, once some kind of revolt begins, but they won't start it. They aren't leaders.'*

*'And we are?'* From Jessie.

*'Yes.'* Nathaniel didn't pause for breath and then he held us both with his gaze, as if to strengthen the conviction in that single word.

He had explained that he had people on the inside, who were expecting our arrival and would keep us sheltered, hidden, until we were ready to take action – although what

34

that action was going to be, Nathaniel didn't specify. Neither did he set out exactly how we were going to get past this wall. And it was only once it appeared before us, blocking the horizon, that we realised the enormity of that task alone.

'How will they know that we've…' I began, the final word – *arrived* – silenced by Nathaniel's actions: he released a flare into the sky.

It created such a light around us that I wondered if we might have been over-exposed – a concern Jessie shared, if I read his glare correctly.

'Don't worry,' Nathaniel voiced, sensing our apprehension. 'There won't be many people looking out. And there!'

He pointed low west and we saw a light flash three times.

It came from within a dense forest of fir trees that sat in front of that endless wall – appearing just as impenetrable as the sky-high fortification. This forest put me in mind of old fairy tales, where spells were cast and barbed, overgrown branches twisted their long tentacles to trip intruders and block the way in.

Three lights winked again through this dark, foreboding greenery – a signal to indicate our next move.

'We're to go towards the east, then,' Nathaniel read in these coded directions.

I started up the boat again and headed east, to the edge of that forest – to a shoreline I realised I'd seen before: in the video of Jessie's parents, posing with the dog at their feet.

As the blades of the boat cut cleanly through the still waters, I thought about Nathaniel's plans for a revolution. How quickly we'd been drawn in, despite some protest about our own quest. I worried we might lose our own purpose in all this. I worried that,

35

Guy A Johnson

despite giving us so many answers already, our new companion wouldn't be able to fill in the blanks that really mattered.

That I wouldn't find out what happened to Albert, my father.

That traces of Elinor were not beyond that wall.

And neither were Jessie's parents – or his twin, Joe.

I feared we'd been lured under slightly false pretences, and yet neither of us tried to turn back. We could easily have overpowered Nathaniel – individually, let alone with our combined skills and strength.

But we didn't – and we let him lead us towards that wall. A wall that kept the water and the dogs inside the rest of the world. A wall that had turned our home into a laboratory and our people into mere lab rats.

*'What's behind it?'*

*'All the luxury you can imagine.'*

'Somehow I doubt that,' I thought, recalling the words we'd exchanged, as we closed in on the shore.

When we got close enough, the water was no longer deep enough for the boat. I thought this odd – wasn't the wall acting as a kind of dam, keeping all the water in?

*'Yes it is, Tristan,'* he told me some time after, when I'd had days to gather up all my unanswered questions. *'And when these lands first flooded, the water level was dangerously high here. But generally it's at its lowest at this part of the wall - just like there are different levels in some parts of your city. Further along, you'll see the levels are much higher. But where we've entered, it's not such a threat at the moment – and it's the safest way in at this time of the day.'*

Guy A Johnson

Two men came out of that thick forest and dashed towards us, grabbing ropes that Nathaniel threw off the side.

'Friends of yours?' I asked, assuming I was as safe as I could be. I jumped off the vehicle and began to haul our transport out of the water.

'I'll introduce you in just a moment,' Nathaniel answered, jumping down to assist, along with Jessie. 'But let's get this thing secured first.'

There was no official mooring, as this wasn't strictly the way into the city – we were taking what Nathaniel called *the discreet, backdoor route.* So the speedboat's front end was pulled out of the water, wedged in the damp crumble of sand and stones beneath it – and we used two thick ropes to tie it to tree trunks a little further in, hoping the knots and the roots would hold it.

'I should be quite safe,' one of two men said to me.

'This is Solomon,' Nathaniel introduced, as we headed into the dark forest, the crunch of sand beneath our feet turning into the squelch of mud.

Solomon was of a similar build to Jessie and me – tall, arms and shoulders thick with muscle, but his hair was shorn within a centimetre of his head.

There was another obvious difference between us and this man – we were still wearing our protective outer clothing, minus the face masks, but Solomon simply had normal overalls over his clothing. Thick cloth, but penetrable.

'Jessie, Tristan – friends of mine, of ours, coming to help with our fight,' Nathaniel said, by way of announcing us.

Friends, were we?

Helping with *our fight.*

37

Guy A Johnson

'So, that's why we're here,' I couldn't help but express – out loud.

Solomon threw me a sharp, cold look.

'You don't want to be here, you take yourself back,' he said, ploughing into the dark green shadows ahead, not even looking back to check if I'd taken up his offer or not.

'We need to move quickly.' Nathaniel addressed Jessie and me, nodding, acknowledging he understood my reaction. He'd kept so much from us – and still was. 'You with me?'

I raised an eyebrow in reply – I'd come this far, hadn't I?

'Good, you might want to lose those protective suits then,' he added, referring to both of us. 'You won't need them here, and their weight might just slow you down.'

So we stopped and shed our rubber, oppressive skins. It should have felt like a moment of freedom – as a set of the authorities' shackles fell away – but suddenly I felt more exposed, more vulnerable without mine. Hadn't we believed that those body suits kept us safe – at least, for a while? What would be keeping us safe now?

Jessie and I shared a look and an understanding – we had each other and would be watching each other's backs like the true brothers we were.

Jessie dropped me a nod, tossed his heavy protective suit aside and moved on into the leafy oblivion. I swiftly followed.

To me, the forest seemed endless and uniform, but Solomon and the other man – Marcus, shorter and scrawnier than his companion, but seemingly just as fearless – strode on with speed and familiarity, reading the map of the land with ease.

Guy A Johnson

Solomon was always ahead, maintaining a pace Jessie and I weren't confident to match. We suspected Solomon knew this, yet he kept to his speed all the same, creating a little distance on purpose. His slighter companion, Marcus, acted as the link in our human chain, keeping us in sight and calling us on with whistles and hand signals. Nathaniel kept to the rear – making sure we didn't stray from the path, or turn back, I guess.

There were landmarks along the way that surprised us and led to questions, although we didn't stop to explore. Small buildings – usually wooden, like the authority laboratories that Jessie had found in the forests near the city, but in complete ruins. Occasional open areas – where the ground had been cleared of trees, as if preparing for the foundations of a building.

There were two discoveries that particularly drew our attention. In the very heart of the forest, we found the crumbling remains of a brick building. Its outer walls were tiled in colourful, cracked ceramic squares and there was the remains of a metal sign screwed into one wall, although the letters had worn away. Moving closer, we looked inside the entrance, although we didn't enter – for fear it might collapse on us. Squinting, we made out a series of turnstiles inside and, further in, a set of wide steps, descending. But these were mainly obscured by fallen rubble – as if an explosion of some kind had sought to block the way completely.

'Once it was a way from one city to another,' Nathaniel said, a little amused by our curiosity. 'Part of an underground train network,' he continued, when we looked to him for more of this story. 'High speed in its day, but a very long time ago. Not many people know about it now. The majority of entrances were buried by a government long dead – and historical records were lost, or maybe hidden. Who knows?'

Guy A Johnson

'You mean, there was another way to get here?' Jessie questioned, his tone turning slightly into an accusation.

'A long, *long* time ago,' Nathaniel stressed, holding out a hand, as if to defend himself. 'You'd struggle to find a single trace of it back home, as all the ways in have been built over. Decades and decades ago, probably longer. Those that weren't built over are generally blocked where the surrounding buildings have fallen or the underground tunnels have caved-in for some reason. And where that's not happened, I'm sure the floods have got in and caused no end of damage to the trains that remain. So – in answer to your question, Jessie, yes, there was another *possible* way to get here. But it wouldn't have been any easier than the way we've come. If you want a better travelling experience, then what you really need is one of those!' Nathaniel was pointing up.

The noise above us seemed to come from nowhere – blades whirring among the clouds above, creating a vortex of fast air around us. We ducked down and looked up through creased eyelids. Helicopters – three in total. Military style, with blades at both ends.

'What the-?' Jessie gasped.

'Don't worry, they won't be looking for you,' Nathaniel reassured us.

'How can you be certain?' I questioned, coming back to my feet, as the airborne vehicles chopped their way north.

'I'd know,' Nathaniel answered, in a tone that reminded us of his status here. *I'm in the Circle,* he'd confessed. He stopped for a moment, looking to where the helicopters had flown, long after they'd faded from sight.

Guy A Johnson

'What is it?' I asked, sensing there was something bothering him – something he might tell us. 'Nathaniel?'

'Nothing,' he said, shaking off whatever it was. 'Let's keep going. We need to get to the edge of this forest before it gets dark – and then we'll use the cover of darkness to get you inside the city wall.'

There was one other attraction that stopped our progress through the trees – another felled area, only this one had been developed on. A vast area, surrounded by chain fencing, it looked like an open prison. Inside, we could see five or six large buildings – brick walls, corrugated iron roofing, like the warehouses down by the Black Sea. I felt a cold shiver down my spine.

'I know this place,' I murmured, and felt a hand touch my left arm – Nathaniel's. 'This is where they brought us. This is where they took us and experimented.'

'It might be,' Nathaniel answered. 'The authorities created many such places like this. I didn't bring you this way on purpose, Tristan. I'm sorry, I'd forgotten this route would take us past here.'

'What is it?' Jessie interrupted, concerned.

I looked on, made out another building – a shower block, recalling some of the humiliation they subjected us to – while Nathaniel gave Jessie an explanation.

I could still see him in my head – Xavier. Strapped to a bench, while they injected him. His blood curdling cries. They'd ruined him, I knew that. Xavier was not to blame for what he'd become. But still, as far as I knew, he'd killed Albert, my father. And so I'd set out on my long-term quest to find Xavier and exact my revenge – funded by the very

Guy A Johnson

government who'd turned him killer in the first place. If my thirst for vengeance hadn't been so acute, the irony would've filled me with shame.

'You said you thought I'd found my father,' I found myself saying, finally coming back to a subject Nathaniel had side-stepped earlier.

'I thought you had,' he answered, looking at me briefly, before turning away. 'We ought to move on, I can see that sky above darkening.'

Following him – oddly reluctant to leave the fenced-in camp of horrors behind – I pursued my line of inquiry as well.

'You don't seem so keen to discuss it anymore,' I argued, my feet catching up with his, matching his speed.

'It was a comment, that's all. I've been watching you, remember. And I've seen the government files on you, Tristan.' He stopped, looked at me, then at Jessie – guessing what I may or may not have shared with my friend about my connection to the authorities. 'I've seen you go in and out of houses. Seen you settle in that city. I assumed you'd found what you were looking for. That is all. Nothing more to my comment.'

I had nowhere further to take this one, but – not prepared to face defeat yet – I picked up another thread I'd let go.

'Who were those helicopters for, Nathaniel?' I asked – this time to his back, as he'd turned, carried on through the forest.

On hearing the threat in my tone, I noticed our other companions – the burly Solomon and the slighter Marcus – turn and look back, wondering if they needed to intervene. Judging that they didn't, they turned away and continued. I felt Jessie's eyes on me – partly concerned, partly wondering if I needed him to do anything.

Guy A Johnson

'You paused for thought, Nathaniel. So I know something's going on – something that's bothering you. Something on your conscience. So, what are they for – what have you kept from us now?'

'They're for the children,' he answered, quickly, like a swipe to my face – like a punishment for my relentless push. 'Children that have been taken, Tristan. From their homes. From their mothers. Something I couldn't stop, no matter how hard I tried. Now, we need to get to the end of these trees before it's too bloody dark.'

He carried on, his pace urgent, his back to me and his tongue still, but I felt his anger at me. Despite the fact I had only more questions whirling around in my head – *which children? any from my city? anyone we knew? is this what happened to Elinor? Billy – had Billy been taken?* – despite these questions and more, I followed on without asking a single one.

And I felt a shift in my feelings towards Nathaniel.

I'd heard the distress in his voice when he'd spat his answer – *They're for the children. Children that have been taken, Tristan. From their homes. Something I couldn't stop, no matter how hard I tried.* Genuine distress for what the authorities were doing – even though he was at the very centre of that government. Finally, I sensed I could trust him – no matter what he held back, no matter that I suspected he wouldn't deliver on many of the personal promises he'd made us.

I even got close to muttering an apology. Close. In the end, I kept it inside – comforting just myself with the notion, as we ploughed on, eventually coming to the end of our long trek through the trees an hour or so later.

43

During this time, Jessie was particularly quiet and solemn – and I wondered if he was silently thinking over what this new *taking* might mean for us. For the people we loved – in particular, for Billy. If he was, he didn't say – and any questions he might have had for Nathaniel, he kept to himself.


We weren't prepared for what greeted us at the end of the forest – for the sight ahead or the smell of it.

'Jesus…' I heard Jessie gasp, raising a hand to his mouth – a reflex as he gagged.

'What is this?' I asked, questioning my thoughts and feelings about our guide once again. Questioning my own sanity – had I really decided to trust this man implicitly?

'I'm sorry, I couldn't have warned you about this,' Nathaniel said to me.

I looked on in absolute horror at the landscape ahead – trying to keep my anger in check, trying to fight back the urge to strike out.

'I don't think you'd have believed me that such a cruel place existed. And how could I have put this into words?'

'Why have you brought us *here*?' I asked, directing my thick growl towards him personally, my eyes reddened with grief and hate. 'Why have you shown us this?'

His answer was calm, measured – but his eyes recognised the fury in mine.

'I've brought you here because it's the safest way in for us,' he said, looking ahead at the scene before us. 'And because now you've seen it, now you've seen what people have suffered, you'll never turn back. Whatever I say, whatever I do, you'll never turn your back on this. On them. Will you?'

Guy A Johnson

'No,' I answered, still a little bitter, shaking my head, taking it all in. 'No, you've guaranteed my commitment now.'

We were stood on a concrete platform that acted like a borderline between the forest at our backs and what lay before us.

Stretching for at least a mile ahead of us, was a barren, muddy landscape – interspersed with rows of wire fencing and topped with curls of barbed wire. In the far distance, I could make out the mighty wall. But closer, I saw and inhaled the cruel determination of the wall's creators to keep others out. Felt the effort of their single-minded, inhumane arrogance.

Past that towering, impenetrable construction, I'd eventually discover the sleek, modern world I'd been imagining since Nathaniel began unfolding his tales. Fortunate enough to get that far in the end – unlike the countless victims I saw before me.

Body after body, in various stages of decay, submerged just below the surface of the endless mire ahead. I could see skeleton hands clutching at the fences, as if hauling themselves out. Could see faces staring up out of the wet earth, eyes open. A thin mist rose off this bog – a foul gas mixing the stench of death with the stench of waste.

'What is this?' Jessie asked, pulling himself up, wiping his mouth after retching a third, fourth time.

'Hope,' Nathaniel answered. 'Or the end of it.'

'Explain,' I demanded, a bilious taste on my own tongue.

But I knew what Nathaniel was going to tell us, even before a single word left his lips. And I knew what was going through Jessie's mind, as he looked out at the massacre

Guy A Johnson

before us. He was thinking of the people who'd fled our city, of the people who'd disappeared overnight, pledging to find a better place to live out their lives.

And he was thinking of Joe, his twin – wondering if he'd come this far. Wondering if his was among the heap of mud-smeared bones. I heard him heave again, and found myself thinking of Albert.

Of Elinor too.

'I think you know what's happened here, what's still happening,' Nathaniel began. 'There have been rumours for years about dry land, about a safer place your friends and neighbours have escaped to. And here it is – the so-called Promised Land. That's how people who live beyond that wall think of it – promised to them, the chosen.' He paused, eyes flicking to me, checking I'd heard the cold dislike in his voice. I had, but I didn't let it show. He continued: 'But there's over a mile of this sodden mire ahead. And anyone who can make it across without sinking below the surface is likely to get caught by the fences. As well as the barbed-wire on top, there's a current running through them.'

'So if they don't drown, they're electrocuted?' Jessie said and Nathaniel nodded.

'The electric current is only intermittent, but there's still enough fences to get through to make the chances of getting past them alive impossible.'

Jessie paled at these words and I thought he might be sick again.

'Jess-.' I said, reaching out to him, as his hands went to his face – covering his grief.

'And you've allowed this to go on?' Jessie accused, his bitter words mumbled through his fingers. 'You and that *Circle* of yours.'

46

'Yes,' Nathaniel answered, shame in his voice, but he didn't offer excuses to cushion his own pain. Just kept to the simple, bare truth of it. Then he added something that surprised us both. 'He's not amongst them,' he said.

'Who?' Jessie asked, lifting his face from his cupped hands, his expression caught out.

'The man you're looking for, your brother.'

Jessie was still, silent for a moment, as he took this in. Then he found his words again:

'You know this, because?'

'I know this for certain,' Nathaniel replied, not really answering though.

'Where is he then?' Jessie asked, exasperation in his voice.

'Not here.'

'What?' Jessie and I spoke in unison, our single voice incredulous – just two small words and a promise we'd been made, a hope we'd been given vanished without trace.

'Sorry. I needed you here. I need your help,' Nathaniel answered and I watched Jessie roll his shoulders back, taking a fighting stance. I touched his right arm, a signal to keep calm. 'It's the only lie I've told you. I promise. But I needed to get you here.'

'What about Elinor?'

'Safe.'

'Jesus.' I shook my head, unable to take in what I was hearing.

'You'll see her soon,' Nathaniel reassured, weakly, and I heard that nervousness in his voice again – that same anxiety I'd sensed when we first encountered him in the forest river.

47

Guy A Johnson

'You've got her?' I asked, feeling my own aggression rise.

'No, I've not got her. But I've seen her and she's safe.'

'Where?'

'She's safe,' Nathaniel repeated and we locked gazes. I couldn't read whether this was meant as reassurance, or as a threat. The quiver in his voice had gone again, though – so it was a threat. 'I promise,' he added, as if to soften it.

An anxious mix of conflicting feelings tied up my tongue; I had no certain idea how I felt about this man or what to say.

'You said this was the safest way in for us?' Jessie posed, breaking our stand-off.

Nathaniel nodded at him. 'Yes, it is. If you want to get in undetected.'

*You,* he'd stressed, but I didn't pick that up when he said it.

'Like these guys?' I snarled, indicating the skeletons in the mud, still thinking over his words, his broken promises, his gall. *I've seen her and she's safe.*

'No, not like those poor souls,' Nathaniel answered, and I heard his sorrow, even if I couldn't trust it. Yes – I was back to not trusting this man, not trusting my own judgement, either.

'No,' Jessie interjected – I sensed a boldness, a certainty in his voice. 'No, because our friend is going to lead the way – aren't you Nathaniel?'

I waited for his look of surprise – the moment we caught him out. But it didn't come.

'I won't be, Jessie,' he answered, his features calm, looking us both over. 'In fact, I'm leaving you here.'

'What?'

Another surprise – another path we'd been misled along.

48

'But Solomon and Marcus will lead the way across. There's a safe route. A way to avoid the sinking pools and the electric currents. If you know the way and how to time it – like Solomon does. You can trust him, I promise you. Trust both of them.'

Jessie went to interrupt, but Nathaniel held out a hand, to acknowledge that his word hadn't been entirely reliable up till then.

'I need to enter this place the way I normally would, so that I don't create any reason for alarm. And so I can catch up on what's been happening in my absence. But I'll see you in there. I'll come and find you.'

'Jesus, you are unbelievable!' Jessie swore, moving swiftly over to Nathaniel, the fingers in his right hand curling to a fist, the elbow drawing back.

'You'd better keep your word,' I hissed, as Solomon stepped between my friend and Nathaniel.

Jessie withdrew his attack, knowing it was pointless. We were strangers in a strange land – lured there under our own volition, with no one but ourselves to blame.

But we did have a choice: go back the way we came, or keep going, hoping, despite all we'd seen so far, that the man who'd led us there – the authority man, this member of the government's secret circle – could be trusted after all.

And we made our choice in bitter silence, looking at the sea of the mud-smeared dead ahead.

'I'll keep to my word,' Nathaniel said, backing off from us, shrinking away into the deep forest of green behind him.

'If you don't…' I called out after him.

49

Guy A Johnson

He looked back, briefly, and we shared a silent understanding of how that unfinished sentence ended.

When Nathaniel was out of sight again, we turned back to the path ahead of us – across a dangerous, corpse-strewn bog-land, littered with killer traps to thwart our progress. And with heavy hearts, we let Solomon and Marcus lead the way – more strangers we'd entrusted our lives to.

As Nathaniel promised, Solomon seemed to know the way, giving us clear instructions as we crossed. *Careful there. Don't step to the left – you'll sink in seconds. Tread in my exact footsteps.* And when we reached the fences, he seemed to know exactly where the gaps were – and when it was safe to go through. *See – there up. Top of the post. Small black box with a flashing red light? When the light goes out, the electric is off. Then you've got ten seconds.*

'Why aren't they on permanently?' I asked, questioning the intermittence of this defence mechanism.

'Because energy is precious,' Solomon answered. 'Even here.'

Gradually we crossed that mile of sinking mud and got closer to our next hurdle – the formidable wall seeming to soar higher and higher, the closer we got to it – crossing the majority of it without incident. No shocks, not even a wrong foot sucked into the pockets of sinking mud that surrounded us – hidden from sight like land mines.

Until we were about two-thirds of the way through, that is.

It was midnight-dark by then and we'd slowed right up, the increasing precariousness of our situation intensifying our caution.

50

Dog-tired, the gaps between the four of us – Solomon and Marcus ahead, me at the rear – had widened, and Solomon kept stopping, looking back, checking we were stepping into his path of footprints, before they melted away. In truth, we could barely make them out in the shadows that engulfed us.

We'd become numb to the bodies around us. They were in varying states of decay, from skeletons clothed in nothing but mud, to recent departures – faces twisted in the agony of their demise, skin greying, eyes dull but staring, hopelessly pleading to be saved beyond the grave. They sickened us – their foul smell, their cruel denial of a chance – but we stopped looking at every face. Stopped looking for those we'd lost – and we'd been looking, despite Nathaniel's reassurance that we wouldn't find any of them here. We were careful where we stepped – avoiding the bodies out of respect – but we'd stopped checking their faces, stopped checking for life. The creep of darkness made this easier.

And we'd complacently assumed there was nothing but death in that soft, shallow grave.

Until the unthinkable happened.

Until life reached out of that thick, earthy gravy.

Just a hand, reaching out like a shoot does towards the sun – twisting about, feeling the air against its muddy fingers, feeling for life.

A hand that grabbed for Jessie, held on fiercely and pulled him beneath that thick, suffocating surface in seconds, as it tried in vain to pull itself out…

Guy A Johnson

*Unfold*

*Remember the first time we met, Esther?*

*Remember that?*

*Our eyes met cross the room at that ball Monty hosted.*

*I say ball – there was no dancing. You complained about that – there was music, but no dancing, just talking.*

*You always denied that our eyes met – you said you hadn't noticed me at all.*

*(I didn't believe you then, and I don't believe you now.)*

*You always said we met when I snuck up on you.*

*In that hidden room with all the machines.*

*And the girl – the sickly one, all wired up.*

*You remember – in Monty's attic.*

*Otterley – that was the girl's name.*

*She's not quite what you think she is, Esther.*

*Like you – not what you think she is.*

*Fold*

Guy A Johnson

3. Billy

I was supposed to just forget.

Supposed to just carry on.

Like it hadn't happened.

Like *he* hadn't done anything wrong.

Like he hadn't left my mother behind to die.

*Billy, we can't! I'm sorry, boy! But there's no saving her! I'm sorry! I can only save you and the others! I'm sorry, son!*

And he'd stopped me from saving her – pushed me off that ladder, when I'd scrambled up it, determined to re-open that hatch and help her down with the rest of us.

*I'm sorry, Billy,* he'd said, like those words – *his* words – would count for anything now.

*I hate you!* I'd sworn at him, picking myself off the grimy, slimy floor of that underground tunnel. *You made us come here! So you killed her! I hate you!* And I'd felt some sore pleasure in releasing those words – they dulled my pain for a moment.

But I couldn't hate this man too deeply.

He had tried to save us, after all. And Mother's final words had instructed him clearly: *'Close the hatch, Gus! Close the bloody hatch!'*

So, while I accepted what he'd done on the inside, I wore a heavy sulk of intolerance on the outside – with an innate feeling that it just might protect me from further pain.

Yet, what was I do to with all my hurt – this sudden loss that ached so badly?

Guy A Johnson

And what was I to do with the terrifying cries in my head – the rabid, vicious barking of those savage creatures, and the blood-curling alarm in Mother's final plea? It wasn't just what had happened to her that frightened me – I felt sick with my own fear. At the thought of how close those enormous dogs had snapped at my heels with their huge, slathering jaws. At the thought of them prowling and howling above us, sniffing the scent of our trail, desperately scratching away, trying to find us.

*At the thought of them getting in,* a voice whispered in my head – a voice I couldn't shake.

I'd seen Augustus lock that door – I knew it was secure. But those beasts had blood in their eyes and they'd seek us out, I knew it. They'd find a way into this underground maze and they'd catch us up – rip us to death in some dark, damp corner where no one else could see or hear us.

As we trudged along in the shadows – the weak light of our single torch eventually diminishing to nothing – there was no time, no place to grieve, to let this all out. And I was too scared to share my fears – too frightened say it out loud in case it jinxed our fortune and came true. I had no one there to comfort me, either – no Aunt Agnes, no Great-Aunt Penny, and no Mother…

Instead, I had Marcie Coleman (not even a friend of mine,) Augustus – the man who'd sealed Mother's fate with a twist of a wheel lock – and the strange, pale girl that Mother and Augustus had insisted on taking from Monty Harrison's house.

Otterley.

That was her name.

Otterley.

54

Guy A Johnson

And whenever Augustus said it aloud – *mind your step there, Otterley; how are you doing there, Otterley* – there was a preciousness in his tone. Like she was special, like she was a treasure of some kind. And I found myself intrigued by her – where had she come from, what was wrong with her (because there was *something* not quite right with her) and why had Augustus insisted we bring her along? I also felt a little resentment – in our group of four, she had swapped places with Mother. This Otterley had escaped from Monty's capture and Mother had been left behind, prisoner to an unthinkable fate.

'Billy? Are you alright, Billy?'

Marcie Coleman – offering me comfort in the darkness that was all around me, swallowing me whole. She meant well, but she wasn't Elinor, she wasn't Tilly, either – and she probably knew it.

'Fine,' I answered, managing nothing else.

Even though it was pitch black, I felt Augustus' eyes on me the entire time – his concern for me and his guilt burning into me, whenever he turned back.

*Is everyone still with me? Keep in close, okay? Careful as you go. Feel the walls. And just small steps.*

Lines he sprinkled like breadcrumbs to keep us going in the one direction.

And, every so often, he'd check in on my feelings too – wanting to know how I was, hoping I'd tell him everything was alright, that he was forgiven. But I couldn't – and I wouldn't have, even if I could. Instead, I replied with questions of my own.

'What's your plan now then, Augustus?' I said at one point, after we'd been inching along in the dark, damp tunnel for a while with no light in sight.

Guy A Johnson

'We keep going, Billy,' he'd answered, his voice echoing off in the distance. 'Keep moving, feeling carefully in the dark, until we find another way out. There has to be a way. The man who designed all this – Mr Cadley – that was his idea. An underground labyrinth to use in times of trouble, to lead us all to safety.'

But it felt like just another story – like the ones I missed from Tristan – and even Augustus didn't seem all that convinced. His voice was threadbare at times, strained and I felt a little sorry for him. I kept that inside, though – I couldn't allow a single chink in my protective armour.

And then the impossible happened.

After hours of moving slowly – step-by-step – in the cold, near-suffocating blackness, a pinhole of light appeared on our horizon. Just a dot to start with and I doubted it at first glance, thinking my eyes were tricking me. But it got bigger, gradually, expanding little by little. But I didn't have the patience to wait for it – I needed to be in that light, swamped by it, hoping it would burn out some of the anguish I felt. Flooding out all the blackness that engulfed me.

So I ran into it, pushing past the others, past Augustus, although I could hardly see the ground beneath my feet.

'Billy! Careful lad! *Careful!*' Augustus cried behind me, but he didn't try to stop me. Probably sensed his old, weaker efforts would have no success.

As I dashed into the increasing brightness, running that race to the light on my own, I felt the tears come quickly and felt some of my pain and anger breathe. I didn't hurt any less, but felt the relief of letting a little of it escape. But when I finally met the light, what

56

I found took that breath away – astonishment somehow mopping up my tears, halting my anguish, like a tap turned off.

'Well I never!' Augustus cried, when he and the others caught up with me, some minutes later. 'You know what this is?'

I shook my head. 'I'm not sure. What is it?' I asked, staring all around, taking in the details.

I didn't quite know what to make of it. It was like we'd stumbled into a cave, yet this was made-man, created on purpose – *with* a purpose. I just couldn't tell what it was for.

The light wasn't natural, but came from lights above us – dull and round, like dinner plates, sunken into the ceiling. And the ground I stood on only stretched a few feet ahead and then it dropped away. I walked to the edge, looked to where the ground was sunken and saw something I recognised: train tracks. Like those I'd played with in Augustus' house, with the toy trains that had the strange name *Xavier* painted on the side.

'It's a station, Billy. An underground station.'

But I'd never heard of such a thing.

My eyes kept searching out our strange find.

There was tiling on the walls – cracked, dirty, and some of it had fallen away, but you could see the colouring underneath: mainly cream, with a line of red and a line of green tiles. To the right of the narrow tunnel we'd come through, there was a wide passageway, with tiled walls.

Augustus peered inside briefly, checking where it might lead, but the way was sealed off – bricked up on purpose, he claimed, suggesting we weren't supposed to go any further.

57

Guy A Johnson

For a brief moment, the voice of my fears returned, whispering in my head – *what if they're*

*behind it, Billy, fighting to get in; what if that's their way in?* Although I knew these

thoughts were nonsense, I went in and pushed against the bricks, testing their resistance.

As I suspected, there was no give – and that was enough to keep my paranoia about the

dogs at bay.

Looking back on the platform, there wasn't much else to find. It stretched along

about a hundred or so metres and there was a bench in each direction, one fixed to the wall

behind it, the second collapsed to the floor, like it had given up its purpose. There was

nothing else of interest, though.

So, I turned my attention back to that railway track.

'There's power?' I asked Augustus, forgetting to be cold towards him.

'And not just that,' he answered, but I was ahead of him with my thinking.

'There might be trains too?'

'Only one way to find out.'

Again, I was one step in front of the old man – launching myself off the concrete

platform, into the narrow lane where the rail tracks had been laid.

'Careful, the lines might be live. The trains would've run off electricity, Billy. And

remember, there's clearly power down here.' Augustus indicated the lights with a jerk of

his head in their direction. 'So, walk sensibly between them,' he warned.

But I knew what I was doing and I knew how trains worked – even if I'd only seen

a model one before. Even if my knowledge was only from old tales Papa H had spun or

from the wrecks piled up in the train graveyard to the north of our city. And I felt my

resentment towards Augustus return a little, my sulky armour reassert itself.

58

Guy A Johnson

'Wait up, Billy. You don't know what's ahead. Wait for us,' he cried out behind me, as I started to walk between the tracks – leaving him behind to help Marcie and Otterley down off the platform. 'Billy, be careful, lad!'

But I didn't listen, didn't heed his warnings – and it wasn't like we had any choices. We couldn't turn back and, as far as I could see, following the train track to wherever it went was the only route forward.

So, I just kept on going – following the track, avoiding its live lines, guided by dim wall lights that were so far apart that we were almost in darkness each time a new one lit the way. And, as I cleared ground along that tunnel – who knew just how many miles we were from where we started, from our flooded homes – I thought back to where our escapade had begun.

How much fun it had seemed – how innocent, how full of adventure – when Augustus had revealed the hidden room underneath his. What a find that had been – the books, the games, the bed, the little kitchen, the luxury bathroom too. Like a magic room – the kind of clean, multi-functioning room I'd dreamed off. And he'd kept it hidden all that time – saved it behind all that clear plastic covering, in case of an emergency.

'We could've just stayed there,' I muttered to myself, bitterly, as the others tried to catch me up. 'We would've been perfectly safe.'

But instead, he'd insisted we go further down – into the labyrinth beneath the city. Another adventure, but this one had turned sour – brought us to those dogs at Monty's house and cost my mother's life.

'We would've been perfectly safe, just there. We didn't need to go any further…'

59

Guy A Johnson

I wasn't conscious that I was sobbing again until an arm reached up to my shoulders and I felt myself shuddering against it.

I instantly stopped walking and ceased crying. Then I looked right to see her beside me – Otterley. The one Mother had traded lives with. The sickly child Augustus had insisted we bring along. I studied her for a minute, taking her in and she let me do this without saying anything. As if I had every right – or maybe she was just used to being studied. There was something in her – something I recognised. A likeness of someone else, but it eluded me at first.

Behind us, there was a cry and I broke my gaze to look back.

'It's okay,' Augustus shouted, over the top of a whimpering that echoed through the tunnel. Marcie had fallen. 'Just a graze. We'll catch you up.'

*Like I'd have waited,* I thought, pulling my invisible, protective cloak about myself, glancing quickly at the younger child beside me – swearing there'd be no more tears. No more weakness.

'Come on, let's keep going,' I instructed, taking her left hand in my right, acting the role of the older boy. Of the braver boy; a brother to be looked up to.

I wondered what Elinor would've made of me – she was always the leader, the braver one – and I had to pull that invisible cloak tighter about myself. 'I wonder what's ahead?' I said aloud, wondering if I could re-ignite the sense of adventure I'd felt before – wondering if this was what I needed to keep me going, to get us all through to wherever this was leading.

'There's shelter,' Otterley said, matter of fact.

Guy A Johnson

'I hope so. And food!' I announced the second line with a forced boom of enthusiasm.

'I can't see that, but I can see the shelter.'

'What?'

'It's made of metal. There are doors. On both sides. And there's somewhere to sit.'

For a moment, I stopped and turned to look at her again. I searched her face again for whatever it was I'd recognised, but couldn't see it at all now.

'I don't understand what you're saying,' I said, my thoughts corrugating my forehead.

'I can see what's ahead. Not all of it, just bits of it. And I can see somewhere that we can rest. Not too far ahead.' When I didn't respond – just stared, trying to take in what she was saying – she spoke again. 'But I can't see food, or drink. But then I can't see everything, can I?'

*Can I?* Like I should know – as if this should all make sense to her ten-year-old companion.

We began walking again, watching our feet.

'Can you really do that?' I asked, after a few seconds of listening to our feet crunch on the loose stones beneath us. Sounding more doubtful than I intended.

'Do what?' she asked, like she'd already forgotten our conversation from moments before.

'See ahead.'

Guy A Johnson

I said it like she had special sight – like her eyes had an amazing lens. But of course it was in her head, wasn't it? Whatever it was – the road ahead of us, or just her imagination – it was all in her mind.

'I think that's what it is. I'm not sure, though. I've been ill for a long time. And I've been dreaming a lot. Seeing a lot. I saw this.'

Otterley waved her arm around her.

'Saw this tunnel and saw us in it.' She seemed uncertain and her mind drifted as she spoke, as if trying to work it out. 'In a dream.'

*In a dream.* Three words that brought me back down to earth. There was no seeing into the future – this was just the mind of a younger child, who had an even wilder imagination than me. I decided to change the subject.

'How come you know Augustus?' I asked.

'I don't,' she answered, which puzzled me.

'But he came for you. That's why we were at Monty's house. He knew you were there and came to rescue you.'

'Rescue me?' she questioned and I wondered for a second if Augustus had made a terrible mistake. A darkness quickly clouded my thoughts as I considered what it had cost us. But then Otterley spoke again. 'It's not the first time.'

'What?'

'Not the first time he's rescued me,' she confirmed, frowning, still not certain, as we walked on in the dim light, avoiding the live lines. I thought she might elaborate, but instead she said: 'it's a carriage.'

Guy A Johnson

'What is?' I asked, trying to hide my irritation – forgetting my earlier pledge to be the older brother, the bigger man.

'The shelter. It's a carriage. A train carriage. The doors. The seats. The metal casing. I see it clearly now.'

'Look,' I began to protest, exasperated by her insistence that she could see into our future.

'Any idea how far, Otterley?'

The question came from Augustus, who'd finally caught us up.

I looked back to him and caught Marcie's tear-stained face in the dull illumination. I glanced down, saw a ruddy knee and felt overwhelmed with sorrow for her. How had she ended up here, miles underground, with a school friend she barely knew, an old man and a sickly child with a crazy imagination? And was this really any better than what she'd left behind – if she *had* been taken by the authorities, whipped into the sky by those helicopters we'd heard cutting up the clouds, would she not have been safer than she was? In the dark, avoiding death by a live rail, with no idea what was at the end of the tunnel.

'Yes,' Otterley said, looking straight at me – and I knew two things instantly.

One, that I hadn't posed my question out loud and yet she'd appeared to have answered it; and two, I realised who it was I saw in her.

Tilly.

'Who's Tilly?' the question came from Otterley, confirming my wild assumption.

But it had to be a trick, right?

'So, how far?' Augustus asked again, interrupting us and bringing our odd exchange to an end.

Guy A Johnson

'I can't tell, I just know it's up ahead. I'm seeing it clearer, though. Which might mean we're getting closer.'

'What's she talking about?' Marcie asked, her tears done. But I found myself too cross to answer – *what made her think it was alright to get inside my head; why had Augustus made such a deal of rescuing this freak?*

Augustus simply moved the conversation on, his eyes watching me, figuring out my mood.

'Let's just keep going – that'll get us to our destination much sooner,' he said, eyes almost burning into me.

I returned the glare, unwilling to relent – keeping my eyes cold with rage.

'And where's that?' Marcie asked – a reasonable question that received a whimsical answer, like this was one of Great-Aunt Penny's old *parlour games*, as she called them.

'The light at the end of the tunnel,' Augustus said, and all Marcie could manage was a deflated *Oh* – as if, in her stupidity, she had missed something obvious. 'Try not to be too angry with me, Billy. I'll explain it all to you – when I find the right moment.' He said this close to my ear, so that only I could hear it. 'I promise you – I'll explain it all.'

I didn't answer – showed no outward sign of acceptance – but continued forth with the others, not raising a single question or objection, until the light truly did appear at the end of the tunnel…

Like before, it began as the smallest dot in the far distance. Because we weren't in complete darkness this time, we didn't see it as quickly – and it felt like every part of our exhausted bodies were falling asleep, so our eyes had lost their sharpness.

Guy A Johnson

'See it?' Augustus eventually exclaimed, just after I'd seen the hazy circle on the horizon growing and glowing wider. 'What do you think? Another station?'

It was.

Smaller than the previous one, but it had the same features – the concrete platform, the cracked tiles on the wall (white and bottle green, this time) and flat, round lights in the ceiling. A rusting, faded sign was screwed into a section of the tiles – only the letters *S* and *k* remaining; I guessed they would've indicated the name of the station stop. There had been three exits at some point, but each way was blocked. And this time, it looked as if the obstructions were caused by an accident – the exits were barred by tightly packed rubble, rather than neatly stacked bricks.

'It's further ahead.'

This came from Otterley, but I hid the urge to sneer at her claims of foresight.

'The carriage, Otterley?' Augustus asked, still using that slightly lifted tone whenever he said her name.

'We need to keep going,' she said by way of an answer. 'There's food too. I can see that now.'

She looked my way when she said that, but I didn't trust her and sensed she'd added that detail to win me over. Choosing not be drawn in, I drew my protective cloak tighter around me and followed as Augustus, Marcie and Otterley continued along the track.

*Let them see your lies,* I said inside, unable to help the maliciousness of my thoughts. I should've been hoping she was telling the truth – it had to be at least a day since we'd eaten – but the irrational bitterness I felt towards her (towards them all) was growing rapidly, consuming any rational thoughts I might have had.

65

Guy A Johnson

It took us another ten minutes of heavy, limb-tired walking before we found it.

At first, we all thought we'd come to a dead end – the brighter light from the previous station had faded behind us and up ahead the lights appeared to have stopped. There was nothing but blackness in sight. But Otterley insisted we shuffle on – *it's just up ahead, I can see it; we're nearly there* – and I reluctantly joined Augustus and Marcie as they let their unshakable faith in the younger girl lead them on.

'There.'

A single word from Otterley that stopped us all.

'Feel it.'

And that's what we all did – first Augustus, then Marcie and finally me. Put our hands out to the shadows in front of us and felt the metal casing of a train carriage with our hands. Felt its bumps and textures, as our eyes adjusted and it materialized from the gloom. Something crumbly gently grazed against my fingers and lifting them to my nose, I smelt rust. Augustus moved quite swiftly, feeling his way around its edges, trying to find a way in.

'Ah, an opening,' he announced, having moved along the left side of it. 'Careful as you come, you need to step into it. That's it, up we go.'

And he held out his hand to Marcie and Otterley, aiding them, as they entered the still dark carriage. I refused his offer and pulled myself in.

'Can you make out the seats there?' he asked us and we could. 'Good. Rest yourselves a minute. I'm going to check something out.'

'You're leaving us?' Marcie, scared she was being abandoned.

66

Guy A Johnson

'No, I'm just going a little further along this carriage. Don't worry. Billy's still here, aren't you?'

I didn't answer, but Marcie didn't protest again, as we listened to Augustus shuffle away from us, his elderly figure ghostly in the grey-light. We heard a handle turn and the sound of a door creaking, suggesting he'd found an exit or an entrance, leading him further away.

'There's four compartments,' Otterley said, breaking the quiet. 'That's why it's dark – they're blocking out the light ahead. And there's a bend in the line of carriages, making it harder for the light to come through.'

'But no food, I see,' I commented, determined not to be impressed – determined to find fault in this strange, sickly girl's predictions.

'We just haven't found it yet-,' Marcie added, quietly, as if doubting who she should side with.

'I bet he comes back with nothing,' I answered, cutting her short – the heavy bitterness I stressed on that last word enough to end the conversation.

For several minutes we were silent in the misty greyness that surrounded us. Shapes gradually formed in the shadows. As you'd expect, the carriage had windows along both sides and there were rows of seats against the walls. There was an open-spaced area too, just a few feet away, and I found myself wondering what this would be for and why the train hadn't simply been fitted with more seating.

I heard Otterley's lips part – a dry, almost clicking sound – as if she was going to answer my thoughts. But she seemed to think better of it and remained quiet.

The skittering sound began about five minutes later.

I'd begun to feel anxious by then, wondering what was keeping the old man. Wondering if he'd been distracted by the contents of the additional carriages Otterley had reckoned were attached to this one. I thought of him pottering with all that old equipment back at his house – the washing machines, the televisions, the recording apparatus. And I imagined him forgetting the food he'd gone in search of – forgetting about us completely, lost in his own mad mind while he stopped to tinker pointlessly with this new, obsolete machine he'd found.

'He's-.' Otterley said, inside my thoughts again, about to defend Augustus. But she stopped there – hearing what I heard too.

Marcie didn't say a word, but sensed Otterley had stopped for a reason – and we all felt a heightened sense of alarm. A sharpness of fear in the misty blackness that engulfed us.

It started a little in the distance – coming from ahead of us, from a part of the tunnel we'd not ventured to. A gentle pitter-patter – like light rain teasing a river road. But then it built-up and I made out the sound clearly – tiny feet, moving at a pace, scattering loose stones as they sped along. Getting louder.

Getting closer.

'What is it?' Marcie asked, but we all knew what it was.

I looked over at the entrance we'd come in by – it was wide open and I couldn't see the door itself.

Guy A Johnson

'It's electronic,' Otterley said, clearly reading my thoughts, but I was too petrified to give this intrusion any anger – to question the fact I was simply accepting this unbelievable skill of hers. 'There's a button to close it, but there's no electricity.'

I saw Augustus in my head again – meddling with the innards this train – and suddenly wished that's exactly what he was doing. Putting his boyish, purposeless pursuits to good use.

The pattering footsteps got closer still and eventually their speed eased up. There was silent agreement amongst the three of us not to move, to barely breathe. So, we simply waited for the inevitable. When it reached us, it paused just outside, as if waiting politely to be invited inside. I heard it panting and imagined a long, wet tongue hanging out over sharp, glistening teeth. Imagined its hunger – trapped down here, with no food, no prey. Imagined it sniffing out our flesh, wondering exactly what our blood would taste like.

Then I saw its eyes.

Red in the dimness – a reflection of the bloodlust on its mind.

Saw them glance around, making out Otterley, making out Marcie too. The latter whimpered and I felt instantly angered by her.

*You'll give us away!* my irrational mind raged – as if the creature hadn't already located us. As if our chances of survival would've been increased by silence.

When it lifted its front left paw up into the carriage, Marcie let out a small yelp. Otterley countered this with a quiet *shush* that shuffled over Marcie's whining and somehow lessened my anxiety too.

Something was different here.

The animal put a second paw forward, eyes glancing back at me again.

69

Guy A Johnson

'It's cautious,' Otterley said. And whether she'd read my thoughts again or not, it was exactly what I was thinking.

'What do we do?' I asked her, forgetting I was the elder – that this strange, poorly child was much younger than me.

'I don't know,' she answered.

But we didn't have to make any decisions about what to do next, as these were taken out of our hands.

It started with a rumbling noise that travelled along the carriage – seeming to shake the whole train. And this was quickly followed by lights coming on – starting from much further down in the carriage furthest away, until it reached us, illuminating all around.

'Electricity!' Marcie gasped.

'He's got it working!' I exclaimed, squinting, adjusting my eyes to the shock of the instant radiance.

I looked around the carriage – at the colours and textures coming to life, at Marcie, and then at Otterley, surprised by just how ill she appeared under the bright glare. The dog had gone – the creature nowhere to be seen, as if it had been scared off by the vessel coming to life.

Next to the open entrance I noticed a large, circular button had lit up. Marcie was closest to it.

'Slam it!' I instructed, pointing, and she did – and two doors slid together quickly, closing up the hole in our safety. Shutting the unwelcome creature out for good. I felt relief flood me as quickly as light had flooded our space – saw this in Marcie too. Otterley was harder to read.

70

At that point, Augustus came back into view – coming down the central aisle several carriages away, he was carrying something in his arms. Once he reached us – nearly dropping everything as he struggled to open the door that linked our carriage to the next one – we could finally see what he had.

'Tins!' he said, joyfully, dropping six or so assorted cans onto a seat next to Otterley, several rolling onto the floor with a clatter. 'Tins of food!' he clarified, as if there had been any doubt.

I looked at the sickly girl – expecting to see a smug look of triumph on her face, but there wasn't one.

'How are we going to open them?' Marcie asked, posing a fair, practical question, but Augustus was already distracted by something else.

'What have we here, then?' he was asking, looking through the glass on the doors – at something outside. 'Looks like we've got company.'

I followed his gaze and saw that, absurdly, he was referring to the creature – the one we thought had scarpered when the train had rumbled and lit up. I could see its eyes in the dark tunnel beyond our metal capsule.

'Another fellow who's lost their way in this underground maze,' Augustus continued, getting his face up closer to the glass, for a better look.

I feared the creature might leap up and show its true colours – the scarlet of its gums and tongue, the poisonous yellow of its teeth. But it remained docile.

'Looks a little hungry too,' the old man added, and shifted towards the door – his right hand moving towards the button that Marcie had pushed only moments before.

71

Guy A Johnson

'Augustus,' I heard myself barely say, dismayed as he did the unthinkable: pressed the button, released the doors and let the creature back in…

### Unfold

*Esther*

*Before I tell you more about me – or about the secrets I know about you – I want to tell you some other things.*

*About what's been going on – right under our noses all along.*

*With the authorities.*

*Esther – if you're reading this, then you're in my flat. Your mother's flat, you'll say. And if you've finally found this note, then I've fled – and you've probably found out a few of my other secrets. You probably know I kept Elinor there.*

*See, she found out about my past – overheard me talking to Papa Harold one day. Recorded me on that damn tape recorder of hers, I'm certain. I was never going to harm her, Esther – I just didn't have an answer. So I kept her at mine – kept her drugged and secure, until I could come up with a plan.*

*But if you're reading this, then that plan failed.*

*I digress though – all this was supposed to come later.*

*First, let me tell you about the authorities…*

### Fold

4. Agnes

From the day that Joe came out of the water, to the afternoon that the skies were ripped apart with the blades from the helicopters, it felt like I moved around in a hazy cloud.

As if, somehow, I was detached from the events that whirled around me.

But that's how it was.

And when Augustus rowed me to Mother's old flat – taking me back to *lay Ronan to rest,* as he put it – it was like I was watching it all from the other side of something. Like through an invisible pane of glass. Looking in, but not part of it.

They all took it for shock – it had been too soon to drag me back to that place where Elinor had been held captive. To the place that was so heavily soaked in blood. In Ronan's blood, so we'd assumed. I still wasn't sure. I knew Joe wasn't lying, but maybe his timings were wrong. And when we returned to bury Ronan, I still couldn't tell if it was his body or another's. I could barely manage to look at the corpse, but when I did, it was in such a bad state that it was no longer possible to tell. The hair was the same colour as Ronan's, the clothes his too. But nothing else – his face, marks on his body – nothing else remained for me to see. A closer search might have confirmed it, I guess, but I'd have had to confess everything to Augustus to justify that. To Esther too – but I'd made Joe a promise to keep his return secret for now. And I intended to keep it.

So I was really no further forward after that, and I continued to walk around, living behind that invisible glass screen – dazed, in shock, unable to comprehend everything that was happening to me – until the afternoon that changed everything.

74

Guy A Johnson

Until that sound came roaring out of the clouds.

I went to the windows and saw the end of something – I didn't get a full view, but it was too low down to be a plane. It had to be a helicopter – although that was equally implausible.

'Where would that come from?' I asked out loud, feeling fully awake again, the fog of the last week or so vanished. 'Who would have something like that? Who'd have the resources, the fuel?'

At first, these questions just hung in the air. But their answers came soon – in a telephone call from Augustus. He had all the answers and more, I was soon to discover.

'It's the authorities, Agnes,' he explained, his tone calm, but his delivery fast – as if he had a lot to tell me but not much time in which to do it. 'I can't say much on the phone, but I picked something up last night. On the airwaves. They're taking them again, Agnes. The children. Those helicopters were headed for the schools. I thought they were coming later – I thought we had time, Agnes. But I'm too late.'

'Billy?' I said, feeling sick with dread.

'No, no I warned Esther in advance – she kept him home. Kept him hidden. But he can't stay where he is. The authorities might come looking when they realise they don't have them all. So, they're coming to you.'

'What?'

'I've said I'll meet them there. At yours. They won't stay. Don't worry – not safe enough, but I might need you to help me convince your sister to let Billy stay with me. See, I can hide him where no one will find him. And who is going to come looking around my

75

Guy A Johnson

old place for the boy? Agnes? Agnes – are you still there? Is everything alright? You heard me say that Billy was safe, didn't you? You heard all that?'

'Yes,' I croaked, barely able to speak – barely able to take it all in.

Esther and Billy were on their way.

My sister and nephew were on their way to my home, where I was currently hiding Joe – husband and father to them respectively. Their irreversibly damaged husband and father, who I'd promised to hide from them for now.

'You have to stay hidden,' I told Joe, as soon as my call with Augustus had ended.

He was resting on the old settee in the kitchen area, a position he'd more or less kept since he'd arrived.

'Esther and Billy are on their way. They'll be here in minutes, Joe. So, we'll need to hide you out of the way. In one of the bedrooms. Do you think you'll be alright, getting up the stairs?'

But Joe didn't move an inch, and I instantly realised the dilemma he faced. If he kept hidden, if he saved them the pain of seeing him like this for just a little longer, he'd be depriving himself – of seeing their faces, of hearing their voices once again for just a little longer too. But if he revealed himself now – while they were faced with the prospect of the authorities on their tail, coming for Billy – well, he knew he couldn't do that. He knew he had to let them deal with their current problem first. He knew he had to delay their reunion – which would be traumatic in itself.

'Can you help me up there?' he eventually asked me. 'My whole body is aching today. Feeling a little weak.'

I nodded; there was no question of my not helping him.

76

Guy A Johnson

'We've got enough time to get you up there and settled,' I reassured. 'And they won't be here long, okay? They're just meeting my friend Augustus and then they'll leave.'

But it wasn't that simple in the end.

Once I'd got him up the stairs, he was a little breathless and I noticed he was shaking too – his hands jerky.

'I'll be alright,' he reassured me, sitting on the edge of the bed that was officially Tristan's, although it had been a long time since he'd slept in it. 'I can do this.'

The words were more to convince himself than soothe my concerns.

'How about I stay with you, till they arrive.'

Joe nodded, so I sat down next to him and we waited in silence. Held hands in solidarity and looked straight ahead, thinking. I squeezed his hand a couple of times and, when it eventually stopped shaking, I felt relieved that he'd finally calmed down. It didn't occur to me that anything else had happened.

It wasn't until I heard Esther letting herself and Billy in down below that I realised something was wrong.

'I'd better go down and greet them,' I announced, standing, releasing Joe's hand and turning to look at him again. 'Joe?'

He was sat upright, but his eyes were closed and his body was slightly hunched forward; he'd fallen out of consciousness.

'Joe?' I asked again, giving him a shake.

And then, like before, he began fitting and expelled a painful, animal cry.

77

Guy A Johnson

For a few seconds, I tried holding him down, but the noise he made – the crying, the thrashing about – attracted Esther's attention. And there was no humane way I could think of to suppress that monstrous yelp.

'Agnes? You up there? What's going on?'

There was distress in her voice – she'd already be worried about Billy, and now she had this added drama to contend with.

I'd been trying to steady Joe with my arms, but I left him momentarily – rushing to lock the bedroom door. But as I did this, Joe's fitting intensified and he fell to the floor – his limbs sporadically drumming against the bare floorboards as they continued to spasm.

Hearing this, Esther stormed up the stairs and tried the door handle, rattling it with insistence.

'Agnes! What's going on? We haven't time for any of this! Let me in! Agnes!'

'Just leave!' I cried out, my body covering Joe's, desperate to get him under control. 'Esther, just take Billy and leave!'

And I ached with the cruelty in those words – she'd fled her own house in fear, terrified the authorities would come for Billy, now that the takings had been resumed – and my tears were genuine. But I had little choice – I'd promised Joe I'd keep him hidden for now and they couldn't see him like this. Their coming back together had to be in better circumstances.

Esther persisted a little longer – jangling the door handle, hoping her frustrated, angry words might somehow see their way to releasing its lock.

'Agnes! What are you playing at! Haven't we all been through enough lately? Open this door! Agnes!'

Then I heard a disgusted sigh and she descended, heavy-footed. I heard her console an agitated Billy. And later, when Augustus arrived, I heard her unleash her anger on him. Joe had finally calmed by then, so I was able to leave him and sidled up close to the door. Ear pressed against it, I listened closely to their conversation. Heard him talk to Esther – reassure her and somehow convince her that she could trust him, that leaving with him was the best option for her son. Heard Billy ask if he was in danger and then Augustus tell him he was going to keep him safe.

My heart ached at the thought of what they must have been thinking of me – hadn't they all been there for me when Elinor had gone missing? Hadn't Esther, in her misguided, religion-muddled way, always put me first? And I knew inside that was exactly what I was doing – putting them first, protecting them both. I just wished they'd known it.

I heard the front door close and they were gone, leaving Joe and I by ourselves again. Looking out the window, I watched the three of them on the river road, sailing towards the Cadley house.


It was the sound of the telephone ringing that drew me out of Tristan's room.

I'd managed to get Joe back onto the bed, covered him over with Tristan's bedding and he'd settled into a calm, deep sleep. There was something comforting about just watching him. Despite the horrific scarring to his body, despite knowing the agonies he'd suffered. Having him there, in that room – I felt his connection to Jessie and could obviously still see his twin in that face, no matter how altered it was. And just having a man in that room, in my house, was an echo of how it felt to have Tristan around. So I

Guy A Johnson

allowed myself to be caught up in that strangely consoling spell – until the shrill ringing in the hallway broke it.

Thinking it might be Augustus – hoping it would be him with news that everything was alright, that my nephew was safe, my sister no longer angry with me – I moved swiftly towards the telephone, grabbing its receiver before it rang off.

'On their way,' a familiar voice said. Distorted, muffled, but strangely familiar.

'Augustus?' I asked, but the line went dead.

Yet it wasn't Augustus at all – a fact he confirmed later that evening when he returned to check on me. He'd had an identical call himself.

'So we both recognised the voice,' he said to me, when I'd reluctantly let him in. He knew something was wrong, straightaway – knew something was going on. But he focussed on the mystery call, sensing my reluctance to engage in anything else. 'We were both warned.'

'But about what, Augustus?'

'I don't know, Agnes. But whoever it was, they want us alerted. Want us to keep our wits about us, and with the very little we know, that's all we can do.'

When Joe cried out again – a softer moan, not the animal cries from earlier – there was no avoiding the subject.

'Agnes?' Augustus asked, gentle concern in his tone.

'I'll show you,' I answered and finally led him to Joe.

Guy A Johnson

Once inside Tristan's room, he gasped at the sight of Joe's disfigured body, sprawled over the bed – the covers I'd put over him having been wrestled away. He was sleeping again, but fitfully.

'Oh, Agnes…' he said, his face pained with the horror of it all.

'I don't know what to do with him,' was all I could think to say, as we both stared at the restless, tortured soul.

'And I don't have any answers,' Augustus replied, but only after a long, silent delay – and it took me a moment or so to make sense of his sentence, to connect it back to mine. 'But I'll be back, okay? To check on you both. I have to get back to Esther and Billy right now, though. Check the boy's alright – and check on your sister too.'

'Check she's not started reorganising all your cupboards,' I added, as we closed the door on Joe and descended the stairs.

A brief, whispered chuckle escaped through Augustus' teeth.

'Well, if I need to keep her occupied, I'll know what to do.'

When we reached the hallway, Augustus gave me a quick peck on the check and then pulled himself back into *this pointless charade* – his latest scornful description of the protective gear we were still all wearing.

'I'll return as soon as I can,' he promised, before descending the slippery steps down to my waterlogged ground floor, where he let himself out.

And although he kept that promise to come back, it was a long while before he was able to.

*'Sorry, I got a little waylaid,'* he'd say to me, when I finally saw him again.

81

With my old friend gone – and Joe asleep – it felt like I was on my own again, with nothing but my thoughts to occupy me.

To keep physically busy, I pottered around the kitchen area. I cleared away china and cutlery, wiped down the sides and the table, smoothed out the creases in the settee, and placed the chairs evenly around the centre table that my family had spent so many days and nights crowded around. Tristan, Elinor, Esther, Billy, Jessie, Aunt Penny and Uncle Jimmy – and Ronan too. So many of them gone away from me, so many of their fates unknown as well.

'Oh, Elinor,' I murmured aloud, standing at the sink, my hands gripping its edge – steadying my frame, as my emotions shook it a little. 'What happened to you, little girl?'

'I'll find her, I will.'

The voice came out of the shadows, from an invisible entity, and I wondered for a moment if it was just my imagination. Just me thinking wishfully that someone would come to my rescue – to *her* rescue. But I hadn't imagined a thing.

Suddenly, there was a form to go with the sound. A body, a face – *his* face.

'Sorry, I didn't mean to startle you, Agnes,' Xavier apologised, stepping in from the hallway.

'Is this how it's going to be now?' I asked him, my breathing suddenly short and quick from the shock of seeing him again. I wondered how he'd got in; Augustus couldn't have closed the front door firmly enough.

'I have to be careful, Agnes. I can't just wander around. I can't announce myself. People are after me.'

Guy A Johnson

'That's not what I meant,' I answered, sharply, but then what did I mean? For a moment, I wasn't sure.

On the surface, having him there felt wrong. Tristan wouldn't like it, I knew that. What had Xavier said last time? *He mustn't know I've been here, Agnes. He wants to harm me, Agnes.* So they knew each other – had a connection I knew nothing about. *He's not to be trusted,* he'd added. But this was from a man who spent most of his time as a shadow – a man who'd faked his appearance to me for months. No, Tristan wouldn't want him here – and neither did I. Xavier was definitely the one not to be trusted.

And yet... and yet there was a feeling I couldn't displace. A deeper, old longing that nagged at me, telling me not to burn all my bridges with him.

'Do you want me to go?' he asked, after a short silence.

I thought for a minute and then shook my head.

'No,' I answered, thinking over the last few days again and the latest developments in the world I could barely make sense of. The savage image of the body on the floor of Ronan's flat flashed in my mind. 'I might need you yet, Xavier Riley.'

'Can I do anything now?' he asked and I shrugged, unsure. 'I could fix us something to eat?'

'You still eat?' I asked, half-joking, but half serious too.

'Yes, Agnes, I do. It's a mind trick – I don't really disappear. You just don't see me, that's all.'

'That's all?' It was hard to hide the bitterness in my tone. And he didn't defend himself – he knew I'd never forgive how he deceived me. *I'm Reuben, and I'm here to talk to you about hope.* No, I'd never forgive that. 'Can you appear as anyone?'

Guy A Johnson

'You don't want food?' he questioned, avoiding the subject.

I stared hard at him – I wasn't letting this one go.

'No, Agnes, I can't. It doesn't work like that.'

'How does it work, then?'

He sighed deeply, drawing his breath in slowly, as if preparing himself for something he didn't want to do, didn't want to say.

'It's down to the recipient.'

'The recipient?' I pointed at myself as I said this.

He conceded with a nod.

'I can only suggest something that might already be there. A need. A want. You saw what you wanted to see, to an extent.'

'With *Reuben*?' I questioned, hardening my voice, lacing it with that lack of forgiveness I was clinging to.

'Yes, with Reuben,' he admitted.

'So, I was fooling myself then? Fooling myself that my twin brother was really there for me? That in times of trouble, I could simply magic him and pretend he'd grown into an adult after all? That he'd survived?' I cried, my voice and anger rising. 'That was all me, was it? All my own stupid fault?'

Xavier's mouth opened, as if to defend himself, but I cut in before he could speak again.

'Who else could I see, I wonder? Who else have I lost that, if I tried really hard – if I really willed it – I could see standing here before me instead of you? Where do I start, Xavier, with my ever growing list of losses?'

Guy A Johnson

'Don't, Agnes. Don't-.'

'Shall we see just how easy it is? I'll just wish my way through that list and see who pops up first-.'

'Agnes! Stop it. Stop this – you're just hurting yourself. Hurting me-.'

'I don't care about…'

He'd moved closer, held my wrists and my focus in one move and was staring into my eyes – holding my gaze, as tears streamed down both our faces.

'Could you be her, Xavier?' I asked, my tearful whisper barely audible.

And he dropped his gaze, the shame in the unspoken answer heavy about him. *Yes.* That was the answer. I felt it in the silence that hung between us – thick and suffocating like a deep fog. *Yes.* If it came to it, Xavier's sneaky little trick could manipulate me that far.

'There's some meat,' I said eventually, breaking our quiet.

Xavier looked up, quizzically. I pointed to the fridge.

'Some vegetables too. You offered to fix some food, remember? So pull something together. I'll be back in a moment. Just need a minute alone.'

And so I left Xavier preparing a meal, while I took myself back upstairs – where I briefly checked in on Joe, before slipping into my own room and closing the door.

Sitting on the edge of my bed, I took some deep breaths again. There really was no escaping the weight of this extraordinary situation. Xavier's and Joe's presence was remarkable, unbelievable and dangerous too. I knew the danger posed with Joe being there – I knew exactly who might come after him. But Xavier? That was less clear – though I had a strong sense he was a dangerous man. And his comments about Tristan – *He's not*

85

*everything he says he is. He came here looking for me* – I didn't want to believe them, I didn't want to trust them. But believe them or not – like them or not – there was no escaping the threat in them. So both my guests were wanted men – both were running from something.

'You coming back down?'

Xavier's voice cut my thoughts. And the oddity of him being there again struck me – absent for so many years, gone for so long he was almost just a myth in my past, and now I'd seen him twice within a short space of time. And he was simply cooking a meal, like he'd been around all along.


'It's not fancy, but it's hot. It'll fill you up,' he said, when I eventually joined him again in the kitchen.

On the table were two plates with a meal of chicken – at least, Jessie had said it was chicken – a few potatoes and some carrots.

'Thank you,' I said and took a place at the table.

We both ate in silence and I was surprised at just how hungry I was – food hadn't been high on my list of priorities. When we were both done, I decided to share the thoughts I'd had while I'd been on my own – the vague plan I'd formed in my head.

'I want you to help me find someone,' I told him.

'Agnes, I've tried. I went straightaway. Tried to find her trail…'

I shook my head – he'd misunderstood.

'Not Elinor.'

'Not Elinor?' he questioned – alarmed to hear me say it.

86

Guy A Johnson

'You looked everywhere you could think of, right? No stone-.'

'Left unturned. Yes. Not one.'

'So, maybe if you stop *looking* for her you'll have a better chance of *finding* her. Maybe if you look for someone else instead – someone who she just might be with, or who might be following her.'

'Who?'

I took in a deep, long breath – steeled myself for what I was about to say.

'He's not dead,' I said, finally admitting to myself that I believed Joe.

'Who?'

'Ronan.'

'Ronan?'

'The body wasn't his, Xavier. He got away. What if he took her somewhere? What if he's still got her, Xavier? What if he's still hurting her?'

'He's not dead?' Xavier questioned, still catching up as my narrative sped on. 'But I saw him too. I went to the flat.'

'It wasn't him, Xavier.'

'But… But how do you know?'

He looked directly at me again – that long, almost mesmerising gaze I'd noticed he did. It gave the impression he was looking deep inside, trying to extract something with his stare.

'What haven't you told me?' he asked.

Guy A Johnson

I knew it would only be a matter of time before Joe made a noise or attracted attention some other way – I'd been lucky so far, as he hadn't stirred at all during Xavier's visit.

'Agnes?'

I answered with a question of my own.

'How do I know I can really trust you?'

'You don't, I guess.'

'How do I know this is even you? Maybe I just want it to be you, eh?'

Xavier managed a short, conceding laugh at this; raised his hands in mock surrender.

'Same answer, Agnes: you don't.'

We were still at the table, opposite each other. Xavier pushed his chair back, stood and reached over for my plate and cutlery. I pushed it towards him, a little chilled by the contrast of this domestic simplicity against the bizarre content of our conversation.

'But I don't think you want me here, Agnes. I'm not the man you most desire under your roof, am I? And he's not materialised – I've not come as Tristan.' He pronounced his name with a little acidity, reminding me of their enemy status. 'So, I think you're pretty safe to assume I'm actually me.'

He ran a bowl of water and immersed our dirty dishes in weak, warm suds. I joined him, taking wet items from his hands and drying them on an old stained towel.

'You still haven't told me how you know,' he said, passing me the last of our knives. 'How you know about Ronan,' he completed.

Guy A Johnson

I paused, tipped my head to one side, deciding what to say. In the end, I told him everything – about Joe's arrival, the torture he'd suffered at Monty Harrison's hands, Ronan's helping him escape.

'And when I went back, I couldn't be certain it was Ronan,' I said, coming to the end of this story. 'They were his clothes, and what I could make out of the body had similar features – but it was… so… badly…'

My voice fell away. The horror of what we'd discovered. The sight of all that blood.

'Agnes?'

My name as a question helped me focus again.

'You really think he has her? That he's taken her on somewhere else?'

I shrugged, and felt tears pierce through my eyes as I dropped my shoulders.

'I'll look for him, okay? I promise. I'll set off and I'll do everything I can to find him. Okay?'

I conceded with what was barely a nod and put down the damp towel on the kitchen worktop.

'I need a rest, okay?' I said. 'A little rest from all this.'

I excused myself from his presence – this man from so long ago, who had just cooked me a meal and cleaned up like a good husband. This man who could appear as anyone, and appear as no one at all. An invisible man.

At the top of the stairs, I considered sleeping by myself – but only for a moment. Hearing Joe moan softly in his sleep, I knew I wanted to be in Tristan's room. Even if he wasn't there. And being near Joe – despite the disfiguration – was still like being near

Jessie. Jessie and Tristan – my true loves, I guessed. So, I crawled onto Tristan's bed, on top of the covers, and fitted into the space Joe had left me…


Urgent whispering woke me.

Xavier's voice.

Opening my eyes quickly, I was alarmed to find him looming over me.

'What?' I cried, shaken.

'I don't know exactly. Saw something from the window that I didn't like. That I don't think you'll like, either.'

'What?' I asked – same words, different question.

'Monty Harrison just went by and he had Esther with him. Heading towards the Cadley place.'

Augustus' house – Xavier's father's house. A connection we hadn't discussed yet.

'Safe to leave him for a bit?' Xavier asked, indicating Joe, revealing he intended us to follow my sister and the man who'd mutilated her husband.

My worry for Joe was only momentary. What if he had another fit? What if we left him and the next attack was worse – fatal? Then again, he'd survived in this state for many years – in the care of Monty Harrison.

'What do you have in mind?' I asked, in the first floor hallway a few minutes later. I was pulling on my protective gear without even a thought.

Guy A Johnson

We took my small wooden boat down to Augustus' house, where a small speedboat was moored – Monty's. As I secured my boat, Xavier leaped onto the other one and checked it over.

'No one on it and he's even left the keys in,' he whispered, stepping back in our boat for a second. 'You know how to drive one of those?'

'I've driven Jessie's before.'

'Okay, take these.'

He handed me a set of keys.

'What are you going to do?'

'I'm going in,' he explained, voice still low. 'Wait in his boat. You hear anyone coming out, you start the engine up. And if it's Monty – even if he's with someone else you know, you drive off. Got it?'

'Xavier-.' I went to protest.

'You have to trust me. I'll be able to get in there without them seeing me. And if they do, I'll make sure they see someone else. But whatever happens, I'll help with whatever's going on. Just wait for me here, okay?'

I must have looked unresponsive, because he quickly – urgently – repeated himself:

'Agnes, okay?'

'Okay,' I answered and did as I was bid.


It felt like forever before he returned. And although the night was still – hardly a sound in the air – I couldn't hear anything inside. Not a shout or a bump or anything.

'What happened?' I asked, when Xavier eventually reappeared, alone.

91

Guy A Johnson

'They've gone under the city,' he answered.

'What?' I asked, perplexed.

'Esther, Billy, another girl who's with them and the old man.'

'Augustus?'

I caught his eye when I said this and he knew what I was trying to convey: that I knew their connection.

'Yes. Augustus,' he answered. 'There's a secret room under this house and it leads to an underground network of tunnels.'

'A network of tunnels?' I repeated, revealing my disbelief, wondering how he knew all this – what exactly had he seen and heard while he'd been in the house. 'If there is such a thing, won't they be flooded?'

Xavier shook his head.

'It leads to part of an old underground train network – long forgotten and most of it's buried. Some people know about it – not many. But *he* does.' He meant Augustus – his father. 'But it's water tight.'

As I digested this information, an obvious question sprung to mind.

'And Monty Harrison?'

'Disabled,' Xavier answered, after a thoughtful pause. 'The old man and I managed some impressive moves between us.'

We shared another knowing look.

'My old man,' he said, finally acknowledging the link. 'He told you everything, then?'

'Yes.'

Guy A Johnson

'But Elinor doesn't know about him?'

I shook my head.

'So, Xavier – should we follow them?'

It was his turn to shake his head.

'No, we've got other business to do, if we're going to find Ronan,' he said, pointing to my right hand – where I was holding the keys to the speedboat. 'I think we should follow his final footsteps – so we're going to check out Monty's place…'

*Unfold*

*Esther*

*I want to tell you about the dogs.*

*You may have been led to believe they were a trick of evolution – an unnecessary evil that was set upon this earth by chance. But that's not the case at all.*

*It all started with good intentions – a few experiments in a laboratory, someone playing God, messing with genetics, just because they can. Then a harebrained scheme that this could lead to some good – create a super-animal, a fighting machine, and use these creatures to control and bring order, discipline and peace to a world increasingly full of crime, violence and chaos.*

*But that was never going to work, was it Esther?*

*This was man's best friend – and it just didn't seem right to turn them into man's worst enemy. And who would control these beasts? What if we needed to reason with them? In the laboratories they seemed like savage killing machines – surely, introduced to the wider world, they'd just wreak havoc?*

*So the program was abandoned – the dogs destroyed and the farms and labs officially closed.*

*But man is curious, Esther – and not everyone in that program was prepared to let go of their project, let go of their baby.*

*And a few not-so-good men set about making sure their dark dreams came true after all…*

*Fold*

Guy A Johnson

5. Tristan


'Jesus!' Jessie cried, as he was pulled down into the mud, hands grabbing both his legs – another person pulling on him, struggling to the surface themselves. Another man? No, a *corpse* my head was telling me – not a person, but a corpse. How could anything still be alive in this thick, airless sludge?

Our guide, Solomon, turned back as my friend went under – so easily, and for a second or so I thought we'd lost him. But his head came back to the surface. And, as he blinked away the wet liquid earth, I saw his eyes in the dimming evening light.

'Can you reach him, Tristan?' Solomon yelled, wading back himself, looking for the map he'd made with his own feet.

Suppressing the panic that fought to rule me, I moved as quickly as I could, careful as I stepped to where Jessie was – so conscious that I could suffer the same fate, that other *corpses* might reach out for me in a vain attempt to return to life.

'Yes, I think I can!' I yelled back, moving as quickly as was possible. As quickly as was safe.

But suddenly the world seemed to move in slow motion – my legs trapped in cement-thick bog – and as fast as I tried to move, the longer it seemed to take me.

Before either Solomon or I could reach him, Jessie was dragged under again by the stranger who was trying to save himself.

'Jessie! JESSIE!' I cried, though I knew merely calling out wouldn't save him – what good could my cries alone possibly do?

Guy A Johnson

Marcus and Solomon seemed to have better luck than me – wading with relative ease through the thick mud – and were somehow at the spot where Jessie had disappeared before me. Delving into the dark pool, elbow deep, they reached in and hauled Jessie to the surface – and with him, they rescued the person who'd dragged him under. Both were pulled to a patch of firmer ground – where they spluttered back to life, coughing up the liquid earth that had sought to swallow them whole. Solomon used some of the water we'd brought with us sparingly – to clear their mouths, nostrils and eyes of the dirt. Used his fingers and dabbed away the external muck – applying it in such a necessary, yet miserly way that I still couldn't easily tell which one of the dirty creatures was Jessie. The darkness didn't help that, either.

It was only when he spoke that I really recognised my friend.

As for the other man – for it *was* a man – I paid him little attention. He was quiet, kept his head down and didn't speak – merely nodding to show us he was still alive, taking the small sips of water Solomon offered him in silence.

I wasn't suspicious, either. Maybe I should've been. But in the darkness, as a skin of mud crusted over his own, I cared little for the stranger, *the corpse*, who'd nearly killed my best friend in order to save himself. I simply felt bitterness towards him – with no interest in who he was at the time.

Once they had recovered sufficiently from their ordeal, the two men came to their feet – the stranger at the rear – and we all continued our journey to that great wall.

As the wall got closer, I could see a way inside – about four or five feet above ground level, there was an opening to a tunnel, blocked by a circular steel door. As we approached, I heard a loud, metallic clunking noise and this round hatch was opened.

I wondered what the next part of our journey would bring. What adventure, what questions – and what risks and terror.

Up very close, a man – hooded, so we couldn't see his face (though it was so dark by then, I'd never have recognised him again in daylight) – up close, a man appeared on the other side and, confident we were the people he was expecting, he reached out with a hand to help the first of us up and in. But he paused, seeing a fifth figure amongst us.

'Came out of the bog,' Solomon explained. 'Bad luck to leave him behind. You've nothing to fear – and the responsibility's all mine.'

Convinced that all was as it should be, the hooded man continued to help each of us climb up into the tunnel. It was a couple of metres in length and we had to crawl along it, but then we were on the other side of the wall. I heard the round steel door close behind us, metal grinding against metal as it was sealed.

The first thing I saw ahead raised more questions – two tiny boats, floating on a shallow river of water.

'I thought the high wall would've kept any water out,' I asked, puzzled.

Inside the main wall was another one – high, but not soaring as much into the heavens as the first. And it was between these two walls that the river road flowed.

'How about we get in,' Solomon suggested, 'then I'll explain. This side of the wall, at this time of the day, we only have the darkness protecting us. We need to get to safety, before it's light.'

'And where *is* safe?' I asked, not for the first time wondering whether we'd made a mistake in entrusting these men with our lives.

'You'll see,' Solomon answered and I swear he smiled, enjoying the mystery and control a little. 'Shall we?' he suggested, indicating the first of the boats.

I nodded – he could answer my questions on the way – and Jessie and I got into a boat with Solomon. The *corpse* – as I was still thinking of him – and Marcus clambered into the second boat and rowed just behind us.

I didn't see what happened to the hooded man who'd let us in, but he stayed behind. Solomon later said that he'd have found his own way in – or that he may even have been waiting to let others in. *We're not the only ones who want to get over the wall, Tristan.*

'So, are you going to explain why a place with such elaborate protection still appears to be flooded?' I asked, as we began to sail along and Jessie added:

'And tell us exactly where we're going?'

'Which question would you like me to answer first, gentlemen?'

When we didn't answer Solomon, he simply chose himself – expelling his tale a sentence at a time, between each pull of the oars.

'The outer wall surrounds the world you've left behind… Goes all the way around it… was built this high to keep out the worst of the floods… The second wall surrounds the city we're headed for… You'll notice the gap between the two widens, the further we go along…'

He took a breath, allowing us both to take this in, before we continued.

'So, this space here,' I began, 'between the two walls, it's…'

Guy A Johnson

'Unchartered territory…' Solomon completed my sentence – then let this new piece of information sink in.

I had an eerie feeling of being exposed and a sudden fear of something coming out of the darkness that was now engulfing us. Jessie's eyes stared across at me, lighting up in the shadows, and I knew he shared my concerns: we'd been misled again.

'It's a vast space… largely uninhabited, as far as I know…' Solomon continued, breaking a temporary silence that had sat between us. 'But we'll be fine… I've done this before…'

'You have?'

'Yes, I have… We'll just follow this river road around the wall that protects the city…'

'And what's protecting us again?' Jessie asked, but Solomon didn't answer.

Instead, he restarted his explanation of the new world we were approaching.

'And when they first came… the people in the city were thankful for the height of the walls…' He stared up at the sky-high brick creations that hemmed us in. 'This space here serves the people in two ways…,' he said, meaning the river road we were sailing along. 'One, as an overflow… If the waters breach the first wall…. They'll all be protected by the second… They'll have time to think… Time to escape…'

'To where?' I asked, wondering if there was another place – a higher ground to escape to. I couldn't imagine a city of protected people taking their chances in the unchartered landscape we were temporarily in – and no one with even a small amount of sense would head back to where *we'd* come from.

99

Guy A Johnson

'As far as I know…' Solomon managed, a little breathy, as he continued to row and speak at the same time, 'as far as I know, there is no… second option or escape plan… But it's made people feel safer… A little story spread around to keep out the fears… to squash the doubts…'

'And the second reason?'

'Ah…' he answered, drawing his arms and the oars back, 'well, a city needs to drink… needs to wash… so, it was built to let a little in… comes direct from the source we sailed across… delivered through a system of pipes hidden beneath the sea of death that we just came through…'

*Sea of death* – that, I later learned, was the local term for the cesspool that we'd risked our lives crossing. A natural mechanism that kept out the riff-raff.

'And this narrow river surrounds the city… Supplying the entire population… No detail was… left out when…. they built this place…'

'Want me to take those for a bit?' I offered, realising that Solomon was out-of-breath – tiring and slowing up too.

He nodded, accepting the offer and we swapped places. I noticed the corpse was rowing the second boat, but had his back to me and it prompted me to check on Jessie, who'd closed his eyes.

'I'm fine,' he murmured when I nudged him, and I left him to his apparent slumber.

'So,' I asked, getting into a rhythm with the oars, 'where is this little sailing trip taking us?'

'Border control.'

'Border control?'

Guy A Johnson

'You didn't think there'd be security checks this way? It might not be the main entrance – and it might not be a very well-known way to get in, but as you saw' – he indicated the boat behind us and the corpse who was rowing it – 'there's still traffic that comes this way. But don't worry,' he reassured me, 'the right security guards are on tonight, if you follow?'

I followed.

It was another thirty minutes or more before we reached *border control* – a long, monotonous ride along that river road, hemmed in by the plain, high walls. But as Solomon had explained, the gap between them grew – as did my fears about just what might be out there in that vast *unchartered territory*. Solomon made this journey easier, though, as he explained more about the city I was about to enter.

'The second wall stretches for miles and miles, enclosing the city. The main way in is heavily protected – and it's not easy to get in and out. You'll get to see that eventually, I'm sure. But the city itself,' he continued, before I could quiz him for more details about that *main way in* – and its doubtless elaborate security procedures, 'it'll surprise you. How modern, how clean.'

'For the elite?' I questioned, hoping to elicit a response that might indicate where he stood politically.

'For the chosen,' he answered, with an undertone of bitterness that satisfied me enough. I assumed Solomon was a paid man – that he wasn't on some crazy, voluntary mission like Jessie and me – but maybe he was a man to trust.

*Just as well,* I considered – glancing up at the walls, in equal awe and fear of their scale – as we were now completely at his mercy.

101

Guy A Johnson

'You'll see that from the off,' Solomon continued. 'Once you see inside the city, you'll wonder if the shortages and poverty you've seen beyond the wall actually ever existed. You'll question how that could possibly be.'

'And it's been here all along?'

'Planned for a long time by the authorities. Meticulously planned and kept secret, Tristan. Like so many things. The ultimate survival of the...'

He dropped the word *fittest* – it wasn't quite right. *Richest? Cruellest? Most powerful?* One of those described it better.

'The very people who were supposed to look after our interests...'

'Just looking after their own.' Solomon finished and gave me a straight smile. 'Basic human nature.'

'How'd they get away with it?' I asked, accepting his last observation some way – for *some* humans, maybe.

'By telling only those they knew who were selfish enough and greedy enough to go along with it. By using their power to keep the poverty out – amazing just how disabling ignorance and poverty are. You only know because you've been trusted, brought in. From the very beginning, the politicians, the scientists, the builders.' He pointed to the city wall again. 'They were promised the world – this world – for their help and silence.'

'And if they broke that silence?'

'Consequences.'

Solomon held my eye after that single word and I felt its weight. I'd been subjected to those *consequences* in their infancy – subjected to the punishments as they'd been invented, when I'd been taken alongside my adversary, Xavier Riley.

'He's risking a lot you know,' he added, referring to our absent mutual friend, Nathaniel. 'How'd he convince you two to come on board?'

'I'm not sure he did,' I answered and Solomon laughed lightly in response. 'What about you?'

'Me?' Solomon asked in a question, like he didn't understand.

So, I set my enquiry out explicitly:

'How'd he get you on board?'

'I've been *on board* as long as I can remember,' he began his answer. 'Wasn't one of the taken, before you ask. Just a little too young for all that. But I had moral parents – *suspicious* parents, who told me who to trust in life and not to be swayed by greed. To think of others. They went missing one night. Just like that.' He snapped his fingers, indicating a trick of magic. 'No trace.'

'You gone looking?'

'No trace,' he repeated, firmer. 'So I had to fend for myself. I was nineteen and got myself the first job I could. Working for another mutual acquaintance.' He drew the word out – *ac-quain-tance.* I pulled a puzzled expression. 'Monty Harrison, a man I believe you know,' he offered, quickly continuing with: 'I know, you're probably thinking I ignored all that wholesome advice from my parents? Well, I didn't really understand Monty's business to start with. He was after security – someone on his grounds, around his home, to keep an eye on things. I just took the job – needed to keep a roof over my head – and didn't question why this man would need protecting. Eventually, he had a young niece come live with him, and I was there to protect her too. And I'd been sheltered from his

Guy A Johnson

reputation. But once on the inside, I quickly learned what kind of a man he was. Saw how cruel he was to those who didn't go along with what he wanted, didn't bend to his will.'

Solomon took a deep in-take of breath here.

'He was a man down for a short while, so had me go out on his extortion rounds – collecting *protection rent,* as he called it, from local businesses. This was before the flooding – before many of those independent companies went under in a very different way. One place we went to sticks in my head. A shop, west of the old city – you know where I mean, where all those smaller, family-owned businesses used to thrive.'

I did – and I was slightly bemused by his reference to the *old city* – telling me he'd left it behind long ago. That *his* city was now the one we were heading into – the protected promised land.

'An older couple owned it. The shop. Proud. A beautifully kept boutique they owned. There was a sadness about them – I picked up on it instantly. Loss, like a sad, low glow all about them.'

Another pause in the tale – Solomon was finding this one hard to recount.

'They refused to pay their *rent,*' he eventually continued, spitting the last word with evident disgust. 'I was there with two other heavies. Being new, they insisted that I delivered the consequences – were explicit about what that entailed. So I smacked the woman about the face – hit her six times, broke a tooth and covered her face and my hand in her blood. One of my *colleagues*' – another word delivered slowly, with bitterness – 'cracked open their cash register and emptied it. Told them we'd be back the following week and that their *rent* would be double.'

Guy A Johnson

'You follow up that promise?' I asked, trying to keep my own anger and judgement out of the question.

Solomon nodded shamefully.

'But they'd given up the ghost. Locked up their shop – had a heavy metal door fitted across the entrance and locked it up with chains and padlocks. The others saw defiance in this and threatened to set the place alight, so I talked them down and they just did a bit of damage to a few of the windows in the end. But I saw something else in that response – I saw two people giving up on all they had. A dream, a life's work – an ambition almost fulfilled and then destroyed by Monty Harrison's cruel greed. By my hand too.'

I was pretty certain I knew the shop he was describing – hadn't Jessie and I come across such a place while sweeping the city for Elinor? And hadn't I seen a face in its attic window? Just a glimpse, if I remembered correctly. If it was the same place, that heavy metal door might not have been in place to just keep Monty out, but to keep something else – *someone* else – in.

'We've all done things we regret,' I said.

'So when one of Nathaniel's men approached me,' Solomon quickly continued, desperate to get to his retribution, 'I didn't give getting involved a second thought.'

'I'm sure you didn't,' I answered, surprised at how deeply affected this man had been by his experiences.

My life to date had been full of good and bad – most of which was my own making – but I'd always learned and moved on. The only looking back I'd done had been in aid of finding out about Albert, my father.

Guy A Johnson

Thinking of him reminded me once again just how far Jessie and I had drifted from our original mission. Reminded me also of what Nathaniel had claimed: *I thought that you'd already found him.* Not that it had really left my thoughts – there just hadn't been a chance to go back to it properly.

'So were you a man on the inside?' I questioned, getting back to our conversation.

'Yes I was – for a while.'

'Just a while?'

'Shrewd old Monty got suspicious. Questioned me about some unexplained absences – didn't like my cover story about visiting an ill relative. *You've never mentioned this uncle before,* he questioned one time – so I snuck out that same night. I've seen what Monty does to his enemies – seen what he does to men who betray him. I wasn't hanging around for a chance of that.'

'Where did you go?'

'Here. To this city. I had a way of getting to Nathaniel if I found myself in need, and he came to my aid. Snuck me in and I've been working for him ever since.'

'Undercover, though?'

'Yeah, but it feels better working amongst the good guys.'

'And are you?'

'Working with the good guys? I think so, yes,' Solomon answered – his *think* not so much showing doubt, but letting me know there was never complete certainty. 'You okay back there?'

He'd turned his head and called out to the second boat that was bringing Marcus and the corpse along. I hadn't paid them much attention while rowing, but noticed then that the

106

Guy A Johnson

gap between our boats had widened. The corpse had his back to us, but he was still rowing and he waved – to indicate he'd heard, to show us that all was fine.

'We're almost there,' Solomon called again, informing us all, 'just around the corner.'

And he was true to his word – about another two or three minutes along the curve of the city wall and we reached a point in the river road where Solomon indicated that we should stop. But our next move was not obvious.

'I take it you've got a good explanation?' Jessie questioned, staring ahead to where the river road simply continued and then looking up, where the wall around the city soared.

'Is this the border control point?' I asked, equally perplexed – a little panic returning in my voice. There was no obvious way in – had we been misled yet again?

'They'll be along in a minute. We just need to wait here,' Solomon answered, but he appeared distracted, looking back along the river, squinting at the darkness.

'What is it?'

'We've lost them – I can't see Marcus and the other guy,' he said, reaching into the boat, retrieving a torch from his belongings. 'Emergencies only,' he added, when I frowned at this sudden appearance – we could've used it before then. He shone the beam across the water, lighting up its ripples. 'Can't see it. Where are they? I don't like this at all.'

'You don't like it?' Jessie replied, and I sensed fear in my friend's tone as well.

'I shouldn't have...' Solomon mumbled, flickering the light around. Then he sighed with deep relief, as the other boat finally came back into view. 'Thank God for that,' he said, momentarily pleased by this sight – but that pleasure was short-lived.

Guy A Johnson

As the boat slowly got closer, we realised two worrying things: it wasn't being rowed, it was drifting; and there was only one passenger remaining.

'Marcus?' Solomon inquired, as the little wooden vessel was almost upon us. 'Marcus?!' he repeated, with more urgency when it eventually bumped against us.

Jessie – having rested for the ride along the river road – pulled himself up. Steadying himself, he stepped into the other boat and checked Marcus out.

The stranger – the *corpse* – had gone, but not before causing Marcus some serious harm.

'He's dead – looks like his neck is broken,' Jessie reported, solemnly.

'Shit,' Solomon cried, instant grief and panic in his voice. 'Shit, shit, shit! I let that happen. I took that risk! Shit, oh god, oh shit! What was I thinking? I didn't even check him out! Shit!'

'Solomon,' I said, keeping my voice calm, raising it enough to get his attention. 'We can't stay here. We need to move. We don't know where that other man might be – or why he's done this.'

I looked out into the darkness – into the vast no-man's-land between the two walls that was inhabited by who-knows-what.

'Solomon, I'm sorry about your friend, but we need you to stay focussed – and we need to keep moving.'

It was enough to get his attention – and he nodded in reply, regaining his composure, although his shock was still evident.

'And we need to carry on with what we were doing. We need to get into the city – yes? And you need to show us how.'

Guy A Johnson

Another nod from Solomon. Then he wiped his eyes, shook his head – as if to temporarily shake off some of what had happened.

'They'll be here in a minute. To help us over. But we'll not be able to take Marcus. We'll have to leave him here.' He paused – a wave of emotion about to swallow him up, but he managed to suppress it.

'Help us over?'

'Yes,' he answered and then *they* appeared – on the very top of the wall. A single flash of a torch beam pin-pointing their position.

There were three of them – shadows in the dark, working in silence. Even their equipment was quiet – an endless ladder rope that we didn't see until it nearly reached us. They rolled it over the edge of the wall, and it hung down like a mane of matted, flaxen hair. Like something from an ancient fairytale.

'You gotta be kidding.'

This was out of Jessie's mouth before he had a chance to consider how thoughtless it might have sounded – given what had just happened and how Solomon had rallied.

'This is *border control*?' I asked – knowing too that I should be focussing on our companion's abrupt loss, on the danger posed now there was a killer in our midst, lost in the water. Or lost in the unknown dark.

'There is no border control as such. I was just playing with you – but there is no other way in for you. If I'd told you before *how* I was going to get you in,' Solomon managed, shaking his head as his eyes rested on his dead friend again. 'If I'd told you before, you'd never have come.'

That was becoming a familiar answer.

Guy A Johnson

'And it's the only way in?'

'It's the only way *you'll* get in.'

I paused, thinking. This man needed time to grieve, time to take in what had just happened – but there wasn't any. A cruel reality we couldn't do a thing about.

'And Marcus – your friend. We leave him here?'

A nod in the dark.

'I'm sorry,' I said, grabbing the top of his arm, squeezing softly.

'Thank you,' he answered, before breathing in deeply – steeling himself for the next hurdle in our journey. 'We must go, Tristan. Jessie – we can't stall any longer. It's too dangerous. For us and for them.' He looked up – at the three shadow men on the very top of that wall. 'They're putting themselves at risk for us too.'

'How high is it exactly?' Jessie asked, and I heard the fear in his voice.

More things to fear at every turn.

'Best you don't know,' Solomon answered. He took another look back at the body in the boat, nodded his friend a silent goodbye – and then turned back to where the rope ladder was dangling. 'Okay – who's first?'

Guy A Johnson

*Unfold*

*About those scientists and their killer dogs?*

*Well, the experiments continued – the genetic meddling, the mutations and the testing. In secret laboratories. Secret to the gullible public, at least.*

*Was this known within the government?*

*Yes and no.*

*The 'no' will apply to the majority – although many suspected, they just turned away, what they didn't know… But a few knew for certain. Some believed there was still justification in releasing those beasts on the unsuspecting public. Our world is over-populated and under-resourced. What an easy solution – release the dogs and allow a natural reduction to occur. A natural selection.*

*So that's what happened, Esther – a small group of mad men decided to set a few hundred of those killers free. And we know what happened next – years of fear. A reign of canine terror.*

*But others had a different plan – others knew there was money to be made here.*

*And that's where I come in, Esther.*

*See, I made killer dogs my business – made them my ticket to a fortune…*

*Fold*

Guy A Johnson

6. Billy

Like before, the creature was cautious about entering the carriage. Shy of us, almost.

'I wonder if we've got anything amongst all this stuff he'd like,' Augustus said, crouching down to the dog's level, reaching out to a couple of the tins of food that had dropped on the floor.

*He* – announced in Augustus' benevolent, easy tone. Not *it*.

I looked over to the others – to read their faces. Marcie looked terrified – stone-still with fear. But in Otterley's pale, thin features I saw something different now – curiosity.

*Should we not be frightened?* I questioned in my head, putting it at the front of my thoughts – looking directly at her, testing her apparent abilities to mind-read.

Her eyes flicked up to mine and she shook her head – there was no need to be afraid.

*How can you be certain?*

'Because it's domestic,' she said, quietly.

'It certainly is, Otterley,' Augustus joined-in. 'There's no need to be afraid of this one. So how did you get this far down, boy?'

'How do you know?'

'What?'

'How do you know it's okay?' I confirmed. 'And that it's a boy?'

Augustus chuckled lightly.

'Well, I'm guessing it's a boy – but I can easily check. As for it being tame, I've seen them before. Just check its eyes – no hate in there. And the bad ones, they're bigger.

112

Guy A Johnson

They're programmed to snarl and bare their teeth at the smell and sight of humans. But this one...' His voice faded and he edged towards the dog, holding out a hand, rubbing his fingers as a kind of welcoming.

Despite Augustus' words and his own confidence, I was still petrified. I'd let him test his theories before I relaxed and let down my guard.

'How did you get here, boy? And who around here would own a pet dog, eh?'

*A pet dog* – I'd never heard such a thing. An alien thought, but it made me think of the puppy my father had brought home. And thinking of Father made me think of Mother. I felt my anger rise up at Augustus – there he was, putting us in danger again.

'You can't help yourself, can you?!' I cried, the words out before I'd barely thought them. And then I stood up, grabbed one of the tins of food and hurled it at our canine intruder.

'Billy!' Augustus roared in reaction, as the creature scarpered back into the dark tunnel.

And then he went back after it. I heard him cooing at it, coaxing it back from wherever it had hidden.

'Come on... That's it, boy... Nothing to be afraid of... That's it... Over here.'

I checked the others again – Marcie still hadn't moved an inch, but Otterley was scowling in my direction. And I felt a little shame, despite the fact my actions had been reasonable.

'They killed my mother,' I snarled at her. 'They nearly killed us all – only she gave her life!'

Otterley dropped her scowl.

113

Guy A Johnson

'No need to thank me,' I added, looking at my feet, quickly looking up again, as Augustus re-entered – with the damn thing in his arms.

I was too angry to protest – too fearful that my emotions would overspill, that I'd lose control of them altogether.

'We'll talk in a moment,' was all Augustus said, and then he walked away – down the aisle of the carriage, towards the next one.

I watched him till he disappeared from view. He returned two or three minutes later, without the dog, and took a seat next to me.

I turned my eyes to my lap, determined not to listen to him. Determined not to believe a word of what he said to me.

'I know you don't want to listen to me, Billy. And I know you're trying your very best not to trust me – not to think of me as your friend, as someone on your side anymore. But I am, Billy – and always will be.

'I did take you all to Monty's house and that did lead us into danger – but I had no reason to believe he'd have packs of those vile animals in his grounds. No notion of what would happen to…'

His voice trailed away here and I heard a sniff. From the corner of my eyes, I saw him wipe his own. But I kept my focus and didn't look at him directly.

'But I've since led us back out and found us shelter and food. Even got this old train running. So, if you dared look at the facts, you'd know I'm not the enemy. That I'm not quite the old fool you're telling yourself I am.

'And I've brought a very special girl with us.'

I flicked my gaze up and saw Otterley looking at me.

'Yes, I know that you know this. That you've worked out – like I have – that there's something a little different about our friend. And I think you know that we had to have her with us. That maybe, just maybe she might be the key to something – the key to saving us.

'And many of us deserve saving, Billy. Many of us are innocent.'

He raised a hand and pointed a finger down the aisle of the carriage.

'Just like that little fella. Lost, alone – innocent of what is going on. He's a sign of hope, you know.'

'Hope?' I asked, still doing my very best to hang onto my hate, my anger, but relenting a small amount all the same.

'Yes, hope that not everything is lost.'

'But you said he *was* lost.'

A small chuckle from Augustus.

'Yes, but the goodness in that creature – which has been eradicated in so many of his species – is still there. That's worth celebrating, Billy. That's something worth keeping.'

'So we're keeping him?' I asked, looking up at Otterley again, at Marcie, who was listening intently, but still looking scared.

'I think we should,' Augustus replied, pausing, thinking for a moment. 'I think he'd be good for us – this symbol of hope. But we all have to be agreed – I won't make you keep his company if we aren't all happy with that. Why don't we vote on it?'

It was still in the carriage for a minute. All quiet. And in that quiet, I sought out sounds that were further away. One in particular – a feint yelping and scratching sound that could only be the dog.

Guy A Johnson

'Okay,' I eventually conceded. 'But you go first, Augustus.'

He nodded in agreement.

'Well, I vote *yes* then.'

I looked ahead.

*Otterley?* I thought, testing her again – and she smiled at this.

'Yes,' she said, aloud.

Marcie remained stock still, staring at me – she was waiting to see which way I swayed.

'And it's got to be a full vote of yesses – right? Not a majority, but unanimous. Everyone has to agree – or the thing has to go?'

'Everyone, yes,' Augustus agreed, but he knew what I was doing.

He knew that I was giving the most terrified amongst us the power to decide.

'Then I vote *yes* as well,' I said. 'So, Marcie – it looks like the decision is all yours.'

And we all looked in her direction.

'Does he stay – or does he go?'


When Augustus claimed he'd got the train running again, it wasn't an empty claim. And it wasn't that he'd just got the lights and the heat going – he'd started up its engine too.

'I can't really claim any glory,' he said to me, almost in a confession. 'This machine was in perfect working order – despite the fact it's probably not been touched for decades, maybe even longer. It's like it's been perfectly preserved down here – there's a bit of rust and a lot of dirt on the outside. But on the inside, it's healthy. And clean – very clean.'

116

Guy A Johnson

'And there's a power source here too?' I said, keeping my enthusiasm muted.

We were both up at the very front of the train – in a cramped compartment that was equipped with all the mechanics to get the thing moving. There was a single, padded seat for the driver – which I took – and Augustus stood behind, leaning over my left shoulder.

'Yes,' he answered, but there was surprise in his voice – like he couldn't quite believe it. 'It's definitely connected to a live source. I wonder...' And he was lost in his thoughts again.

'What?' I asked. 'What do you wonder?'

'Whether this machine is working so well, because it's been kept in use after all.'

'But it's underground – and we got in through a secret way. No one could get down here easily – and why would they need to use it? And shouldn't it all have been cut off years ago anyway – to save energy?'

Augustus nodded, as if agreeing with all my protests. He thought for several seconds before giving me an answer.

'Yes, we did, but we came *that* way,' he said, throwing a thumb over his shoulder to indicate the direction we'd come. 'But we don't know what's up ahead, or to the left or right.'

I gave him a quizzical look.

'You didn't think there would just be one long tunnel, did you? It'll be like a maze, going off in all directions. There'll be junctions and cross overs, no doubt. Just like-.'

'On the model railway,' I interrupted, joining him in that memory. Letting him know I was forgiving him – just a little bit.

117

'And you don't imagine our friend found his way in here via a secret tunnel with a locked door, do you?'

I looked left and down, at the creature who was sitting patiently on the floor – looking up with big, brown eyes whenever I glanced his way, expectant of something.

'He's hungry, but not starving. So, he got in here and not *that* long ago.'

'What does the map say?'

Augustus and Mother had brought together two halves of a map that marked out all the hidden entrances to the underground tunnels. *Including one under our house,* Mother told me – although she'd not found it before we'd left our house behind.

Augustus let out a short huff.

'We fell off the map a long time ago, Billy. I checked it when we came across that first station, just in case, but none of these tunnels or tracks are marked on it. So we're on our own here. Completely in the dark.'

'Not completely,' I said, indicating a small bright light above our heads.

'No, not completely,' he echoed, smiling at me and we both sensed a little of what we'd lost coming back.

'So what's your plan?'

'Plan?' Augustus answered, throwing part of my question back at me. 'You think I have a plan?'

He paused – reading my face to see if his flippant tone was a little too flimsy. Judging it wasn't, he carried on.

'No plan, Billy – but I have a few ideas. Maybe we should head back to the others. Talk through what we do next?'

Guy A Johnson

I agreed with a nod and stood up from the driver's seat. As I did, our new companion looked up hopefully, stood and wagged his tail. Augustus was right – this creature wasn't like the others we'd encountered. It was harmless, timid – although it shared some of the features of its ferocious relatives. And even though its jaw was small, I still feared the sharpness of its teeth and the hard, relentless clamp of its bite.

'You'll have to stay here,' I told it, as Augustus opened the door to the carriage behind us. 'We promised Marcie, after all,' I added – but it continued to thrash its tail about excitedly.

That was the deal – Marcie voted *yes,* but only because we agreed to keep the tiny beast in another part of the train. 'Thought you said these things were intelligent?'

'They are,' Augustus said, letting me out, shutting the door behind. We heard a muffled whimpering once it was closed. 'They just don't speak our language, but they can be trained to do many things.'

'Like kill?' I asked, still testing him on occasion.

'Kill. Fetch. Roll over. Guard. Protect. Many things, Billy. He wasn't known as man's best friend for so long without reason.'

'Hard to see it now though, isn't it?' I questioned, my tone soured.

'Yes,' Augustus conceded. 'Yes it is. Usually.' He nodded at our friend, when he expelled that last word.

As well as the small driver's compartment, there were four carriages in total. It was in the third carriage along that Augustus had found the tinned food; there were five boxes in total.

119

Guy A Johnson

'No dust, no rust and hardly damp,' he explained, touching the boxes and their contents as he spoke.

'What does that mean?' I asked, not clear on his point.

'If these had been down here any length of time, Billy, I'd have expected some kind of decay – even very slight. But there isn't and that suggests-.'

'It hasn't been here long? That someone brought it recently?' I questioned, jumping ahead.

'Maybe.'

He thought for a minute, wondering whether to share more with me.

'None of it quite adds up, though. If this was being used by someone, why leave it here in the tunnel?'

'Maybe it broke down?' I suggested, but the instant the words left my mouth, I realised that couldn't be the reason.

'But it appears in perfect working order,' Augustus answered, confirming my error.

'If that's the case, it doesn't make sense. Why would you leave it abandoned here – especially with the food? Why would you do that? Do you think…?'

My question petered away.

'What?' Augustus asked, reading a flash of fear in my face.

'What if they were chased away? Hounded way?' I tipped my head back towards the driver's compartment. To the sound of scratching and whining.

Augustus shook his head, softly.

'If there were any true beasts down here, we'd have encountered them by now,' he said. '*He'd* have encountered them too – and not lived to tell the tale, either.'

120

Guy A Johnson

'They'd kill one of their own?' I asked.

'They kill *anything* – and don't be fooled into thinking that the poor fella back there is *one of their own*. Far from it.'

I huffed out a sigh – confounded by our mystery.

'Then why leave the train here – in perfect working order and with supplies?'

Augustus grinned suddenly, like a light had gone on in his head. His smile was child-like, almost out of place in the dark, enclosed space we'd found ourselves – but it still drew me in.

'What? What is it?'

'Us,' he answered, mystifyingly.

'Us?' I repeated, corrugating my forehead.

'Yes, Billy, us,' he said – and I wondered if I'd ever get a clearer explanation. I did. 'What if they left it for us, Billy?'

I was no less puzzled by this answer.

'How would they know we were coming?' I asked, but he simply shrugged.

'It's not a bad theory, though, is it? Apart from the question you just raised. Yes – how would they know?'

*Whoever they are,* I thought to myself, but I kept that inside – Augustus seemed pleased with himself and I didn't want to destroy his enthusiasm by raising too many questions, revealing too many flaws in his theory.

'Who knew we were coming?'

*No one.*

Guy A Johnson

'And why would they want us to get in the train – to wait here, wait to be rescued, or to drive it on?'

*Or to stop us going any further – to trap us?*

'And just where did that creature come from?'

*From a killer pack, Augustus. It's just a trick – it'll turn on us any second and the rest of its breed will descend. It'll be carnage!*

'What?' Augustus asked – and I realised a few words must've come out without me realising.

'I don't know, Augustus. I can't answer any of your questions. You really think someone left this here for us?'

Another shrug, but he gave me an answer of sorts.

'The only thing we do know is that it *is* here for us. It works and there's enough food to last... Well, there's enough food. And we can't go back, Billy. We can only go forward.'

'In this thing?' I questioned.

'Yes, Billy – I'm suggesting we go forward in the train. So in the spirit of democracy...'

I finished his statement for him.

'We talk to the others and put it to the vote?'

He nodded.

'Very sensible, Billy. Very fair.'

And with that, we headed down the remaining carriages back to Otterley and Marcie.

Guy A Johnson

The vote wasn't unanimous this time, but only because Marcie didn't want to decide – she just left it up to the three of us and Augustus said that was fine. That it was a lot to put on young shoulders. She annoyed me a little – Tilly and Elinor would've stood up and been counted. But I guess it wasn't her fault she wasn't one of them.

*Try not to be too hard on her,* Otterley said, planting the words directly into my head – so that only I heard them.

*That's a great trick,* I thought, staring into her gaze. *Like whispering but no one will ever overhear.*

*Someone might,* she answered, but I let this odd comment go, as Augustus was demanding my attention.

'Right Billy,' he said, standing up. 'Time to get this machine on the move!'


It was decided that Augustus needed to take the controls – but that I'd ride up front as his *right-hand man.* Which meant I was also in charge of making sure the dog kept still.

'You might also have to take it outside for it to do its business if we make any stops,' he told me – a statement that he had to explain as it made little sense to me. 'Might not be a bad idea to do this ourselves – go out in pairs.'

Otterley and Marcie didn't mind me being up in the driver's box – Marcie was happy for others to take the responsibility and Otterley was completely unfazed.

So once everyone – including the dog – had *done their business* (Augustus' words) my old friend and I made our way back to the driver's compartment and set about getting the train moving.

Guy A Johnson

It wasn't entirely clear how Augustus got the engine going again. He seemed to fiddle about underneath the control dashboard and called this technique *hot wiring.* It was a bit hit and miss and took several attempts before the train hummed back to life. And it seemed that all the time he'd spent tinkering with old machines at his house had finally paid off.

'Right, here we go,' he said, as the train rumbled. 'I'm not entirely sure what *all* of these switches and buttons do – but I've got a pretty good idea about most of them. We'll take it slowly just in case I need to stop, or I press the wrong thing. Or something else decides to come the other way, towards us!' He winked at me when he said this, showing me it was a joke – but part of me did fear that it might just happen.

'You driven one of these before?' I asked, surprised he was so assured about what he was doing.

'No but I worked on machines like this a long time ago. Fixed them up! In another life…' He winked again, enjoying the mystery he was creating about himself. 'Now, let's try turning that up…'

He reached out to a dial and twisted it clockwise – instantly filling the room with a hissing sound that came from speakers hidden above us.

I put my hands to my ears to block out the sound and even the dog seemed a little distressed.

'I'll turn it down,' Augustus offered, before explaining: 'but it's best we keep it on. In case we get a signal.'

'A signal?'

Guy A Johnson

'I'm assuming it's the way the control centre used to contact its drivers. So it's a way of getting any messages to us. I'll leave it on, in case we pick anything up.'

Once the hissing was reduced, it was bearable and after a while I forgot about it.

'Do you really know what you're doing?' I checked, as the vehicle began to move, picking up a little more speed than I'd expected. In my head, I could already imagine the lights of another train coming towards us and Augustus panicking, as he fussed with the wires under the dashboard – unable to get them to disconnect. Or worse – he disconnected us, plunged us into darkness and an on-coming train crashed into us all the same.

What had he said? *I worked on machines like this a long time ago. Fixed them up!* He hadn't said he'd been a driver though – nothing close to it.

*Have faith. He won't crash it. He'll keep us safe.*

Otterley – reading my thoughts and dropping her own into my head, even though we were a distance from each other – in different carriages. I wasn't sure if I was disturbed or impressed.

*What if I don't want you listening in?* I thought back and she answered quickly.

*Fair enough. I won't.*

And I didn't hear her in my head again for a while.

'What you thinking?' Augustus asked, noticing my introspective gaze.

*I'm wondering if you'll lead us into danger again.*

'Just about Otterley. She's a bit different,' I said, keeping my thoughts as just that – thoughts. 'How do you know her?'

'I don't. Not really. I tried to rescue her once. From a place where they took children – you know all about the takings, don't you? A long time ago, though – and Monty Harrison

125

got to her. Stole her away, I guess is the best way to put it. Yes – stole her away,' he said, satisfied, eyes out front again, squinting into the darkness ahead of us.

'A long time ago?' I questioned, thinking this an odd statement. 'How old was she then?'

And then he gave me the oddest answer – and the widest grin accompanied it, showing he enjoyed its peculiarity, its impossibility.

'Same age she is now, Billy.'

'What do you mean?' I asked, perplexed, but somehow certain he was telling the truth – at least as he knew it.

'Exactly that. She looks exactly the same age as she did when I last saw her – and that was many years ago. I can't explain it – at least, I can't yet. And I don't know why she was so precious to Monty Harrison – why he had to have her, why he kept her locked away, wired up to machines all these years. She's clearly fine without all that fuss.'

'Wired up?' I repeated, wondering what I'd missed – something back at Monty's house, perhaps, when Mother and Augustus had left us in a bedroom.

'I said she was special, didn't I? And I just know she's the key to something – I just haven't found what to yet.'

'She can read minds,' I told him – thinking this revelation might help inspire him, but he didn't seem to hear me, instantly distracted by something else.

'What have we here then?' he questioned to himself and I felt the train slow, as Augustus fiddled with the controls. 'See, up ahead Billy. Which way do you think this thing'll take us?'

126

Guy A Johnson

'What?' I said, looking through the window, trying to make out what Augustus had seen up ahead.

'Which way do you think we'll go?' he repeated, as everything became clear. 'And quickly – before the moment has gone and it's too late. What do you think, Billy?'

We were heading towards a split in the tunnel, with the track running off left and right.

'I don't know!' I said, unreasonably panicked by the sudden responsibility.

'It's almost upon us, son – can't leave it much longer!' Augustus continued, his boyish tone suggesting he was enjoying the drama and excitement. 'What's it to be? Which way does our future lie?'

*Otterley!?*

*Left, Billy – tell him left.*

'Left!' I cried, and Augustus laughed out loud, enjoying game of it – laughing louder when it turned out I was correct. That Otterley was correct.

'Left indeed, young Billy. So let's see where this takes us!' the old man cried out, his mood still light, as if the game had relaxed him a little. He reached out to the dog and ruffled its head – which prompted it to stand and yelp playfully, wagging that skinny tail.

*It's where we're supposed to go, Billy. It's all happening the way it should. And we'll be safe.*

Otterley – back in my head, but I was okay with that, as I'd asked her in.

*Good,* I thought back, reassured by her weird talents, perplexed by so many things about her that didn't make sense.

127

Maybe Augustus had got it wrong about her age? Maybe he'd rescued a child that had simply looked like her. I'd *think* that question at her later, I told myself. Once we'd got to wherever we were heading.

But until we did, I decided to keep my eyes on the road ahead – watching out for shadows in the darkness, just as Augustus had.

'Two pairs of eyes are better than one,' he said to me, once he realised what I was doing. 'Might even let you have a go at driving the thing in a bit,' he added, giving me a friendly wink.

We were definitely back to where we had been – two friends at opposite ends of the age spectrum. I considered pulling my protective sulk about me again, but I'd punished Augustus enough. And I needed this friendship, much more than I needed my anger.

We continued in quiet harmony for some time – side-by-side, looking ahead – content with each other's company, with the dog at our feet and the fizzy hum from the speaker system almost inaudible.

And then the oddest thing happened.

An unexpected thing that threw our concentration and threw our settled mood.

A voice.

Coming through the speaker, intermittently, between the hissing sound.

Just three words.

*On... their... way... On... their... way...*

Repeated, over and over, like the recording was hiccupping.

Guy A Johnson

'That again,' Augustus said, his tone and frown puzzled. 'I had that in a call. Your Aunt Agnes too. Thought I knew the voice. She thought it familiar too, but neither of us could put our-.'

'I know it,' I said, certain. Even though it was distorted, the recording not clear – as if other, outside noises were interfering with it or swallowing it up.

How could they *not* know it – not recognise it?

'What?'

'It's Elinor,' I answered, feeling a cold shiver all over my body. I knew instantly Otterley was back in my head, listening in. 'It's Elinor's voice.'

And, as the words flew from my mouth, the lights in the carriage eerily cut out – the train hurtling us on in complete darkness...

### Unfold

*There are other things I should tell you about, Esther.*

*Other experiments the authorities conducted – on humans.*

*You know about the takings – I know that, because so many of your friends and relatives were taken. Agnes. Tristan. Joshua and Ethan, your cousins. Joe – although not his brother, Jessie. Ever wondered about that? That's another tale in itself...*

*And you'll know that some of them were subjected to terrible things – experiments and tests, all under that dubious umbrella of progress. They only did the very worst of things in order to save the world – that was their claim then and it's their claim now.*

*But that's not where the experiment began.*

*The children were being manipulated from the very start – before the very start. In the womb, Esther. Agnes, Tristan – all of them were twins. Did you know that? Yes, every single one of the children taken had been a twin. And every single pair had been genetically modified while still in the womb – unbeknownst to their mothers.*

*But not you, Esther.*

*You were not one of a twin.*

*You were not tampered with in that way.*

*And I bet you are wondering why...*

### Fold

Guy A Johnson

7. Elinor

Nathaniel, the man who seemed to be in charge of everything, left us just two days after he'd introduced himself.

Two days after he'd told me – matter-of-fact – that I, Elinor Taylor, was going to *save the day.*

I don't know where he got these ideas about me – or *how* he even knew me. I'd never met him before. Neither had I met my other strange companion before – Ethan, who'd taken me from the bloodbath at Grandad Ronan's flat.

Grandad Ronan – the man I'd trusted, who'd lured me back to his home and held me captive there, for little or nothing, as far as I could see.

I was still struggling to accept this – what he'd done, that he was dead (probably at Ethan's hands) – hoping all the time that there'd be an explanation, that, inexplicably, it might all turn out not to be true. *Your head made a mistake, Elinor – none of these things happened.*

And now I was held captive again – on the boat which Nathaniel appeared to be captain of.

'You're my guest,' Nathaniel insisted, when I'd confronted him.

We were up on deck, a day before he departed and left others to care for me – or keep me prisoner, depending on your view. We were on a wide river-road in the midst of thick forest. The boat was still – not moored, but the engine was off and I felt the tide move us back and forth, gently. My stomach was just about getting used to the constant sway.

'Then why can't I go back to my mother?' I asked.

Guy A Johnson

'It's not that simple,' he answered.

'She'll be worried. She'll have been worried for months. And what if they find all that blood at my Grandad's flat. What if they think it's…'

'Elinor, I'm not going to hurt you,' Nathaniel said, his voice a little soothing. He reached out to touch me, but I flinched, and he rescinded this ill-judged act of affection. 'But I can't simply send you back. It really isn't that simple. And we've all got our part to play – me, you, and your mother too. And others that you know. All got a part to play in saving the day.'

That phrase again. *Saving the day.* I gave him a questioning look, but he didn't offer further explanation. Instead, he made a bargain to appease my worries and homesickness.

'What if I could you could send her a message?' he suggested.


It wasn't quite what I expected – the message I got to send. Neither was the way I got to send it.

'What were you expecting?' a man said to me a few minutes later. A man whose name I didn't know – one of a handful of people on the ship who were helping out that I hadn't been introduced to properly.

We were below deck, in a small cabin where – among other things – there was a black box he claimed was recording equipment. Like something Old Man Merlin kept in his crazy house, it was a flat oblong, cased in black metal, with no buttons or knobs to get it working – just a remote control that caused lights to flash up on its otherwise black exterior.

Guy A Johnson

'I don't know,' I shrugged, somehow disappointed and let down by what was being presented.

'Did you think you were going to send a message in a bottle or something?' he scoffed.

But when he said this, I realised that this was exactly what I'd had in my mind – something to put in a story, something a little more romantic, a little more poetic than a digital recording. Something that would've made Tristan smile. Further sadness filled me as I recalled another loved one still lost to me – another who I longed to send a message of love in a bottle.

I'd thought about Tristan a lot – knowing he'd have gone looking for me. Knowing he'd have been wretched with guilt at being the last one to have seen me the day I was taken.

'You should think yourself lucky – not many people could get their hands on this kind of technology,' the nameless technician continued. 'Not today. A privilege to be able to see it, let alone use it. You ready to start recording?'

'I guess so,' I answered, looking at my hands, where I held a sheet of paper.

When Nathaniel had suggested sending a message, I'd thought I'd simply get the chance to write my own words – and that it would be making its way just to my mother. But Nathaniel said we had to be clever about it. Resources were scarce – even to those with privileges like him – and he couldn't waste them on a message to one person alone. We had to be more efficient than that.

Guy A Johnson

'So,' he said, handing me something he'd already composed, 'how about you send something that would appease your mother's fears – as well as helping me get word round to others in the same breath?'

I didn't like the way things had changed – Nathaniel had suggested one thing, then once I'd agreed with it, turned it into something different. Something that wasn't about me at all. But it was this or nothing – that I could see very clearly. So I took the script he'd written and followed the unnamed man down below deck, to the small cabin with the recording equipment.

'What you going to do with it?' I asked, hesitating before I started. 'Once we're done, how will it get to my mother?' He gave me a small sneer. 'And the others – how will the message get out to the others?'

'Airwaves,' he answered, pointing a finger and whizzing it around the room, suggesting invisible lines of communication. 'We'll put it out there – transmit it and infiltrate various bits of technology. Radios mainly – residential ones and government ones too. Jam the authorities' lines with it, if we can. We'll get it down telephones too. Your mother got a telephone?' he asked, finally conceding that this was personal to me.

I nodded.

'Well, that's how we'll get it to her. Not sure how clear it'll be though.'

'Why?' I asked, suddenly a little concerned.

'It's not exactly quiet around here – lots of background noise, wherever you go. Need a soundproofed room really, but not practical – not on a boat. I'll do my best, though. You ready?'

Guy A Johnson

There was no further stalling – I'd agreed to do this, albeit with reluctance. And hopefully – once Mother heard my voice – she'd be reassured of my safety. Reassured I'd got away from Grandad Ronan alive.

'Okay.'

'Good. When I give you the nod. Like this.' He demonstrated with a tip of his head. 'When I do this, it's a signal I've started recording – then you start reading it out.'

About thirty seconds later, he relayed the signal and I began.

*'This is a message to you all. To let you know that things are going to change. To those of you who have made it your business to oppress the people – we are going to reveal the truth and make you stand up and be counted for what you've done. For those of you who want to fight for what you know is rightfully yours, you'll get your chance. And for those of you who've lost the will to fight, don't worry – help is on its way.'*

He put up a hand for a second – indicating I take a dramatic pause – then he nodded again and I delivered the final line:

*'Your people are on their way.'*

The man shushed me out of the cabin at that point.

'I've got a few technical things to sort out – need a bit of peace and quiet to concentrate,' he said, as if I was somehow creating noise and fuss.

So I left him and returned to the deck. There, Nathaniel was waiting, staring out at our horizon of dense greenery.

'It's quite beautiful, isn't it?' he said, keeping his eyes on the forest.

And it was – more beautiful than anything I had seen, apart from pictures in books at Papa Harold's or Old Man Merlin's. In my home city, the only greenery was the grass

135

covering the hill our school was built upon. And the trees were dead – leafless, grey skeletons marking where plant life had once thrived.

But I hadn't come this far and suffered as much as I had already to talk about the view. I wanted some answers – I wanted to know what was going to happen. I wanted to know why I'd been brought there.

'You're very sure of yourself, aren't you?' Nathaniel answered, when I began an assault of questions. 'For someone of your age – fifteen?'

'Thirteen,' I replied, realising I'd gained another year without mother. Something else Grandad Ronan had denied me. 'Only just, though.'

'Well, even more impressive.'

He said nothing for few seconds and I had to resist the urge to badger him for answers. But given his impression of my maturity, I decided to wait while he contemplated.

'I'm a person of some privilege, Elinor,' he began, still looking out into the fertile oblivion. 'Someone who has had access to luxuries, while others have suffered. Someone who has access to information that others are ignorant of. Someone who has worked their way into a position of power, while others have suffered a powerless existence, daily. Someone wh-.'

'You're in the authorities?' I interrupted, an act that surprised him and his rehearsed words stuttered to halt.

He nodded. 'There's no fooling you, is there?'

'You're high up then, if you've got power?'

'Almost as high as you can get,' he said, but he wasn't bragging – just indicating the level of his authority, of his influence.

136

Guy A Johnson

'So you could stop it all, couldn't you? All this poverty? The way people are treated too – the way the authorities have abused their…'

I stopped – my words crumbling away, as I considered the danger I might be in. This man was part of the authorities – a shadow to most of us, like the God that my Aunt Esther spent so much time praying to for all our salvation. An unseen body that controlled through fear and rumour – its very invisibility the reason it kept control. And you watched yourself, because you never knew who was watching you – who was listening and reporting back. At least, that's what Tristan had led me to believe – and Mother had never countered any of his claims.

'You don't need to be afraid, Elinor. You don't need to watch what you say to me. And you're right,' he reassured me, finally landing his eyes on mine. 'I can stop it all. It's been my plan all along. I've been playing a long game, you might say. Using my position to listen in on people – to their conversations, to get an idea of who they are. But not to trap people or to oppress them further – no, I've used my privileges to work out who I can trust. Who'd be willing to join me if I choose to rise up and fight.'

'You've been listening in on us – listening to Mother, to Tristan?'

'Yes, I have, for my sins.'

I thought for a moment – mulling over a few things.

'If you're so high up, why didn't you just change the rules? Change the laws and make everything fair?'

Nathaniel chuckled and I wondered if he was mocking me.

'Oh, Elinor, how I dreamed of doing that, especially in my early days. Before I entered *the Circle*.'

Guy A Johnson

I looked at him quizzically.

'*The Circle* is the highest level in the government – and not many people know about it, or even know who is in it. The authorities have secrets within secrets. It's all very cloak and dagger.'

I pulled a half-smile, as this last phrase reminded me of the kind of thing Tristan wove into his stories.

'Yes, as I made my way up through the ranks, I imagined how I'd make so many changes when I got to the top. Simply – as you say – change the laws. Reveal the truth about what had really happened and make things right. But there was no *simply* about it, Elinor. The further up I went, the greedier, the more selfish my peers became. There was not a single one among them who showed any care for the underprivileged. I was on my own. And I had to be careful, Elinor. Had to watch who I shared my sympathies with – who I trusted with my opinions.'

'And who did you trust?'

'No one, Elinor. I had to look outside *the Circle,* outside the authorities to find my allies. I used the surveillance technology at my disposal to find them. And then I slowly built up my network – using others to help me grow it in secret. Even now, not too many people under my influence know that their leader works so high up in the authorities. Just a few privileged ones. And I've purposely kept it that way.

'But my network is huge now, Elinor. Made up of families like yours, going about their everyday business on the surface – but if you secretly peek beneath it, they're waiting for the right time. They're waiting for the right signal. And then we'll strike – then we'll make those changes. That time is almost upon us too.'

Guy A Johnson

He stopped speaking, giving me a chance to take in what he'd said. Giving me the opportunity to think through my next set of questions.

'You said that I had a part to play. But I'm only thirteen – what makes you think I can help? And Mother – how is she involved?'

'Those are big questions, Elinor. Big questions, because what I'll ask of you is big too. I'll start with your mother, though. She's been involved without knowing it for so long. Tristan was sent your way many years ago – by the authorities. They sent him to look for someone in your city – not under my orders, I might add. He didn't find who he was looking for – but he did find your mother. And then he joined a family that turned out to be full of potential allies.'

I was confused.

'Tristan worked for the authorities?' I asked, worried that Tristan might not be who he claimed. That – like Ronan – he might not be a good man after all.

'He was hired to do a job,' was how Nathaniel answered – giving me neither a yes nor a no. 'To find someone. That's all – and, as luck would have it, stumbled upon your family.'

'Who was he looking for?'

Nathaniel paused, drawing his breath in slowly, turning his eyes back to the lush forest before us.

'I don't know how I lost track of you,' he eventually continued, choosing not to answer my question – going down a different conversational path. 'Didn't realise that Ronan had taken you until the very end. Sloppy of me and I feared the distraction of your

Guy A Johnson

absence would mean I could no longer rely on your family's help. A shame, as you were the ideal unit.'

'We were – are?'

'Yes. Every single one of you. You mother with her fighting spirit. Tristan with his adventurous nature – and willingness to go in search of those he believes have wronged him.'

I frowned and wondered if he'd explain this comment, but he simply continued – revealing family members and secrets I knew nothing of.

'You have cousins out there too, who had already joined my cause. Ethan to start with.'

He was caught by my surprised look.

'You didn't know?'

I shook my head, my feelings for the blood-covered man who'd saved me from Grandad Ronan suddenly turned upside down.

'How is Ethan my cousin?' I asked.

'You have an aunt and uncle, much older?'

'Great-Aunt Penny and Great-Uncle Jimmy?' I questioned back, and he nodded.

'Yes. Ethan was taken as a child and, well – it didn't end well for him. You really didn't know about him?'

I shook my head and Nathaniel paused for a second, thinking through what he might say next.

'Well, I met Ethan years ago, when he was living in a place for lost children. Only your great-aunt and –uncle found him, took him home – and then he became yet another ally I lost track of.' He took in a long, slow breath. 'There's a lot to take in, Elinor, isn't there?'

I agreed with a tip of my head – which was spinning inside, as I tried to keep up with all the half-finished revelations.

'But then a little luck came our way when Ethan found you – and then, before I knew it, I'd found you both again. In that little boat.'

'Luck?' I questioned, the word seeming an odd choice. What was lucky about any of what had happened?

'Ethan tells me he only stumbled across you, Elinor,' Nathaniel began to explain. 'He was lost in the city and simply looking for somewhere to shelter. Tells me the door to Ronan's flat was wide open. Lucky for him and lucky for you. Seems he got there just in time.'

I pulled a puzzled frown. 'Just in time for what?'

'To save you, Elinor.'

'From Grandad Ronan? Ethan killed him, didn't he?'

To my surprise, Nathaniel shook his head.

'No, Elinor. Ethan says he didn't kill Ronan. When he entered the flat, he found the body already in that terrible state. Already dead. But he might've scared off the perpetrator. Saved you from a similar fate. So, like I said, a little bit of luck.'

He paused, reading my face, as I took in this chilling thought.

'Who do you think killed Ronan?' I asked, deciding to drop the familial tag.

Guy A Johnson

Nathaniel's lips parted slightly, but then he stopped again. Thinking. But how he'd intended to answer my question, I'd never know. Instead, he changed the conversation – taking us back to the story of Ethan, sounding a little more rehearsed as he spoke.

'Ethan has a twin, you know. Like so many of his generation. Another cousin for you. His name is Joshua. He's out there somewhere too – fighting the cause, I hope. Although, I've lost track of him as well. Something I seem to do a lot of.'

He stopped again, caught up in his own thoughts, his eyes scanning the vast forest that was our view.

'Nathaniel?' I said after a while, interrupting his reflecting, trying to bring him back to our conversation.

He pulled a brief, straight smile and began speak to again.

'You've quite a family, Elinor – whether you are aware or not,' he said. 'Your mother, father, cousins, aunts and uncles. Quite a crowd.'

'My father? I don't know my father. Surely you mean Tristan?'

There was another pause, and I saw my question had caught him off guard again.

'Tristan's not your father?' he asked, but there was something false in this question – the pause preceding it too long, the surprise in his tone a little fake. And hadn't this powerful man claimed he'd been watching us for years, making it clear he knew so much about us? Yet I was to believe this vital piece of information was unknown to him?

'You know he's not, don't you?'

Nathaniel said nothing, turning his head further away from me, avoiding my stare. And I felt my heart beat a little faster in anticipation of what I was going to ask next.

Guy A Johnson

'You said my *father* – you know him, don't you?' I asked, my tongue feeling heavy, as my mouth dried up a little. 'You know who my father is?'

My already spinning head was suddenly pirouetting with possibilities, but Nathaniel continued to look the other way, remaining silent on the matter.

'Oh my God – it's Jessie, isn't it?' I reached out, grabbing his arm, pulling on it to get his attention – to get a reaction, as a crazy excitement whipped me up into a wild frenzy. 'Jessie's my real father – I'd guessed that all along! It was a family whisper, one I kept over-hearing! It's why he's always been there! It's why he's-.'

'No, Elinor,' Nathaniel softly interrupted me. 'Jessie Morton isn't your father.' He turned his face towards mine at last, finally catching my eyes with his. 'I can assure you he isn't.'

'But you know who is?' I questioned, trying to keep the anxiety and excitement from my voice.

For several seconds he simply held my gaze, but eventually he gave a reluctant nod.

'Is he someone I know?' I asked, one of far too many questions that were swimming about in my head.

A shake of the head this time.

'No, you've never met him.'

'But you know where he is? You do, don't you? And you could take me to him – you could let me finally meet him? Does he know about me? Does he know he has a daughter?'

This time, Nathaniel kept his face neutral, letting me ramble off my questions, until I ran out of steam and into his silence.

143

Guy A Johnson

'Please tell me,' I pleaded, my heart beating as violently as my head was whirling.

After another long pause and a deep, reluctant sigh, Nathaniel gave me just a few details.

'He does know about you, Elinor. And you will get to meet him, once this is all over.'

'Once you've defeated the authorities?'

A nod in reply. 'Yes. Once that's happened, or maybe sooner. But for now he has a very important job to do and I can't – I *won't* – risk anything that might jeopardise his success. I'm not expecting you to understand, but you'll have to tru-.'

'Does Mother know where he is? Has she seen him at all? Does she know what he's doing?' I unleashed another set of inquiries and saw a surprising reaction in Nathaniel's face – he flinched at the mention of Mother. 'She does, doesn't she?'

'Elinor,' he said, trying to pacify my excitement.

'Nathaniel, please tell me the truth! It's not fair! You've brought me all this way – further away from my family. Said I can't go back until I've done whatever you want me to do. So you can at least tell me what you know. At least tell me what's going on back home.'

'Elinor,' he answered, his voice gentle and low, as he reached out and patted the sides of my arms. 'I can't tell you anything else. It's just not safe – and I'm sorry I've said as much as I have already. It was careless of me to slip up – and now I've raised all your hopes and expectations.'

I went to reply – to plead that he *hadn't* raised my hopes and that I *could* handle whatever else that he was holding back – but he quietened me with a finger to my lips. As

144

he did this, tears I'd held in the bottom lids of my eyes spilled through my lashes, splashing on my cheeks.

'So, I'm not going to make any further mistakes – but I will make you two promises. One, I'll get that message you recorded out on the airwaves, making sure it gets to the people you care about. The people who may well be worrying that you are harmed or in danger. If I can, I'll get that message to your mother – but that I *can't* promise.'

'And your second promise?' I asked, hopeful it would meet the expectations that were trying to burst out of me. It did.

'That when this is all over, you'll get to meet him. And then he can explain where he's been all this time – and why he had to spend so many years away from you. Okay?'

I nodded, wiping away my tears, allowing myself to be appeased by these small assurances – although I had one final question:

'What's his name – my father?'

'Xavier,' he answered, quickly, as if revealing that didn't matter much and then he began to walk away. 'I have things to attend to Elinor – will you be okay if I leave you?'

I nodded a reply and he disappeared below deck. But the strange name – my father's name – left me a little stunned. It was weird – hearing it, and finding it so odd, so foreign, and yet it was instantly so personal. So *mine*. But there was something else as well. Something familiar – I'd seen it somewhere, maybe? And this bugged me for a long time, before I eventually remembered where I knew it from…

When I awoke the next day, Nathaniel had left us and I wouldn't see him again for a while.

Guy A Johnson

'He left you this,' the unnamed man who'd recorded my message on the black box said to me, handing me a folded over piece of paper.

I'd been awake a while, but was still lying down on a bench below deck, a rough blanket covering me.

I unfolded it.

*Dear Elinor*

*I always keep my promises. I'll see you soon, but for now stay safe. And Robert will look after you. Do as he says – he's one of the good guys. He'll tell you exactly what we need you to do – how you'll play your part in saving the day.*

*Nathaniel.*

I looked up to his messenger.

'Yep,' he said, reading my thoughts, pulling half a grin. 'That's me.'

'You're in charge now?' I asked, slightly scornful.

'No, little lady,' he answered, gently sarcastic himself. 'I'm not in charge – you are.'

He said those final two words without a hint of mockery, putting the fear of God me in – a phrase I could hear my Great-Aunt Penny using.

'What do you mean?'

'I mean,' Robert continued, 'that you'll be leading on this particular part of our mission.'

'And what does that involve?' I asked, fearful of the answer he'd give.

'Winning over some lost souls,' he said, grinning a boyish, almost devilish grin…

### Unfold

*Of course, not every one of that generation of twins was taken, Esther.*

*I think if <u>every</u> child had been taken by the authorities – even if sometimes it was only for a few nights – I think if <u>that</u> had happened then the government's secret would've been exposed much sooner than it was.*

*As it was, the unsuspecting public was kept in the dark for some time. In the distant past, Esther, rumours and conspiracy theories would've spread like wild fire – but the authorities took full control of the media and all people had left was word-of-mouth. Observations and tales passed gradually over garden walls and along telephone lines – when they were working, that is.*

*So, it took a long time for everyone to realise what was happening – for people to cut through the lies and realise their children weren't simply running off and coming up with tall stories.*

*Not every child of that generation was taken, though – but they were all tested. And some of this happened in plain sight – pills and injections from doctors, blood extracted by a nurse, extra tests or questionnaires set by teachers, social workers assigned to families for no reason. This was all part of a plan to monitor the development of a generation of modified beings. And those who showed particularly interesting traits – like your sister Agnes – well they were plucked from their families.*

*Some of them were quickly returned, when further testing revealed little else of interest.*

*But others they kept for longer – like Tristan, like Xavier Riley. You know that name, don't you, Esther?*

Guy A Johnson

*And some were never returned.*

*Like your cousin, Joshua. But I can tell you what happened to him, Esther. I can tell you what he's been up to. And, depending on your perspective, it's good news.*

*Yes, Esther – it's very good news for some of you...*

**Fold**

8. Agnes


When Xavier said we were going to check out Monty Harrison's place, I first thought he meant his house – a sprawling mansion that was built on a huge, guarded estate to the north-east of our city.

I'd never been there, though I knew Esther had at least once – invited to a fancy party that she'd dismissed as *dull,* and had not been prepared to share any details of. That was before the floods, before Joe had disappeared.

But Xavier didn't take me to Monty's house – not at the start. Instead, we went to what he referred to as his *headquarters.*

'We're going to *Breakers,'* he said and I felt a chill go down my spine – remembering what Joe had said about that place.

'That's where they kept him,' I told Xavier. 'That's where Monty kept his dogs too. Held his experiments.'

'I can take you back home. I can do this on my own, you know,' Xavier offered, reading the terror in my face.

But I shook my head.

If he turned back just for me, we'd lose time. And how had he described the state Monty had been left in? *Disabled.* That was it – *disabled.* That suggested it would only be a matter of time before Monty *enabled* himself again and called for help.

'I'm with you,' I confirmed, taking long deep breaths, as we sailed along the river road towards *Breakers* – stealing myself for whatever lay ahead.

149

Guy A Johnson

The risks we were taking – the leap of faith that I had taken with Xavier – kept washing in and out of me, rinsing through my thoughts like diminishing waves on a beach. And I felt sick with this mental unsteadiness. The thought of entering Monty's headquarters – going in search of evidence of what Monty had been up to. Of entering the place where Joe had been held and tortured. Where Joe had said Monty kept those vicious creatures in cages.

And we were relying on a sleight of hand – a mind trick I barely believed myself – to get us inside. In the blink of an eye, it could all be over.

That had been our biggest risk too – Xavier had repeatedly warned me that his strange ability wasn't certain to work. Wasn't one hundred percent guaranteed. Sometimes it required a little assistance – something slipped into a drink, an enhancer mixed into food.

'Is that what you did to me?' I'd asked, as we discussed the options.

Heading north-west, we'd reached the fork in the road that had been called *Destiny's Point* for as long as I could remember. You took a left on the river road for the police station, the hospital and similar honorable services – and a right turn to sail along a different, darker path altogether.

Xavier didn't answer my question – hearing the restrained anger in my tone, he just dropped his head.

'What about these guys – Monty's people?' I added, moving us on. 'You need them to see you as Monty immediately?'

'I do,' he answered, lifting his head back up to me, catching my gaze. Then, right in front of me, he disappeared. I couldn't decide if I felt reassured by the ease with which he

Guy A Johnson

created this deception – or shocked at how easily my own mind could be manipulated. 'I'll just have to catch their eyes,' he finished, coming back to me.

'Here's hoping,' I said, as our destination came into view.


I'd never been to *Breakers* before – I knew of it, but I'd never been tempted to visit bars, even before the floods. And, even if I had been tempted, I'd heard that Monty's was a sort of *boys only* place.

There was a mooring space with a plaque indicating it was Monty's personal parking spot. As Xavier secured the speedboat to it, I looked up at the place we were about to enter. The way in seemed to be by an external fire escape – a set of metal steps that twisted out of the water and up the side of the building.

The water was shallower at this end of the city, so part of the notorious ground level – where Monty's sick secret had been locked away – was visible above the waterline.

Two big men – dressed in black protective gear, with masks covering their faces – were placed on the steps at first floor level. The return of Monty's boat had caught their attention – and the whole time that Xavier set about the business of mooring the thing, they kept their eyes on him.

'Hey, what's going on there?' one of them asked, moving his bulk down the steps towards us, making the metal staircase rattle with the weight of his steps.

I feared this was it – our mission over before it ever began – but that changed the moment Xavier turned round and looked the man in the eyes.

'Is there a problem?' Xavier asked.

After a momentary frown, the man shook his head – an apology in that movement.

Guy A Johnson

'Sorry, sir, didn't realise it was you,' the guard said, retreating back up the steps, looking back a couple of times, his frown slightly puzzled by something he couldn't pin down.

'There's two of them,' I whispered to Xavier and he quickly looked up at the second man – gave him a brief wave, locked his gaze.

'Sir,' the second man answered in response and both went back to their work of guarding the entrance.


Joe had given us a very accurate description of the layout of *Breakers*, to the point that Xavier moved very confidently from floor to floor, room to room, as we headed to the apex of the building – allowing him to focus his thoughts, and keep Monty's workers under his spell.

And it was the oddest thing, watching Xavier seek out the eyes of the men at each point inside that place – how every one of his henchmen simply waved us in, nodding respectfully at Xavier and muttering a clipped *boss* or *sir* at him. A couple of them looked twice, a small question in their faces, like that first man at the door – but it never came to anything.

My presence invited a completely different kind of look – a disrespectful leer, as if they knew exactly why the big man had brought me along.

'Good,' Xavier said, when I protested about this. We were on our own, having made our way to Monty's private office at the very top of the five-storey building. 'If they think old Monty's brought someone back for a bit of fun, they're unlikely to disturb us – wherever we go.'

Guy A Johnson

Despite the fact this would buy us time and privacy, I didn't like the insinuation.

'Come on, we've work to do,' Xavier said, brushing my indignation aside.

Monty's office was small, yet plush – decked out with a sense of luxury that was out of place in our city, and, even though he was absent, I felt a sense of Monty's vulgarity as if he was in the room with us. As if he were breathing down our necks.

The floor was carpeted in a thick, dark red weave. *Blood red,* I reflected, imagining the colour had been chosen carefully – chosen for its ability to hide evidence of violence. The furniture – a wide desk, a drinks cabinet and two tall chests of drawers – were all made of mahogany wood, gleaming with a rich polish that was out of place in our city. Behind the desk was a large wing-backed chair covered in dark green leather. I could just see Monty in this environment, sitting smugly in that luxurious seat, counting up his illicit earnings.

Our first task was to look for keys.

'Any sort – find them and pocket them.'

Xavier's intention was to get us into the basement – to get a look at what Joe had described to us. The thought terrified me – what if those wild creatures were loose down there? What if Ronan had set them free too?

'Then he wouldn't have made it out alive himself,' Xavier reasoned. 'And neither would Joe. And not one of Monty's men mentioned any trouble to us. So, my guess is Ronan got in here and got Joe out, but left everything else as it was.'

Feeling reassured, I set about my task in an orderly fashion, trying to stay as calm as I could. We worked methodically around the room – Xavier working clockwise, me the

153

Guy A Johnson

other way, searching through drawers and feeling along surfaces, until eventually we found what we were looking for.

'Here we go,' Xavier announced, his hands patting the underside of the large leather chair behind the desk. 'I can feel something under the surface.' I heard a ripping sound – not a tear, but the parting of a Velcro join. 'A clever hiding place,' Xavier said, pulling himself up straight, jangling a set of keys on a metal ring.

'What next?' I asked.

'See if they unlock the ground floor.'

As we made our way back down through Monty's club, I felt the sickness in my stomach fold over several times. Any second our cover could've been blown. And as every one of those seconds passed by, it meant we were closer to those savage beasts.

Before we left Monty's office, Xavier had insisted we loosen our clothing, making it obvious what we'd *been up to.* And so I'd had to endure the knowing looks on the faces of Monty's men, all of whom stared where the buttons on my shirt were open, before looking into my face with a mix of desire and scorn.

But, along with Xavier's dubious mind trick, it worked as a distraction and we made our way to the well of the building without a challenge.

'You taking the lady in there, boss?'

At the entrance to the notorious ground floor, one of Monty's men finally challenged us. It wasn't a confrontational exchange, more a show of concern. But it jolted my senses and I wondered if it might have the same effect on Xavier.

'She insisted,' Xavier answered, a twisted smile crawling across his face – as if to suggest that something equally twisted might happen once we were beyond that door.

154

Guy A Johnson

The man smirked back and nodded, and then proceeded to unlock and open the door for us. I heard about six bolt locks retract and noted the door was heavy and thick – about five inches deep. With the entrance open, we were immediately hit with a dense, unpleasant smell.

'Allow me,' the man said, sweeping the door open as wide as possible – sneering and leering at me as we walked through, noting my dislike of the stench that filled the air. 'Lock you in boss?'

Xavier shook his head at the question, making sure he caught the man's eyes and held them.

'Leave it unlocked. It'll be fine,' he said and the man nodded, closing the door behind us.

'Jesus!' I cried, as soon as the door clicked shut – throwing my hands up to my face, shielding my nose as best I could. As much as Joe had filled me in on what this place had been like, he hadn't prepared me for that thick, foul aroma.

We couldn't see the dogs at that point – or hear them, for that matter. We found ourselves in a small utility room, with several doors leading off it.

Xavier nodded, acknowledging my disgust, but somehow remaining unaffected. 'The smell of animals cooped up together. Their sweat, their urine and their faeces. You didn't think Monty would be the kind of man who regularly had his animals cleaned out, did you?' he asked, opening a door to our right.

Inside, we found animal food supplies, stacked tightly on shelves.

No, I didn't. Still, the overwhelming stench might have prompted even a man such as Monty to take action.

155

Guy A Johnson

A door on the left led to a small shower room and I wondered if Joe had been allowed to clean up in there over the years. It wasn't something he had mentioned. There was also a washing machine and a row of hooks from which hung several protective suits. I wondered if we needed to put these on before we went any further – maybe the animals we were about to encounter carried some kind of contagion. We'd taken our own suits off as soon as we'd entered *Breakers,* leaving them with a member of staff.

'I think we'll be safe enough,' Xavier said, when I shared my thoughts about the garments. There was a certain irony about his words, as we were, after all, about to enter a place of great danger. 'So, are you ready?' he asked, pointing his eyes straight ahead – to another door at the end of the small anteroom.

I noticed it was padlocked in three places.

'We still can't hear a thing,' I answered, my stomach sick with nerves. 'Don't you think that's odd?'

'Yes, I do.'

'They could be asleep, or maybe Ronan finished them off. You think he might have? Joe didn't mention that.'

'No?'

Xavier kept his sentences short – keeping his cool at the same time, as he allowed me to stall the inevitable. Allowed me to put off facing what was in the next room.

'So – we could stay this side and always wonder,' Xavier eventually challenged me. 'Or take a look at what we came here to see. What do you say, Agnes?'

I took a deep, slow breath and felt my stomach turn again, as my nerves curdled in my guts. For a moment, I thought I might faint, but managed to steady myself.

156

Guy A Johnson

'Yes, let's get this over with,' I said, taking another long breath, hoping I could hold it together – that my body wouldn't let me down, my legs buckle or my insides liquidate.

Xavier nodded at me and then used the keys we'd found to release the padlocks. Seconds later, he pushed it open and the smell around us intensified.

I gagged, but managed to keep steady, whereas Xavier bent over and dry-retched.

'You okay?' I asked, half of my concern with him, the other half with what lay ahead.

'Fine,' Xavier answered, hands on his knees, breathing deep, composing himself.

It was dark in the room – lit just by the light coming through from the anteroom.

'Should we find a switch?' I asked, suddenly wondering what the right thing to do was.

I thought back to what Joe had said about how the dogs were housed. *They're in cages. Together in packs. But the cages are sturdy. In all the years I was down there, they never broke free. There was the occasional accident – a door not locked securely that led to a fatality. But the animals were largely obedient – they knew where the food was coming from. Yeah, their instinct to survive made them behave themselves.*

And Joe's words gave me a small amount of confidence – he hadn't known we'd be checking the place out when he'd told me, but there'd been earnest reassurance in his voice. Still, as the light from the smaller room behind us bleached the darkness away, I doubted just how safe it was to venture further.

Suddenly, I heard a buzzing sound and tubes of lighting flickered across the ceiling, flooding the space with brightness. I turned quickly to Xavier – his hand was on a switch,

Guy A Johnson

left of the entrance. Then I turned back to the room itself and took in the vast space before me.

'Xavier...' My voice trailed away.

'I know,' he answered, moving close to my side. 'Come on,' he said, gesturing we move further in.

I nodded, slowly stepping into the room of cages, almost lost for words, as I took in everything around me.

'They're... All... Asleep...'


It was set out like a maze.

That's the best way I can describe it.

A maze of metal cages, stacked three up. They were secure – locked with heavy padlocks – and the creatures were all sleeping. But it was eerie in there, seeing all those dormant beasts – up to three per enclosure, depending on their size. Accompanying the thick, nauseous smell was their heavy, sonorous breathing – the sound of their sleep reverberating around the room in unison.

And it was vast – that space. As we walked along the rows of cages, it seemed to go on forever. It seemed so much larger than I'd guessed it would be from the outside, as if it was some kind of optical illusion. I didn't count the number of cages or the animals in that place, but there were hundreds of them.

'An army,' Xavier mouthed at one point and the thought made me shiver. *An army.* Is that what Monty was building? But if that was it, what would he do with such a thing? It didn't make sense.

Guy A Johnson

'Can we get out of here?' I asked, after we'd been there a while. I'd no idea how long we'd been in that room, but it felt uncomfortably longer than I'd intended. 'I don't want to be here when they wake.'

'I don't think they'll do that,' Xavier answered, and suddenly I got the feeling there was something he hadn't told me – something he knew, but had purposely held back.

'Why do you say that?' I asked, stopping where I was and staring at him. He turned away, examining one of the cages. 'Xavier, why do you say that?'

'Come, look at this,' he finally answered, signaling me over. One of the dogs was close up to the grating of the cage and he'd put two fingers inside and managed to part its fur. 'See that?'

I moved a little closer – not wanting to get up as close as Xavier. It was the size of a full adult human – as long as Tristan was tall, with huge paws and sickeningly muscular legs. And I could smell something off it – a rotting, bloody smell.

Ignoring my reticence, Xavier coaxed me further forward.

'See – there. On the skin. See that mark?'

Where he'd separated the fur, I could see a small dark red spot on the pink skin. A puncture mark.

'These animals aren't sleeping – they're unconscious. They've been put in this state. So they won't be waking any time soon, I imagine.'

I should've felt relieved – the very thought of them waking up had terrified me from the moment we'd stepped in. And I couldn't imagine the volume of sound if the booming snores transformed into a rowdy uproar of barks. It would've been deafening. Deafening and petrifying. Although the cages were secured – both to the floor and each other – I imagined the dogs rising and rocking their cages in defiance, determined to get out. Determined to get to us – to rip us apart, as was their savage nature.

But seeing them like this – in this coma-like state – was somehow just as bad. Just as unnerving.

It made me think of what Tristan had told me – about the bodies they'd uncovered in that old government laboratory he and Jessie had raided. He'd described them as puppies and said they'd looked preserved, but maybe they'd been drugged. Poisoned, even. Injected with something that had killed them off?

But that wasn't what was happening at Monty Harrison's club. These creatures were sedated. Sleeping, but very much alive.

'I just don't understand it.' I said, suddenly feeling dizzy and suffocated by the smell, the sound and the stillness in that room. 'I can't get my head around any of this.'

'Me neither,' Xavier confessed and I felt a sense of disappointment. I'd hoped he'd have some kind of answer, but I could tell he was genuinely mystified. 'But I think we should get out of here. Maybe we should head to where Augustus and your sister were heading.'

'Monty's house?'

Xavier nodded.

'I don't think there's anything else for us to see here – and there's nothing we can do. But there might be answers where they've headed. And if there aren't, we can at least see if they need our help.' He paused a minute, thinking. 'You think Joe will be okay on his own for a little longer?'

160

Guy A Johnson

I thought of Joe's erratic fitting and wondered – but I didn't think my presence had made a difference. And something told me Joe had been having those episodes a while, probably locked in one of the cages that were hemming us in.

So I nodded, but I had a question of my own.

'How do you feel about seeing your father again?' I asked, watching Xavier's reaction carefully. 'Will you fool him into thinking you're someone else, to get out of it?'

For a second or so, he simply looked up at me and held my gaze with his. It occurred to me that something strange might happen – that he was playing a mind trick on me and he'd change before my eyes, deny that *Xavier* had ever been there. Then I remembered what he'd said – it was mainly in my head. It was about seeing what I most desired to see.

Nothing happened, though. He just kept his stare steady and eventually answered.

'Not sure if I'm ready to see him, but I will. I have to face him as myself sooner or later. Can't run from the past forever, can I?'

There was suggestion in that last sentence that I picked up on immediately.

'No, Xavier – you can't run away from it forever. Someday you'll have to face it.'

'Agnes-.' he said, reaching out to me and I heard his voice break with emotion.

Of all the times and places to be thinking of *her*, to be discussing any kind of future involving *her*.

'You okay in there, Boss?'

A deep bark of a voice, coming from the anteroom interrupted the moment, forcing our emotions to sober.

I caught a look of alarm in Xavier's eyes. Whoever was calling was out of sight – not in his eye-line. *What if I can't trick his mind,* Xavier's look said. *What if he sees me for*

161

*who I am?* If that happened, who knows where we'd end up – possibly in one of the cages?

On our own, if we were especially lucky; in with one of those mighty canines, if we

weren't.

'We're fine,' Xavier answered and saw his face wince when the other man answered

with:

'Who's there? Is that you, Boss?'

The voice got louder as the man got closer and I realised I needed to intervene, cause

a distraction. So I did the same thing I'd done earlier – loosened my clothing, to make it

look as if we'd been intimate, opening my shirt a little wider this time, suggesting the level

of our activity had accelerated. Then I took steps towards that voice, covering myself up

with my hands in feigned shock when we came face-to-face.

I hadn't seen this one before – but he was tall, bulky and dressed in black, like the

other men Monty had scattered about *Breakers.* I noticed he had something poking out of

his trouser pocket on the left – the butt of a pistol.

'I'm sorry,' he said, instantly apologising, but looking beyond me, curious to catch

a glimpse of *Monty.* 'Boss? Is that you back there? Can you just step forward, so I can

check you're alright?'

'What is it you think I've done to-,' I began, sounding as indignant as I could, but

the man held up his right hand to signal I shut up. His left went instinctively to the gun,

feeling it through the fabric of his trousers.

'Come forward, sir,' he continued, dropping the *boss* tag, suggesting he hadn't been

fooled by Xavier at all. Suggesting we were about to get into a whole lot of trouble. 'Come

Guy A Johnson

where I can see you. I'm armed, and the lady here can confirm that. Step forward so I can see you clearly, before I take action we'll all regret.'

My heart was in my mouth, wondering what would happen next. Wondering – once he came into sight – if Xavier could pull off his mind trick and convince this man that he *was* Monty Harrison, the criminal mastermind in charge of this place. Or wondering if his stepping out of the shadows would simply be coupled with the quick drawing of the pistol and the crack of a bullet – cutting through the muffled choir of animal noises that hummed around us.

'It's me,' Xavier's voice announced, just behind me.

I kept my eye on the man, on his movements – on that gun.

'There's no need to be worried or concerned.'

'You?'

The single-word question confirmed what I most feared – Xavier hadn't lured this man in with his eyes, hadn't manipulated his mind at all. And I expected that hand to reach for the pistol any second, but it didn't. Instead, the man stepped forward, walking past me, with his right hand held out in front of him. I turned around, just in time to catch Xavier and this man shaking hands.

'You know each other?' I questioned, buttoning up my shirt and tucking it back into my trouser waist. I felt a mix of relief and nagging alarm – relieved to find myself out of danger, but alarmed that Xavier was friendly with one of Monty's employees. 'What's going on here?'

I'd meant what was their relationship, but the man took my question literally.

163

Guy A Johnson

'Monty Harrison's been breeding these creatures here for years,' he began, giving me information I already had. 'Had a small handful, but the pack is now over several hundred. Two hundred plus just in here.'

'He's got them somewhere else?' Xavier asked, while I was still wondering who this other man was and what their relationship was.

'Been moving them for months. Drugging them, like this,' he continued, indicating the somnolent brutes that surrounded us.

'Where does he take them?'

'I don't know. He took a few up to his house, but something went wrong.'

'What happened?'

He shrugged.

'I've not seen, but I've heard they got out. That the tranquilizers wore off too early and some of the men were torn apart. A few of the dogs have turned up in the river roads, but others are running free.'

'Yes, I'd heard,' Xavier answered, while I was distracted with thoughts of Billy – the day he'd fallen into our river road. The body of a puppy that Tristan had pulled from the water. And there'd been another occasion, more recently – a waste collector had told Jessie and Tristan about another dog found drowned in the waters.

'Are they still at his house?' I asked the stranger, no longer caring who he was – more concerned with the welfare of my sister, my nephew and Augustus. 'Xavier, they've headed for that place. Billy, Esther and your father!'

Xavier reached out, touched my arm to reassure me he'd heard. Before he could say anything, the other man spoke up.

'You need to get out of here, Boss,' he said. So we were back to that – Xavier was his superior after all. 'Both of you. Did you lock eyes with all the other men?'

Xavier nodded.

'Good. Hopefully there shouldn't be any trouble. But I'll follow you out, be ready to take action if you need a little help getting back out.' He patted the bulge his gun was making. 'You've got Monty's boat, right?'

'Yes.'

'So you've got Monty somewhere too.'

A nod this time.

'No time to explain, right?'

'No time to explain,' Xavier answered the man, but he was looking at me – as if the message applied to me too. *No time to explain.*

*Don't think I won't want some answers,* was the reply I hoped to convey with my eyes, before we made our way back out of that kennel – leaving the noise and stench behind for now.


We made our way back up to the first floor of *Breakers* and out of the building without a single challenge. But that didn't mean my nerves were any less frayed. If anything, knowing what was caged beneath us – and knowing that some of those creatures had been let loose on Monty's home ground – left my emotions more fragile.

'We don't know that they're in danger,' Xavier reassured, once we were back in the boat and his ally had waved us off – maintaining the pretence that he was seeing off the club's boss and his latest mistress for the night.

165

Guy A Johnson

'But we don't know that they're not,' I fretted. 'You saw the size of those things. You saw those jaws, the muscles on their legs.'

'Agnes, we don't even know if they found their way there. We don't even know if they got onto Monty's land – let alone whether those creatures are still roaming his grounds. If you were set free from captivity, would your instincts tell you *not* to stray far?'

He took my silence as conceding.

'No, you'd get the hell out of there. So wherever they are, they'll be long gone by now. Okay?'

'Okay,' I answered, allowing my anxieties to lessen a little.

But he was wrong.

Those creatures hadn't fled the home of their captor.

And when we finally arrived at Monty's remote mansion, still on the north-west side of the city, we realised just how wrong we'd been.

Guy A Johnson

*Unfold*

*There's so many things to tell you, Esther.*

*So many beginnings to so many different stories – and I want to tell them all to you in one go – for fear that one or another will lose your interest and you'll ball this note of mine up and throw it away.*

*So much to impart about you – about secrets that have been kept from you. Secrets I will reveal, if you'll bear with me.*

*And I promised to tell you about your lost cousin, Joshua, and what he's been up to. I'll come to that too. Brave boy – or terrible nuisance, depending on how you see things.*

*But first let me tell you about something very close to your heart – Joe.*

*During all those years of exchanging your letters, I couldn't tell you where he was. For your safety, and Billy's. But not for Joe's – I lied saying I was protecting him. It was too late – the enemy had him. Yes, Esther – Monty Harrison had Joe all along. Kept him locked up like a dog – kept him in the same place he kept those puppies of his. Experimented on him too, Esther. A terrible cruelty, beyond imagination.*

*And I'm sorry – but I never tried to save him. Not even for you. See, I was too busy saving myself. But I make you a promise here and now – as soon as I get the chance, I'll save him. Yes, I'll finally free Joe and help him make his way back to you.*

*Why would I do that, you might ask? Well, that's a fair question. It's so you won't think me entirely bad, Esther.*

*So you'll forgive me when you discover the truth about me…*

*Fold*

167

Guy A Johnson

9. Tristan

Jessie was the first of us over that wall.

The first to step onto the rope ladder and climb precariously to the top – where a trio of strangers would eventually haul him over into the place we'd been promised held all our answers.

But as he slowly scaled that unstable ladder, I could only stare up and wonder if he'd ever make it. At roughly fifty feet, I lost him – the darkness swallowed him up completely and all I could do was pray we'd get a signal to let us know he was safely up and over.

Ten minutes or so passed before a torch flashed three short bursts of light at us – exactly two seconds apart.

'He's arrived safely,' Solomon interpreted, but while I felt reassured that he'd made it, I wasn't certain about his safety. 'No time to waste, then?'

It was an instruction posed as a question – and he held the rope ladder away from the wall, where its flaccid rungs hung.

'Up you go,' he added, as if there was any doubt that I was to go next.

I emptied my head of every thought, every question, every doubt, as I made my way up that wall – focussing solely on the task in hand, knowing that any distractions would be costly. Fatal, even. I just held on tight, as I inched up the rungs, squeezing violently as if strangling a tiny neck. I chose a good pace too – enough momentum to feel like I was making progress, but not fast enough that there was a chance of missing a step and falling back. And to remain attentive, I forced every thought about slipping and crashing against that wall from my mind – along with all the other thoughts I'd banished.

I don't know how long it took me, but by the time I reached the top of that wall, I could feel a numb ache in my hands, arms, shoulders and back that I knew would feel worse in the coming days.

'Just one more to come,' I said to the three men who were waiting for me.

'Not two?'

'No, we lost one,' I answered, keeping it simple, but even through the dark I read the understanding their eyes.

'Okay, let's get this last one up,' one of them said, and I slumped next to Jessie and watched as they gave Solomon the three-flash signal to say I had *arrived safely*.

And as I watched, I realised how precarious our journey had been up the façade of the fortress – the rope ladder was secured to the three men, but nothing else.

'Don't think I'd have taken my chances,' Jessie commented. 'If I'd have known.'

*If I'd have known.*

How often had we said and thought that so far – and how often would those words spring to mind again?

I shook off this thought and just prayed for Solomon – prayed that the three *security guards* had enough strength left to haul a third man up that purpose-built rock face.

'Almost there,' one of them eventually said in a strained voice, and seconds after Solomon came tumbling over the top, landing in an exhausted heap a metre or so away from us.

Guy A Johnson

'What happened to Marcus?' another of the men asked and Solomon spent the first few minutes of his arrival recovering his breath and explaining his companion's absence.

While he did this, Jessie and I kept quiet and discreetly took in our surroundings. When we'd rolled over the top of the wall, we'd fallen onto a ledge about three feet down and that ledge was about ten feet deep as well – a measurement that directly reflected the depth of the wall itself. And on the inner circumference of the wall, there was another waist-high edge to stop you simply falling over. I looked over this, cautiously – I didn't want to give myself away or cause any of my companions concern – but I couldn't see very much. There were some lights below, but they were dull, muted somehow – and everything that was going on below appeared in a blur. I could see movement, though.

'There's a roof over the top of the whole city,' Solomon explained, joining us, after he'd finished debriefing the other men. 'A reinforced glass roof, keeping out the rain and pollution.'

'And keeping out the riff-raff,' Jessie added, his tone heavier, more bitter than his choice of words.

'Like the Atrium, in our city,' I said, recalling the enormous commercial centre made of glass and steel that had once been the pride and joy of our now decimated city. 'My father had a small business he ran from there.'

'I remember that place,' Solomon responded, acknowledging my comparison. 'It is a bit like that – like a huge greenhouse. But you'll see for yourself over the coming days. Tonight, we have to get you inside – somewhere safe, before anyone sees you. Then we can prepare you for *tomorrow*.'

Guy A Johnson

'Tomorrow?' I questioned, wondering why Solomon had intonated such importance on the word. 'What's happening tomorrow?'

'Tomorrow we'll introduce you to city life,' he answered, exchanging brief looks with the other three men – brief enough that I couldn't really comment on it. 'But now – right now – we need to follow these men, get you past the last hurdles before you're truly safe. Come on.'

He indicated we all stand and we followed this instruction, both slightly hesitant as we wondered what these *last hurdles* were likely to be. Picking up on the hesitancy in our movements, one of the group said:

'Nothing to worry about boys,' in a sarcastic feminine tone and I caught a sly smile flash at me through the darkness. 'We'll look after you.'

So – one of our rescuers was female.

I tried to hide my surprise, but the others noticed and chuckled, including Jessie who tapped me jovially on the shoulder, whispering: 'Don't worry, I'd assumed they were all men too.'

It served as a light moment during an otherwise tense evening, but it also highlighted how vulnerable we were – in the darkness, about to enter a city we were not welcome in. A city we'd been given very little detail about. I also questioned the sharpness of my own wits – how had I *not* noticed one of our party was a woman? Not that her gender mattered – just how had I not realised this obvious fact? But later, I'd discover I'd overlooked far more important and obvious details along the way.

We walked along the top of the wall for another ten minutes, before we stopped.

Guy A Johnson

'The last of your hurdles,' the female in our group announced, briefly switching on her torch and flashing it across the ground – revealing a square, metal door embedded in the brickwork. There was also a computerised panel of some sort cut into it and the woman knelt down before it and tapped in a code. She stood up and we all listened and watched as a series of bolts automatically unlocked and a thick steel hatch slowly opened up until the door was at a 90 degree angle.

'Your last hurdle,' the woman repeated again, staring into the space in the floor and it seemed like the entire group held their breath in unison, as we waited for whatever this hurdle might be. Kneeling down again, she leant forward and turned her head to one side, as if she was trying to listen.

'Any signs?' Solomon eventually asked, breaking our silence.

'Sounds like it's safe to go in,' she answered. 'Right, we need to be quick. This door will automatically close in another few minutes and the sentries will be back in a similar time period. So, in we go.'

As I processed these two details – the automatic door (which would lock us inside, no doubt) and these *sentries* she spoke of – the woman and one of the men stepped into the hole in the ground. She switched on her torch again. Next, Jessie and I were encouraged forward, with Solomon – who was also carrying a torch – and the last of our companions at the rear. Inside there was a staircase – a tight, claustrophobic stone staircase, which we were expected to descend.

'There are over three hundred steps,' Solomon explained, his voice low, as if he feared being detected. 'And they're steep, each one deep.'

'And we're taking them all?' I asked.

172

Guy A Johnson

'Yes,' he answered. 'Every single one. Once we're at the bottom, we should be fine. They don't guard the bottom – just the top. Once we're at the bottom, the darkness will keep you covered and we'll get you to the safe-house.'

*Safe-house.* Another new concept to digest.

'What do you mean by *they* don't guard the bottom?' I questioned, deciding I'd come back to the details around this safe-house later.

'The sentries,' Solomon explained, just as we reached a concrete landing, a mere fifteen steps down. 'See here?' He flashed his torch left and right and I saw a passageway on both sides. 'Those tunnels go all the way along the wall and there are guards patrolling them night and day. The entrance we came through is one of many along the way – built-in in case of emergencies.'

'Emergencies?'

'Think of it like a fire exit.'

'A fire exit?' I queried. 'Does it unlock *without* a code from the inside?'

A slight chuckle from Solomon.

'No, you still need the code to get out.'

'So not a very safe fire exit then?'

This question prompted Solomon to continue his explanation.

'The code changes every thirty minutes and is only known by the few that need to know it.'

'The sentries?'

'Yes, the sentries and those high up in the authorities.'

'Nathaniel.'

Guy A Johnson

'Yes, but don't speak his name here, not unless you must. It's not safe to. Just as we have people on the inside, those corrupt in the authorities no doubt have people spying on us, infiltrating our group. We have to be careful, at all times.' *Those corrupt in the authorities* – this suggested the government had people working for it that *weren't* corrupt, a concept I was still struggling with.

'So, did one of *your* spies get us the code tonight?' I asked.

'Yes, and promised us the coast would be clear for the time the code was active. But we don't have a lot longer before that code is replaced and the sentries' likely return – so we need to keep up our pace and get further down, so they don't glimpse our light.'

There were no other landings on our descent – which also meant no further passages holding the threat of these sentries. But the narrow stairway left me dizzy as we went down at an increased pace. Like the precarious crawl up the rope ladder on my ascent, I did my utmost to focus on the end goal – to escape the airless cylinder whose walls felt closer and closer at every step – ignoring the nausea that nagged in my belly. At one point, I broke from a trance just in time to grab Jessie, who stumbled forward, as if he'd fallen asleep for a second.

'Sorry,' he apologised, righting himself – relieved not to have caused any harm to those ahead of him. He stopped for a second or so, but the woman in front turned her head back and hissed:

'We've not time for this,' before annexing it with a softer. 'Sorry. If we delay, we increase the danger of being caught.'

We completed the rest of our descent without incident. But, by the time we reached the end, we were wet with sweat and made sick by the suffocating atmosphere. Despite

174

Guy A Johnson

Solomon's reassurance we'd meet no resistance or security at the bottom of that steep, stone flight, I was still surprised to simply find an arch in the wall taking us from the narrow stairwell out into the city.

*'Aren't they worried people will try to get out?'* I asked Solomon later.

*'Nobody has ever tried to escape, Tristan. Many have tried to get in, though – so they just secure the very top.'*

'So, this is it?' Jessie said in a whisper, as we took our first steps inside the city – finally on the other side of the wall.

'Yes.' The woman answered this, mirroring his volume. 'Welcome to *Elysium*.'

'*Elysium*?' I questioned, and she gave me a quick look that suggested I was interrupting something.

'It means heaven,' she answered, as if it was a secret, rather than an obvious translation she was revealing.

'And is that really where we are?' Jessie asked, regaining her attention. 'In Heaven?' He questioned her with less skepticism than I expected.

'Well, there is only one sure way to find out…'


We didn't see much that night – when we left the enclosed stairwell in the wall and entered the city streets, it was densely dark and lights that may have lit up our surroundings at an earlier hour were extinguished. Our companions were keen to get us off those streets and into their *safe-house* – promising we could play at tourists another day.

But what I do remember is a series of alleyways – one after another, the end of one leading to the beginning of the next, like a maze. And I recall speeding along streets of terraced houses – not even appreciating the fact that we were on foot and not treading water until later, when we were behind closed doors.

The place we were to stay – a place where we remained hidden for three days – was a three-storied house, tucked away at the end of an alley. Later I'd find it was neighbour to a funeral home on the left and a coffee shop on the right – the latter only a bygone concept in the city where I'd left Agnes and her family. And the rest of the street was made up of small shops – one that sold cards and newspapers, a butcher's, a hairdresser's, another café. So, this safe-house was an anomaly where it stood and should've stuck out. Should've attracted some attention for its misplacement. Yet the authorities showed it no interest – as if it were so obviously out of place it couldn't possibly house any kind of threat.

'And yet,' Nathaniel said to me, three days later when he returned. 'It is the headquarters of my little rebellion.'

'What took you so long?' Jessie had asked, irritation evident in his tone.

We'd been prisoners since the night we'd arrived – hiding in the basement of the house the entire time, wondering what the darkness had hidden from us. Wondering exactly what was in this secret city of *Elysium*, which had been so expertly concealed from the rest of the world.

*'Our city doesn't even have a name,'* Jessie had said, quietly devastated, when we'd heard what the metropolis behind the wall was called.

*'That's because it's not a city, Jess,'* I reminded him, thinking of what Nathaniel had told us. *'Not anymore. It's just one giant laboratory – for one giant experiment.'*

The basement was well equipped – a living room with a kitchen area, a small bedroom for each of us and a bathroom. But the door at the top of the stairs to the ground floor was locked soon after we crossed its threshold.

And Solomon's promise that we'd see the city – see Elysium – *tomorrow* came to nothing, seemingly another lie in a long string of deceptions. We didn't see it until after Nathaniel had visited us.

'I'm sorry I've kept you waiting. Kept you like prisoners. I've had to settle a few official affairs, and something unexpected came up. Something I couldn't leave,' Nathaniel said, in answer to the question from Jessie about his whereabouts. 'One day I intend to devote all my time to the people that deserve it, Jessie. But until the time is right, I still have a day job to do. I still have a cover to maintain.'

We were at the kitchen table – Jessie, Nathaniel, Solomon and I. We'd just eaten a meal, when Nathaniel and Solomon arrived together, the former carrying a clear bottle (containing vodka) and four glasses with him. Jessie helped himself to three consecutive shots, holding Nathaniel's gaze for the entire performance – making a point in silence.

'I know I haven't told you every detail you need to know,' Nathaniel said, breaking from the lock of Jessie's eyes and looking to me. 'And it may seem like I've taken you from one enclosed space to another.' He fluttered a hand in the air, indicating he meant the basement we were currently occupying. 'I've deceived you along the way too – I know that. Made promises I've not made good. I've deceived a lot of people over the years – a whole government of people, a whole city of them, and others, like you. I make no apologies for this. My focus is always the greater good. But the risks I take mean I can't be as open as others might like – as you might like, or even feel you need.'

Guy A Johnson

He gave both of us a measured stare at that point – to ensure we were listening to the speech he had clearly rehearsed in advance. We both nodded to acknowledge he had our attention and he continued.

'The unfortunate incident with Marcus,' he said, looking mournfully in Solomon's direction, whose gaze was downward. 'The death of our friend – putting our grief aside – has me worried about our security. Someone knows you've been smuggled into this place. And, while I've kept you locked up here, I've been trying to find out who.'

'Surely his killer was another desperate soul, taking every measure he needed to survive?' Jessie asked, but Nathaniel shook his head at this.

'From everything Solomon tells me, you were offering that man safe passage – and he chose a different path. None of you recognised him, right?'

'No,' I answered.

'So why did the man feel the need to flee – to kill? And he'd got so far – you were minutes away from getting him over the wall. Why would he risk it all – at the last moment, having got so far?'

We were silent – none of us had an answer. So Nathaniel gave us his.

'Maybe he'd got as far as he needed – over that first wall.'

He let that sink in a minute. I thought of that vast, unknown territory between the two walls, swallowed up by the darkness when we'd been briefly exposed to it. And I wondered just exactly what was out there – and why a man would so desperately seek it?

Nathaniel continued:

'You'd saved him from drowning and got him over the wall that surrounds *your* city – but maybe that's all he needed. And I believe he was someone we'd have recognised –

178

Guy A Johnson

Solomon said he was still covered in the mud and it was dark by then? That even Jessie wasn't recognisable in that state?'

I confirmed with a nod, glancing at Jessie simultaneously.

'So I think it was someone we knew. Someone who didn't want to be seen by some of us. Someone not on our side.'

As we took this in, Solomon pulled a puzzled expression.

'Solomon?'

'If that's the case, Nathaniel, I don't understand why he was in the mud. I don't understand why he chose to take that route into the city.'

'I think whoever it was thought he could get himself over the first wall – to wherever he was heading. And once he got into trouble, took a chance with our little army. But then he hadn't bargained on who'd be in our party.'

Solomon and Nathaniel shared a knowing look and then glanced at Jessie and me.

'What? You think it was someone who didn't want *us* to see him?' Jessie asked and Nathaniel nodded.

'There's someone in our group. Someone we put among you – a former member of the government who was known to you. Someone we thought we could trust. But I've since found out that he betrayed us – betrayed you too. And I fear that the enemy has been in our camp all along.'

'Who?' I asked, concerned – racking my brain to identify this man, wondering how we had been betrayed.

A single name from Solomon left me cold.

'Ronan,' he said.

Guy A Johnson

The tale that followed aroused a whirling circus of feelings in Jessie and me – hate, foolishness, anger and bitterness. Ronan – grandfather to Elinor and Billy – had been a secret government agent in his early years. A fundamental member of the authorities who'd overseen the takings and been a part of some of the dark, heinous crimes to which I'd been subjected in my teens. Once he'd retired, an apparently repentant Ronan had approached one of Nathaniel's associates and made a connection. And for more than a decade he'd been one of the Nathaniel's men on the inside of our city, keeping an eye on what was happening, looking out for potential recruits – keeping a particular eye on Agnes' family and associates, having judged them as perfect candidates. As potential leaders. But doubts were now well and truly cast on his character – and his loyalties.

'If you haven't worked it out already, you'll soon realise I don't trust anyone – not entirely. But I almost made an exception for Ronan. He seemed genuinely remorseful for his past – utterly disgusted by the actions he and the authorities had taken. For the torture he inflicted.'

I felt his gaze on me at this point, but I didn't look up. I didn't want him to see what was in my eyes – the pain I kept buried so very deep.

'*Almost* made an exception?' Jessie interjected.

'Yes. I had someone keeping an eye on him – not high security. Just a trusted friend who would report any change in Ronan's behaviour. And he was apparently acting a little jumpy. So, I had Ronan watched a little closer and I made a discovery.'

'What?'

'He had Elinor.'

Guy A Johnson

I looked up at his point, shock draining the suffering from my eyes.

'Yes. Ronan took her. She found out about him – about his past – and he held her captive. I don't think he was going to harm her, but when I learned this, I sent a man in to free her. But Ronan killed that man and fled, leaving Elinor behind. Luckily, another ally had stumbled upon Ronan's place and the girl is safe.'

'Where is she?' I asked, wondering if he'd tell me this time. But he didn't.

'Safe,' was all he was prepared to say. 'From what I understand from a contact that is close to your friends and family, everyone thinks Ronan is dead. They mistook him for the man he'd killed. But he definitely isn't dead. He's on the run.'

Nathaniel gave us another moment to take all of this in, to see if we had any questions.

'I know he's committed a terrible crime,' I managed, keeping my bitterness at the back of my throat, restraining my fury in order to remain logical – to be able to think, 'but why do you think he's betrayed *you?*'

'Because Ronan's one of the few people in the authorities who knows my name – knows what I'm involved in, what I'm planning. And I got word today that I'm under investigation. Nothing official. Just a whisper – but a whisper I can usually trust. I think Ronan cut his losses and decided betraying me – betraying our cause – was the only way he could survive. So, if he was the man you pulled out of the mud, then we're in big trouble.'

Solomon poured each of us another glass of vodka. He and Jessie knocked theirs back, but Nathaniel and I left ours untouched.

Guy A Johnson

'It's a lot to take in and remain focussed,' Nathaniel said, looking at me – a stare that told me he was relying on me. Relying on my trust and cooperation. 'Have you ever tried to count up the number of times you've been betrayed, Tristan?'

'I haven't a head for those kind of numbers,' I answered, finally raising my glass and slowly consuming the clear liquid. 'But I have a question – what does this mean for us all? What does this mean for whatever you've been planning?'

'A good question, Tristan. A good question – and it's the other reason for my visit tonight.'


While Nathaniel didn't explain *everything* to us over the hour that followed, he did explain more than before – and we finally knew how we fitted into his plans and what he needed us to do.

We were to lead an army of his men out of the city – an army of supporters who were finally prepared to put their lives on the line and rise up against the authorities. There was transport to get us out, but there were also a number of vulnerable citizens that we needed to rescue and get to safety first.

'Vulnerable citizens?' Jessie asked and I could tell by his tone that he was suspicious of this phrase.

'Please tell me these *vulnerable citizens* are not a bunch of old cronies you're protecting?' I asked and a look from Jessie confirmed this was exactly what he was thinking too.

Nathaniel raised a hand in soft protest, realising where our minds had taken us.

'No, not at all. They're the children.'

Guy A Johnson

'The children?'

I immediately thought back to the *taking* he'd mentioned as we'd headed to the wall.

'Yes, Tristan – the children. You remember the military helicopters we saw,' he continued, as if reading my mind. 'And you thought they might be looking for us?'

I nodded.

'And I said they were carrying children. Children taken from their families – something I hadn't been able to stop?'

I gave him a second nod – listening intently, hoping he'd answer all the questions circling in my head again.

'Well tomorrow, part of our mission is to put that right,' Nathaniel continued, acknowledging the concern that now flooded Jessie's face with a nod of his own. 'To stop it happening again, like it happened to you, Tristan. Like it happened to your brother, Jessie. But I'll need you to stay level headed. To keep focussed. Both of you. It's going to be dangerous. Very dangerous.'

'Were they taken from our city, Nathaniel?' A question from Jessie – one he'd no doubt kept inside since Nathaniel had mentioned this new *taking* a few days earlier. One he dreaded the answer to. 'Did they take my nephew? Did they take Billy?'

'Yes, they took them from your city. Hundreds of them. Took them from other places too. Cities isolated by the floods and by the authorities, like yours, within the enclosure. And they probably have your nephew, Jessie – but I don't know that for sure.'

Jessie drew in a sharp breath – an attempt to still his anger.

'Is there anything else you haven't told us, Nathaniel?' A question from me.

A too long pause and a shared look with Solomon suggested there was something.

183

Guy A Johnson

'Nathaniel?'

Eventually, he looked at Jessie and I coolly and simply shook his head – if there was something else, he wasn't prepared to tell us. He'd shared enough.

'Tomorrow morning, you'll finally get to see this city,' he said instead, as if we hadn't asked our question at all. He poured out the last of the vodka into our four glasses. 'But you'll need something to get around the place. Something to get you past all the security checks and reach your destination.'

From under the table, Solomon produced a small bag and took out two metal bracelets.

'These are your fake identification tags – they're new today, created by an ally I think I can trust.'

'You *think* you can trust?' Jessie asked, his exasperation rising again. And I knew that news of the takings – news that Billy was probably in grave danger – was killing him inside.

'They'll get you into the places I've talked about – the places I need you to be. They'll quite literally open all the doors you need – just as long as you're wearing them. But I can't take any more chances or leave things any longer, just in case. So tomorrow we take action.'

Nathaniel didn't elaborate this point – *just in case* was left to our imaginations to figure out.

'Before I leave you two for the night, do you have any questions?'

Guy A Johnson

An odd question, given it was clear he was still holding something back. We shook our heads – yes, we had many questions, but they weren't the ones he would answer. At least, not with the truth.

Once both Solomon and Nathaniel were gone, we retired to our beds and I was surprised to find sleep came easily for me. The following morning, Jessie confirmed as much for himself. I guess there was little else we could do – our fates were sealed. We had no other choice than to follow Nathaniel's instructions – follow his lead into whatever the next day would bring us.

We woke at 6am, left the tall, cramped confines of the terraced house – squashed between the funeral home and the café – and entered the bright light of *Elysium*, dazzled by its illuminating beauty.

'No wonder they wanted to keep it to themselves,' Jessie announced, unable to hide the sense of awe he was feeling, as he looked up high to the glass dome that covered the entire city – a dome that reflected the bluest sky and a honey-coloured sun back down on us. It was unnatural – like a movie of a perfect horizon – but still we were drawn in by its fakery, warmed by the man-made glow.

'Seems almost a crime to destroy it, doesn't it?' I said, as we were ushered away from the small street of our recent place of residence – by the woman and two men who'd helped us over the wall. Aside from Solomon and Nathaniel's visit, they'd been our sole companions over the last three days.

Guy A Johnson

'But destroy it we must,' the woman answered, sending us both a brief, sharp look – a warning we weren't to fool around with her. That even comments made in jest were not acceptable. 'We have to bring this all to an end.'

'Yes,' I answered, nodding soberly back at her and we made our way into *Elysium* – a city that reminded me of a tale I'd told Elinor and Billy over and over. 'The story of the *White City*,' I thought to myself, recalling the details.

*The White City was a quiet, sacred place. Cold to look upon, but warm in spirit all the same... From the enormous angel statues that kept sentinel at its grand, wrought iron gates, to the soft sand on the shore of its icy sea, everything about the place was crystal white... The White City was pure white through and through...*

That wasn't how I'd tell the tale in the future – I'd correct the details that had been elaborated *(the enormous angel statues)* and the obvious lies *(warm in spirit all the same.)* But there was a lot of truth in what I saw. And there was a part of the story – a particular line – that I wouldn't need to alter. A line that gave the whole tale a sense of prophecy.

What was it again?

*And then one day, a lone black cloud appeared on its snowy horizon, casting a shadow of grey.*

That shadow was us – it was the task that Nathaniel had drawn us into.

Elinor had always asked me if the story was true – if the White City really existed. I'd always side-stepped answering, always been vague, just told her to listen. But as I stepped out into it, I promised myself the next time I saw her, I'd finally answer that question.

Guy A Johnson

'No, Elinor,' I'd say. 'It doesn't exist, but only because Jessie and I helped bring it to an end…'

'It's quite something, isn't it?' Jessie – at my side, drawing me away from my thoughts.

'Yes it is,' I answered, back in the present, looking up into the ocean blue dome that covered the city, protecting it from the real world beyond.

We were still in the street where our safe-house was, but in the daylight it seemed different – the buildings that closely surrounded us were painted white and the stones of the ground were such a pale grey that they too appeared almost white, shimmering as the sunlight caught them.

For a moment, we were silent together, simply looking ahead at the new world we'd been led to. And though we said nothing, I still got a sense we were thinking of the same thing – of the ones we'd left behind. Of Agnes, Billy, Esther – and Elinor too. Elinor, who was no longer lost, but still lost to us for now. Thinking about what they might be doing, what they might be feeling – particularly about us, as we'd been gone so long. Much longer than we'd anticipated or promised. And thinking about how all of this – the *White City* ahead of us – was nothing but a rumour, a legend to them.

'So,' I eventually said, turning my head to the woman in our group, beginning a question, 'which way do we go?'

'Just follow me,' she answered, taking the lead, striding ahead along an alleyway of near white – before turning a corner and leading us into a residential maze.

Eventually, we would reach the core of the city.

And there we would be even more amazed at what we saw.

187

Guy A Johnson

There we would discover exactly what Nathaniel had refrained from telling us the night before.

We'd get our answers too – after all the promises and lies from Nathaniel, we'd finally get the answers to our questions.

Every.

Single.

One.

### *Unfold*

*So, I've told you what happened to Joe, Esther – finally making up for some of my lies. But that can't make up for a lot of what I've said and done, I know.*

*I'm guessing by now you'll have learned a few other things about me.*

*You'll have discovered more about the crimes I committed in the past – and no doubt some of those I've committed more recently. And you'll doubtless be thinking very badly of me.*

*You have to understand, though, I'm partly just a victim of my generation. Back then, when the authorities were desperate to save our world and made some of its cruellest decisions, it was a case of sink or swim. Join the government ranks and become a survivor – or lag behind with your everyday man and get left behind for good. So, while I chose my life's path, I didn't get much of a choice.*

*But I wasn't the worst of the men – there were others who committed crimes greater than mine. Others who became power crazy. Others who wanted to play God, Esther.*

*There's one man in particular you should know about.*

*A man you know very well.*

*A man I should've warned you about sooner.*

*The man who kept Joe captive and tortured him, Esther – Monty Harrison.*

*I know that you're aware he's no saint, Esther, but Monty Harrison committed the most monstrous crime of all of us…*

### *Fold*

Guy A Johnson

10. Billy

When we were plunged into darkness, I thought for the first few seconds that we would crash into something, but the train continued to hurtle along at full speed. And I felt a certain thrill, once I'd got over shock of the sudden dark – felt exhilarated for the first time during our adventure underground.

I thought Augustus might mess with the controls, slow us down, but he either couldn't find the right buttons without the light – or perhaps, like me, he was relishing the thrill of it all, reveling in the danger.

Yet, we weren't travelling blind for long. The lights gradually returned – flickering above us intermittently for a while, before regaining a full beam.

'Why do you think that's happened?' I asked, trying not to show any concern in my voice.

'Maybe there's a loose connection up there,' Augustus said, pointing at the ceiling of the driver's compartment – pointing at the blinking lights. 'But it'll be nothing to worry about,' he added, sounding as casual as he could to dispel any anxiety I might have felt. 'I should check how the others are doing – make sure they weren't too spooked by that. You happy to hold the controls, while I nip back for a minute?'

When he said this, his eyes fell to the canine who was curled up on the floor – who was somehow oblivious to the excitement we'd encountered.

I was getting used to our unconventional companion – no longer fearful that he might turn on me at any second and rip out my throat, like his species had my mother's.

Guy A Johnson

But I'd not been left alone with him until that point – and I didn't have Augustus' instincts and confidence in these matters.

'Or you could go instead, and I'll man the train,' he offered, as an alternative.

But I shook my head – I didn't want this to be a big deal.

'Do you think they heard that announcement in their part of the train?' I asked, referring to the voice that had come over the speaker system – a voice I was convinced was Elinor's. *On their way,* she had said – the message repeating several times, stuttering, like the recording was catching.

He shrugged.

'You really think it's Elinor? You know, neither her mother nor I thought it was her for a moment – though we were certain it was a familiar voice.'

I *was* certain, though.

'There was just lots of other noises surrounding it – like she was in a crowd or something. And I know what her voice sounds like when it's disguised or distorted – when we used to play, sometimes we'd do kind of silly voices.'

I felt a little stupid after I'd given this explanation, but Augustus just nodded thoughtfully.

'Could be the background noise,' he said, finding some sense in what I was saying. 'But if it is our Elinor, what does that mean?' *Our Elinor* – that seemed like an odd phrase from him. She was *our Elinor* – but he wasn't part of that *our*. He wasn't family. Much as this niggled me, I didn't make a big fuss about it – Augustus and I had made good progress since those dogs had taken Mother.

'Billy?'

191

Augustus' question drew me from my thoughts.

'Are you okay, boy?'

I nodded, a little too quickly.

'Yes, go check on the others, Augustus. I'll man the ship.'

And he smiled a small smile – at my use of his name (I hadn't said it out loud before) and my joke about driving the train.

'Okay. I'll be back in a while.' He went to leave, then paused, looked back at me and pointed to the creature on the floor. 'You know, we really should give him a name.'

'A name?' I questioned, thinking it the most absurd of things – and typical of Augustus to flit from one apparent random thought to another. 'Why would we give it a name – it's a dog.'

'It's what we humans used to do,' he said, finally heading out of our small compartment, talking with his back to me. 'We used to name our pets…'

'Pets?!' I questioned, the air ringing with another alien concept. 'What do you mean *pets*?'

But Augustus was gone – into the next carriage, probably occupied by a completely different thought already – and my question went unanswered.

While he was gone, I mulled over the many strange things we'd discussed while we'd been up front, driving the train.

The dog. The things he'd said about it being trained to do things – *fetch, roll over, guard, protect,* he'd said. More like some kind of strange toy than a wild creature. And the fact he now suggested we name it, like a person – a family member. What had he said

192

they'd been known as, the dogs? *Man's best friend.* More odd concepts that my head was struggling with.

*They killed Mother,* I dared to remind myself, holding my feelings steady, staring at the dog, who looked up at me with sad eyes. He was different from those beasts at Monty Harrison's house, but still I couldn't completely trust it and I felt my nervousness at being left with it return.

There were other things that played on my mind.

The road ahead, in particular – or the lack of it.

*We fell off the map a long time ago, Billy,* Augustus had said – offering no reassurance about where we were headed, where we might end up. And I still feared the weight of the water above us. Surely, sooner or later, the drowned world overhead would make its way down – cutting the electrics, swallowing up our thin air and flushing us out. Yet, Augustus had been utterly convinced of our safety on that front. And it was dry underground – as he'd pointed out, there was no rust or damp on the tinned food he'd found. Although that simply led to another puzzle, as Augustus had suggested the food hadn't been down there long, that maybe someone had brought it there recently – even left it specifically for us. That seemed a wild idea, though – how would they know we were coming?

But these weren't the biggest of puzzles, these weren't the strangest questions I had in my head. No, those were reserved solely for my new friend – the strange little girl who could get inside my thoughts and read my mind.

'Otterley,' I mouthed, thinking over what Augustus had begun to tell me, before he'd been distracted by the split in the tracks and we'd heard Elinor's distorted voice.

193

Guy A Johnson

What were his words?

*'She looks exactly the same age as she did when I last saw her – and that was many years ago. I can't explain it – at least, I can't yet. And I don't know why she was so precious to Monty Harrison – why he had to have her, why he kept her locked away, wired up to machines all these years.'*

And then there was what I already knew – the mind-reading.

I decided there and then to let her back in again – to let her read all these thoughts and see what she had to say.

*Otterley? Otterley?*

But I didn't get that weird feeling I'd had before – I didn't sense her invading my head space. I tried again.

*Otterley? Otterley?*

Still I felt nothing, so I was simply left to wonder about it all – the girl who hadn't aged, who Monty Harrison had kept *wired-up* (whatever that meant), who Augustus had said he'd rescued once before, years ago. The girl who could see what you were thinking.

'The girl who looked like Tilly Harrison,' I said to myself, recalling my own observation – and that's when I felt it. Like a sudden, sharp feeling – like a gasp or a shock of some kind. Otterley was back in my head – my words about Tilly had drawn her in.

I asked my single word question once again: *Otterley?*

*I don't know,* she replied, dropping these words in my head. *She's the other one.*

*The other one?*

The other what? This wasn't making sense.

*The one in my dreams. The one I see doing things I haven't done. The other me.*

194

I thought for a minute and then posed another question in my head for Otterley to read.

*Like your twin?*

She was gone from my mind for a second or so, but then I felt something, as she returned.

*Yes. Maybe. But that doesn't feel quite right. She doesn't feel like another person. She's just the other me. I can't explain it any better. I'm sorry.*

*She looks like you,* I offered, elaborating: *the Tilly I know. She looks like you. Similar.*

*She saw you in the water, Billy. The Tilly in my head saw you fall out of a boat. There was a dead dog in the water.*

*A puppy?*

*Yes. A puppy. The dreams I have – I think they are hers too. We share dreams, I think.*

*That happened, Otterley. I fell in the water and Tristan saved me.*

*And your mother was frantic, screaming, like you were going to die. Like you'd been poisoned?*

*Yes, yes she was!*

And suddenly I felt myself overwhelmed – with Otterley's unreal revelation, with the memory of the dog in the water and Mother's hysteria. How I missed it now – how I'd hated her at times, her hard ways with me, but how I wanted that back more than anything else. How I wanted her back.

After a few minutes, I recovered myself and drew my friend back into my thoughts.

195

Guy A Johnson

*Otterley? Otterley?*

But she was gone again – out of my head, like she'd switched her ability off.

Respecting my privacy, I thought at the time. But it wasn't that at all – she didn't want me to see what she was thinking, what she'd seen in one of those strange dreams she somehow shared with Tilly.

*Tilly,* I thought, my mind drifting off, as I wondered what exactly had happened to my friend since she and the rest of the school had been taken away in those helicopters…

When Augustus returned, he seemed a little more preoccupied than usual – his eyes flitting around as quickly as his thoughts, never staying on me for more than a second.

'Is everything alright?' I asked him, wondering what was up, but he reassured me it was nothing.

'Just wondering about the journey ahead, where we're headed exactly,' he said, but I wasn't quite convinced. The road ahead of us hadn't bothered him before – he'd been confident we'd be alright, even though he had no exact idea of our destination. So this didn't quite ring true.

'You sure?' I checked and he simply nodded, avoiding my eyes completely.

'Now, I wonder how far we've come exactly,' he said, moving the conversation on, focussing on the vehicle's dashboard.

I saw no point in trying to make him tell me what was concerning him, so I took an interest as he eyed the dials and buttons that controlled the train.

'I didn't note the mileage when we started this journey, Billy – maybe I should've,' he said, pointing to a counter on the dashboard. 'But see here?' He pointed to a dial – like

Guy A Johnson

a clock face – that was measuring our speed. 'We're doing fifty miles an hour according to that. And we've been travelling, what – an hour, maybe longer?'

I had no idea – neither of us had a watch to tell time by and there was nothing on the train to indicate it, either. But I wanted to play along, to pretend at least that I'd been making a note of these important things.

'An hour and a half, Augustus,' I announced with confidence and he grinned, looked my way, holding my gaze for a moment or two – seeming to relax a little. 'That's about 75 miles, right?'

'Yes, good maths, dear Billy. Good maths.'

We were quiet for a while, both of us simply looking ahead – into the dim view of the lowly lit tunnel before us. There was nothing to see – just a blurred glimpse of the close brickwork as we went past it. I kept thinking that the view would change any minute – that we'd come out of the tunnel we were in and into another station. But we didn't – not for ages.

'This is clearly taking us somewhere specific,' Augustus said – I listened for that nervousness he'd spoken of, but his voice was calm again. So, he really *wasn't* concerned about where we were going – that had been a white lie to cover something else up.

'Any thoughts on what that specific place is?' I asked, letting his deception go – I'd come back to that later.

'I don't know – but we've been travelling some time, with no other splits in the track, offering different directions. And no other stations have appeared. Remember when we came across that fork in the road?'

I nodded: yes, I did.

Guy A Johnson

'And the train veered left – the tracks taking us in that direction.'

I thought for a minute and made a few leaps with my imagination.

'Do you think someone is controlling this? That we're being watched?'

Augustus took a moment to think over his answer – considering how best to explain.

'In the past, there'd be someone – someone outside the train itself – in control of the tracks. Overseeing the many different trains using the network – and it was their job to make sure there were no accidents. No trains crashing into each other.'

'Like me and Elinor, when we played with the model railway at your house?'

'Yes, Billy – just like that,' he confirmed, a chuckle in his voice. 'But this is all different here. This is all locked away, forgotten about. I don't think anyone is overseeing this or in control of our journey. It's just us down here.'

I took in what he'd said for a moment.

'You said you thought someone had been here recently,' I said, recalling other theories he'd suggested. 'Said they'd brought that food, and that it had to be recent because of the lack of rust on the tins.'

'Yes. Maybe someone. Maybe this train is used for something, and used regularly, but I don't think someone is controlling it – not outside of the train.'

'What then?' I asked, a little confused.

'I think the train *automatically* went into the left-hand tunnel. – like it was pre-programmed to do so. And I think maybe this train *only* goes down this route. Billy, I think the journey we're taking – the destination this train is headed for – is the only journey it takes.'

198

'But why? And there's nothing at the other end,' I said, thinking about where the journey had started. 'At that first station, and the second one we came across, there was no other way in. There was nothing to see there. It was all blocked up. And only we know the way – from your house, from Monty Harrison's house – because of the map. This was all buried – forgotten about, you said.'

'I did, Billy. That's true. But maybe we missed something. Maybe there's something back at those stations we didn't see. Maybe we missed entrances to other tunnels – to other ways in and out.'

Augustus held my gaze for a moment and read something in my eyes.

'You're frightened, Billy?'

I nodded. I couldn't deny it – what had begun as an exhilarating adventure into the unknown suddenly felt a little more unnerving.

'Me too,' Augustus said, still looking into my eyes. 'Just a little bit. But.' And then he paused, making me think he wasn't going to finish his sentence. 'But Billy, we've lived in a frightening, unpredictable world for a long time. A world where the water washed away our homes, leaving many homeless or dead – leaving everyone living in impoverished conditions. And we lived in a world before that where those bloodthirsty dogs terrorised everyone, where governments kidnapped children – and mistreated them terribly.'

I thought over what he was getting at.

'So putting ourselves in this situation – in the firing line of more danger – is okay?' I said, testing out one possible meaning.

He laughed dryly.

Guy A Johnson

'It's one way of looking at it. But, no, I was thinking differently. Do you see the water down here, Billy – do you see the floods?'

I shook my head. No, it was dry – water-tight, we'd been assured.

'And no one's been abducted so far, have they? No one has gone missing from our party?'

Apart from Mother, I lamented in my head – but outwardly I agreed with him.

'And,' he said, like it was the last thing on his list, 'and the only creature we've met down here has been as tame and docile as you could imagine. *Beyond* your imagination, I suspect, Billy.'

I didn't commit an answer to this – not while I was still thinking of Mother. But Augustus didn't need my confirmation to know his point was clear.

'So, despite feeling anxious about the unknown ahead – about what might be in the darkness out there – all the omens so far are good. And we should take some comfort in that. Shouldn't we?'

The last two words made me wonder if Augustus was really sure after all.

'We should?' I said back, also in a question.

'And yet...' Augustus concluded, his sentence drifting off unfinished – suggesting our fear might be justified after all. 'Is it your turn to check on the others?' he asked, his demeanour and focus both changing suddenly. 'Me and thingy here will be alright on our own for a bit.'

*Thingy.*

He was still expecting me to name it.

'Okay,' I said, leaving them both.

Guy A Johnson

As I closed the door to the driver's compartment behind me, the lights started flickering again and – making my way along the four-carriage train – I struggled to remain steady.

Returning to Otterley and Marcie, I caught a strange look from both of them.

'Did Augustus tell you?' Marcie asked me, with a childish eagerness, and Otterley immediately broke her gaze from me and glared at the other girl.

'Tell me what?' I asked, puzzled.

'No, he didn't,' Otterley answered, indicating she'd been in our minds again – in Augustus' at least – and could confirm that whatever information the old man might've imparted hadn't passed his lips.

'Tell me what?!' I repeated, my voice firmer – my pulse quickening.

Augustus *had* seemed a little odd, nervous, when returning from the girls last time.

'Marcie – what should he have told me?'

But the girl was suddenly reluctant to say anything – looking to her lap, shaking her head.

'Otterley?' I said, turning to the other one. She remained reluctant to start with. So, I tried a different tact. *Otterley – I've trusted you with my thoughts. I've let you in my head.* And I did exactly that – let her in, allowed her to communicate with me telepathically. *I've let you see my feelings. The things I kept hidden.*

'Okay.'

A single word concession out loud.

*Okay. I'll tell you. She dreamed something.*

*What?*

Guy A Johnson

*She dreamed something,* she repeated, while Marcie watched our silent interaction, trying to work us out – not really understanding that we were communicating.

*Who?*

*The other one. The other me.*

*Tilly?*

*Yes. Maybe. Tilly. Yes – Tilly dreamed something.*

*And what did she dream?*

For a moment, Otterley left my head and dropped her own. But after a second or so, she took in a slow breath and I sensed her back inside me.

*She dreamed about your mother, Billy. She dreamed about your mother.*

I felt the tears instantly sting my eyes and streak down my cheeks.

*Tell me what she saw.*

Another pause – but a short one, like she was just preparing the task, not avoiding it.

*They find her, Billy. Two people – they find her.*

*Who? Who?*

My anxiety levels and my heart rate had increased further and I could feel a film of sweat rising through the surface of my skin.

She shook her head and returned to speaking, as if the telepathic concentration had been too much for the emotions in hand – as if it had exhausted her.

'I don't know, Billy. I'm sorry. A man and a woman, that's all she dreams. I didn't hear any names.'

Guy A Johnson

'And is she alive?' I asked, hoping beyond hope that she'd say *yes* – and even though it was only a dream, I was relying on it to give me hope. Hope of finding that which had been lost to me for good.

'I don't know, Billy.'

'But what did you see, in Tilly's dream – Otterley, what could you see?'

And under pressure, she said two words that diminished the tiny flame of hope I'd blown oxygen into.

'A body.'

'Hers?' I asked, as the final sparks ebbed.

'Hers.'

I remained with them for the rest of our journey on the train. Took one of the carriage seats and simply sat quietly as we sped on, the lights continuing to flicker, occasionally going out completely. Marcie would gasp when this happened, but that was the only sound that escaped from the three of us. Apart from that, we were silent.

Otterley stayed out of my head too – I didn't ask her in and she didn't invite herself, either. I guess she knew what I was thinking – it was written all over my sullen face – and she allowed me the privacy I needed. I doubt it would've helped for her to see those thoughts, to understand that I wished she'd never told me – not that Marcie gave her much choice. That telling me about some stupid dream had been pointless, and only achieved in stirring up my grief – in making me relive it all again – when what I really wanted to do was forget it all. Forget what I saw, forget Mother, forget that Augustus stopped me going back for her, because that was easier than trying to live with it – easier than trying to understand its meaning.

Guy A Johnson

'We've stopped.'

These were the words that killed our quiet – from Otterley.

Numbed by my dark thoughts, I hadn't noticed us gradually slowing down – but she was right. We *had* stopped – the lights in the carriage were on, but the vehicle was no longer juddering along, although the engine was still humming.

'Where do you think we are?'

This was from Marcie – a pointless question, as none of us had any idea, but I held back from pointing this out.

'I don't know,' I said instead.

'Should one of us go to Augustus – find out if he did this?'

'No need,' I said, tipping my heading towards the window, looking into the next carriage.

He was heading towards us, the nails of four small feet clicking along the floor behind him. I saw a nervousness rise in Marcie, when she saw the dog approach.

'He's fine,' I reassured her. 'He really is. Hardly even barks.'

'What's happened?' Otterley asked, as soon as Augustus was over the threshold and with us in the carriage. 'Why have we stopped?'

'We seem to have reached the end of the line,' Augustus answered, brushing his hands over the dog's ears, to which it reacted by furiously wagging its tail.

'What do you mean?'

'Exactly that – there's no more track. I felt train the automatically slow down, like something kicked-in – which was just as well as I don't think I'd have stopped it in time.'

Otterley and I gave each other a quick look.

204

Guy A Johnson

'So where do we go now?' I asked, feeling my anxiety levels rise – wondering what lay ahead of us.

'There's something here, Billy. Something I want to check out.'

'What?'

Augustus shrugged.

'An entrance, an exit, a way out, or just another way further into wherever we are, but it's definitely the way ahead.' The way he said this – talking in almost a riddle – reminded me how well he was suited to that name we'd known him by for all those years. Old Man Merlin – it had never suited him better. 'Are you coming?'

'Will there be dogs – more dogs?' From Marcie.

'Like this one?' Augustus asked, but she shook her head. 'I doubt it, but I can't guarantee it. Can't guarantee anything.'

'I'm coming,' I confirmed and Otterley stood up, showing her intention was likewise.

'Marcie, I'd suggest you stick with us, but if you don't want to, you could stay on the train. Lock the doors. There's food here and I doubt we'll be gone long. I could leave…' His sentence trailed, as he looked down at the creature at his feet.

'I'll be fine. I'll stay here, but *that* can go with you,' Marcie said, almost visibly shrinking away.

'Okay, okay,' Augustus agreed, although you could tell he wasn't entirely happy to leave her. 'You two ready?'

We nodded in unison.

Guy A Johnson

'So what have you found, Augustus?' I asked, as we stepped out of the train, back into the dark, damp tunnel and made our way along the last part of the tracks – carefully avoiding the live lines. The doors closed behind us, as Marcie immediately pressed the button that locked them. 'What have you seen?'

But Otterley answered for him – entering both of our heads, as if to just remind us of her strange ability.

*A door. He's found a door...*

Guy A Johnson

### Unfold

*Monty Harrison knew all about the experiments that had gone on, Esther. Knew all about the twin program and the DNA manipulation that had occurred. Knew all about the government's secrets, as someone like Monty Harrison had fingers in every pie – even back then.*

*He wanted a part of it too – wanted to have a stake, a very personal stake, in the future the authorities were creating. Wanted to see his own reflection in that future.*

*Something I very much doubt you'll know about Monty is that he lost the love of his life when he was in his twenties. Rose, her name was. They were due to marry, but she was killed in an apparent accident – knocked down by a car outside the front of her home. Monty's grief was immeasurable – and made worse by the fact that he suspected it hadn't been an accident at all. That someone with a grudge – there was a long line of potential suspects, even back then – had hurt her to get at him. And it worked.*

*Monty never looked at another woman. Rose would always be the only one for him. And, as the years went by, he grew lonely. So, when he heard about the experiments the authorities had sanctioned, he had one of his maddest ideas – he wanted a child of his own. A child created in the image of Rose – using his DNA, of course.*

*And, applying his usual persuasive methods and putting pressure on his high-level contacts, Monty got his way. A child was created for him – a replica of his sacred Rose. But Monty lost sight of what was motivating the government and their scientists – to them this was an experiment, a chance to try new things – to push the envelope further than before.*

207

Guy A Johnson

*So when the girl who had Rose's looks was presented to our gangster associate, Esther, he didn't quite get what he bargained for.*

*And he didn't suspect for a minute that they'd created more than one girl.*

*That they'd created twins.*

*Not at all…*

**Fold**

11. Elinor

With Nathaniel gone and Robert at the helm, we travelled further along that river road, further amongst the dense, green forest. While Robert had stated that I was in charge – not him – he still took the practical lead in deciding where we were heading and giving the others on the boat instructions. And, as I had so many thoughts to distract me after my chat with Nathaniel, it was just as well.

There was so much churning over in my head – some of it making sense, allowing me to tie up loose ends in my mind. But other things had me in turmoil – had me wondering exactly who I could trust.

*I'm a person of some privilege, Elinor. Someone who has worked their way into a position of power... as high as you can get.* It made perfect sense that Nathaniel was a senior member of the authorities – it explained his apparent wealth and the huge boat, which made Jessie's speedboat seemed tiny. It also explained why he commanded the compliance of others so effortlessly – maybe they feared him more than they trusted what he said, what he promised.

It didn't surprise me that he'd been watching us and listening in on our conversations – there had been rumours for a long time that the authorities were tracking our every movement. Great-Aunt Penny would shush you every time if you cussed the government, for fear the officials might swoop in and lock you away for your rebelliousness.

And I'd always imagined that the senior people in the authorities were all bickering with each other – so when Nathaniel said he hadn't trusted any of his colleagues with his mission to bring justice, it rang completely true.

209

Guy A Johnson

But his other revelations had left my head dizzy and my heart racing.

What he'd said about Tristan.

*Tristan was sent your way many years ago – by the authorities... he found your mother. Joined a family that turned out to be full of potential allies.*

Tristan was a spy? Tristan working for the authorities? I wasn't sure I could believe it – this version of Tristan was so far removed from the one I knew. Tristan was the person I trusted above all others, even Mother. Tristan who had been...

'Like a father to me,' I thought, staring out into the dense, dark green forest we continued to sail alongside.

*Like a father.* And that was Nathaniel's other bombshell – he knew my father. He even promised I'd get to meet him, once all this was over. And he revealed his name too – Xavier. The strange name that had been inscribed on Old Man Merlin's tiny trains on the miniature railway Billy and I had played with. Could there be a connection to that crazy old hoarder and the Xavier who was my father? That seemed too much, but then it was such an unusual name, not one I'd heard before. Were they related – father and son, even? Could it be that Old Man Merlin was actually my grandfather? I shook my head – it was a ridiculous idea.

This had been Nathaniel's biggest revelation about my family – but it wasn't the only one. Ethan – the odd man who'd come to my rescue – was in fact my cousin. He and his lost twin, Joshua, were my Great-Aunt Penny's children. Another family secret, locked away. And Ethan hadn't killed Grandad Ronan, as I'd suspected – not according to Nathaniel. *When he entered the flat, he found the body already in that terrible state. Already dead.* But Ethan *had* saved me from the same fate. And, as I tried to take stock of

210

everything Nathaniel had said, I found this comforting – and it made me determined to get to know him a little better. Yet my cousin didn't make that easy.

'The times I've met him before – long time ago now, though,' Robert explained to me, 'I've found him a bit distant. A bit damaged by all that's happened to him. Bit of a loner, you might say.'

And this seemed true. Ethan very much kept himself to himself, in spite of my efforts to get a little closer. He'd been cleaned up once we'd boarded the speedboat and looked less frightening in a clean shirt and trousers, but whenever I approached him and attempted to pull him into conversation, he'd almost flinch and withdraw himself. And he had a quiet glare in his eyes that watched you like an animal watches its prey – considering its opportunity to strike.

'I did warn you,' Robert had said, one morning when I'd retreated from my cousin, disappointed yet again that I couldn't make any progress with him. 'You'll just have to keep trying and make allowances.'

I'd pondered this thought, thinking back to the scene in Ronan's flat – I'd dropped the *grandad* by then. I was still wondering about that blood-soaked scene and what had actually happened. Still wondering if Ethan – damaged, withdrawn Ethan, with that cold look in his eyes – might still have had a hand in Ronan's demise.

'You think he could kill someone?' I asked Robert. 'You think he's suffered so much that it's turned him into a killer?'

Nathaniel might have claimed Ethan wasn't responsible for Ronan's murder – but he'd been soaked in his blood – and he had the motivation. There was no denying those facts.

Guy A Johnson

'Anything's possible, especially when you've been through what he has.'

Robert meant the takings – I'd learned that my cousin had endured worse than many, as had his brother, Joshua. The latter had never made it home, never seen my great-aunt and –uncle after he'd been abducted. Although, Nathaniel had suggested he'd seen him – kept tabs on him for a while. As he had *all* of us.

'Just give Ethan time,' Robert advised. 'Let him come to you, maybe?'

I agreed and kept a little distance between myself and my cousin.


The solidity of the forest that hemmed us in on either side of the river road was unforgiving. The thickness and closeness of the greenery was almost suffocating, but it was also endless. I kept expecting to come to the end of it, to come out into the open – to come out into sea. But Robert said we were going far, far east – as far away from my city as we could get and to the far side of the city where the authorities lived.

'They have a separate city?' I asked.

While I'd always wondered where the government hid itself, I'd always imagined it was nearby – hidden in a privileged part of my own town that I'd never been to. Somewhere in the far north, past the police headquarters and the hospital. I didn't imagine that they were this far away – on separate land.

'Yes. In the east. A protected city. A white city,' he added, with a hint of the story-telling flare I recognised as Tristan's. Tristan, who I missed so much, but whom I also trusted a little less now.

When we eventually stopped the boat – after so many days and nights, I'd lost count – we were still enveloped by mighty trees on both banks, their curved branches meeting in

212

the middle to create a natural arch. It was nighttime too, and Robert said we were to leave the boat – step ashore into the unknown territory under the cover of darkness.

I was terrified, but Robert insisted. So we moored the boat and stepped onto solid ground and Robert led a group of six of us – including Ethan – through leafy undergrowth, without a torch or any kind of light to illuminate the way.

'We'll use the torches we have when we know it's safe,' Robert scolded me lightly, when I complained about it, stumbling almost purposely over the bony roots of a tree to make my point. 'Once we know it's safe – once we know that no one else is here, I'll hand you your very own light, Elinor. But for now we must follow the path in darkness. And don't worry – I know the way. I've been here before.'

Yet I didn't feel especially reassured, as we stumbled on. And I worried that we might be blindly walking into a trap – that our enemy would be waiting to ambush us as soon as we reached our destination.

I'd still not been given any more details on my specific role in all this. What had Robert said I'd be doing again? *Winning over some lost souls.* But what did that mean? When I'd asked him, he'd just grinned and said I'd find out soon enough, like it was some game. But as we made our way through that forest land, shrouded in blackness, it couldn't have felt less like a game.

We eventually reached the end of the forest, where there was high link-chain fence surrounding a vast clearing in the middle of the wood. Adjusting my eyes – the promised torches still hadn't materialised – I could make out the shapes of buildings on this bare landscape.

Guy A Johnson

'This is where we go in,' Robert announced, as one of the others used a pair of metal cutters to create an opening in the fence. 'But before we do, let me tell you exactly why we are here – and exactly why you, Elinor Taylor, are such an important part in it all.'

Even in the dark, I could read the utter seriousness in Robert's face – his game playing was over. This was the real thing now.


The plan sounded simple enough – when you weren't responsible for its success or failure.

'This place is where we're bringing the children,' Robert began.

'What children?' I asked, confused.

'The ones the authorities have taken.'

'Takings?' I said, hearing my mother's voice and the terrifying tales she'd told me of her own childhood. 'It's started again, like before?'

Robert nodded, but quickly spoke again, reading the alarm in my face. 'But it's not like before, Elinor. And that's why we need you.'

'I don't understand.'

'You will,' he said, taking a deep breath and rubbing one of my shoulders with a hand – the closest he'd got to a gesture of affection. It was welcome too. And I was beginning to like Robert – especially as he was starting to be straighter with me. 'We're intervening, Elinor. The authorities have already taken children from your city, and from other cities.'

'Other cities?'

'You didn't think yours was the only one, did you?'

Guy A Johnson

I shook my head – no, I wasn't that dumb. And yet part of me did think that my city had been the only one.

'If the authorities have started the takings already, why are we here – why have we come to this place?' I'd asked, looking out into the night, to the open space we'd come to, to the shadows that were buildings. A thought suddenly came to me. 'Are the children here? Are we here to rescue them?' I looked worriedly back at our small crew.

Robert shook his head.

'No, they're not here, but they will be.'

My corrugated brow showed him I didn't quite understand.

'As I said, we're intervening, Elinor. That's what Nathaniel left us to do. He's got another team together – they'll be rescuing the children and bringing them here. All of them.'

'They're not here yet?'

'No, not yet.'

'So,' I began, realising there was still one big question he'd not answered, 'why did you need me?'

'Trust, Elinor,' he began, looking me straight in the eyes, as if to gain mine. 'The children have already been taken by one group of adults, only to be taken again by us – another group of adults. They'll be confused. They'll be frightened – be worrying about their families, about their lives. But we want them to feel safe, to understand that we plan to put things right, to reunite them with their loved ones. Why should they trust us?'

'But you think they'll trust me?'

Robert nodded.

Guy A Johnson

'Some of them know you went missing, Elinor – the ones from your city, your school. So they'll think you'll have first-hand knowledge of whom to trust and whom not to. And they'll listen to you, we're certain. You'll keep them calm – you'll convince them we're the good guys. And we need their trust, Elinor, because we don't know how long we're going to be out here.'

'What do you mean?'

'Things are going to happen, Elinor. A rebellion.'

'Against the authorities?'

Robert nodded.

'Yes. Once the children are here and safe, there are plans in place to bring them down. There'll be fighting.'

'A war?'

A shrug.

'Maybe, but definitely danger. So, it might be quite a while till these children see their families again. If at all.'

As he said these last three words, Robert was watching me closely, checking if I could handle such realities – if I understood the implication. I nodded quickly, a confirmation that I did.

'But they're not here yet, Elinor. And we've another job to do first.'

'What?'

'We need to check this place is clear. Need to check the enemy hasn't found out about it. And then I've just got to hope I can radio a message through to Nathaniel.' He paused, turned away and spoke to the others. 'You all ready?'

A chorus of yesses confirmed they were.

'Are you ready, Elinor?'

'I think so, yes.'

'Good. In which case, maybe you should take this.'

Robert handed me a small black torch. I instinctively switched it on and a strong, bright beam flooded out the dark. I switched it off just as quickly.

'Use it sparingly – and only when you really need to. Right, in we go.'

And with that, we made our way through the hole in the chain fencing and quietly, gingerly, made our way across the huge compound.


Once we were all through the fence, we ran lightly across the open ground till we reached the first of ten or so building shadows. It was strange moving on dry land – albeit the earth was muddy. But it was really solid – not even marshy, like the train graveyard was back home. The only dry land I'd walked on before was the hill on which *St Patrick's* was built.

Thinking of that filled me with brief sadness, as I thought of my times with Billy – at the train graveyard, on the school hill. I wondered if he'd been one of the children who'd been taken – and whether I'd be reunited with him. The thought lit a spark of joy in me. I thought to ask, but then thought again. Robert might think it a childish thing and I didn't want to seem childish. So I kept this little wish to myself.

Initially, the six of us kept together – prowling around in the shadows. Fear had triggered my adrenalin and that in turn was keeping me alert and on the move. And all the

Guy A Johnson

time we were out in the open, I kept expecting us to get caught. For someone to step out from the dark and question our presence. Or worse – no questions, just action.

'We're looking for any signs of recent life,' Robert said, as we crept along. And I allowed his words to distract me from my worries. 'As far as we know, no one has been here for months,' he reassured. 'Not since Nathaniel last sent people here to check it out. So there shouldn't be anything here. This is just a routine check. Just to make sure.'

'What should I look for?' I asked, needing a little more guidance.

To my surprise, Ethan answered.

'Lights. Voices. Any movement. Marks in the ground – footprints, tyre marks.'

'Tyre marks?' I questioned.

'Land vehicles.'

I nodded, trying to catch his eyes in the dark, but he kept them averted, as he continued to list what we should look for.

'Food waste. Empty bottles. Packets. Wrapping. Signs people have been living here. Warmth. Water. It should be cold and dry here, if it's not inhabited.'

'That's right,' Robert interjected, an attempt to gain control of the conversation again.

'Things for washing. Soap. Towels. Toothbrushes. Things for cooking and eating. Pans. Plates. Cups.'

'Knives and forks?' I offered Ethan and I got a flicker of reaction. Progress.

Robert cut in again.

'Let's get to this first building ahead and then decide how we're going to split the group.'

Guy A Johnson

*Split?* I thought, but I said nothing, as no one else seemed surprised by this announcement. Ethan picked up on my silent worries, though.

'It'll be fine,' he said – short and with purpose, but little emotion.

'Thanks,' I answered, offering a small smile, but he didn't return it. *Small steps,* I told myself. *Small steps.*

When we reached the first of the buildings, we didn't split to start with.

'Let's enter the first one together – agree a process for checking we're safe and then split the rest of the buildings between us, replicating the process in each one,' Robert suggested, as we reached two large doors which I assumed were the way in. 'Sound like a plan?'

We all agreed with nods and murmurs.

'Right – Michael?' Robert's question was put out to the member of our group who'd cut through the wire fencing. 'Want to cut through the lock?'

As he asked this, Robert turned a torch on and flashed it at a thick chain lock that was looped between the handles of the doors. But something was immediately clear – the chain was already broken and was simply hanging between those two handles.

'Someone's got here before us, Robert,' Michael said, stooping down and picking up the lock part from the ground. 'I was part of the last visit here. And I secured these locks personally and destroyed the keys, as we agreed then.'

'Why did he do that?' I asked Ethan quietly, not expecting an answer – surprisingly I got one.

'So anyone who came back here would have to damage the locks. So, even if one of them sneaked back – maybe with the enemy in tow – there'd be no covering it up if they tried to get in.'

'Unless they used new locks,' I observed.

'There is that.'

*One of them* – that was a phrase that stuck in my mind. Suggesting he didn't feel like one of the team, but considered himself an outsider – like me. I liked that; sought some comfort in it.

'I doubt whoever came here is still around, but let's be cautious, okay?' Robert addressed the group with those doors still pulled together. 'And I'll have to get a message to Nathaniel, now that this place has been discovered by someone else-.'

'The authorities,' someone affirmed.

'The authorities? Probably, yes,' Robert continued. 'It won't be safe to bring the children here now. We'll have to find somewhere else. Right. Ready? Good. In we go then…'


That first building we entered was identical to all the others in its layout – apart from one unique structure, which was essentially a shower and toilet block. But the others – Robert said there were ten in total – were the same on every level.

As we entered, straight ahead of us was a huge area that looked like a cross between a hospital ward and a laboratory. It was filled with bed after bed, each surrounded by monitors. And everything was sectioned-off with rubber curtains and all the equipment was covered it plastic – like it was brand new or had been cleaned and sealed-up. There were

220

also a series of long benches, with stools tucked underneath them. And on top of these were all sorts of scientific paraphernalia, similar to what I'd glimpsed in Old Man Merlin's back kitchen – only these items were new or clean, the apparatus covered in a transparent film, like everything else.

Above this area, there was a small room tucked away in the roof, but it was completely empty.

'You know what this is, don't you?' Robert had said to Ethan, and my cousin had nodded. 'You remember it then?'

'What?' I'd asked, but Robert had gravely shaken his head at me and I pursued it no further.

Underneath the laboratory/hospital, there was an expansive basement – with a floor covered in mattresses. The group weren't surprised by this – they'd set them out here on a previous visit, Michael (the lock-cutter) confirmed. But they were alarmed by the disarray – the bedding covering each and every mattress was disturbed.

'As if someone has been sleeping here,' Robert said, concern in his face and voice.

'As if people, lots of people have been sleeping here,' Michael emphasised and Robert conceded with a nod.

There was further evidence of habitation through this dormitory area: *food waste, empty bottles, packets, wrappings.* In my head, I checked off Ethan's list. *Things for washing. Things for eating.* There were signs of this everywhere.

'Someone left in a hurry,' Robert thought aloud. 'No attempt to cover up, apart from the lame attempt to put that lock back in place. 'Let's keep going.'

221

Guy A Johnson

Off the main area we found some smaller rooms, which Robert described as *examination rooms.* We found signs of use here too – damp paper towels and used syringes in a *clinical waste bin* (Michael's description.)

We also found a set of steps that took us further underground and this sub-basement led us down into a maze of small rooms. The first ten or so of these looked like private sleeping quarters – each had a bed, a chest to put personal belongings in, a sink to wash in and a sense of comfort about them. But thereon, the rooms were much narrower and had a very different feel.

'They're like cells,' I muttered to Ethan.

Like a prison, each room was a compact oblong, with a bed, maybe a table, a light, but little else. And in each door there was a grill and a metal plate that slid cross it. But it didn't look like anyone had been down there – at least, not in the first building we entered.

After we'd scoured that first block, Robert split us up into pairs – he with one of the others, whose name I wasn't sure of, Michael with another and me with Ethan. I was pleased to be paired with my cousin, who was gradually thawing, I felt – the cold look in his eyes lowly warming. But I hid these feelings – I didn't want my enthusiasm to put him off, cause him to retreat.

Of the remaining buildings, we were given three each. And the first one Ethan and I entered by ourselves, we found a similar set up: the laboratory areas all sealed up, the room in the roof empty, the bedding on the floor of mattresses disheveled and the maze of cells unused. But our second building threw up something different altogether.

Guy A Johnson

Gaining confidence that whoever had been there was long gone, we decided to split up – Ethan covered the first floor and the room in the roof and I did the basement. He then promised to join me in the sub-basement. And it was there that I found her – the girl.

She was lying on a bed, turned away from me, her face buried in a pillow.

'Who are you?' I asked, but she didn't answer and I suddenly felt unsafe. Suddenly vulnerable. I had no idea who she was or what she might do – what if this was a trap?

*Ethan! Hurry up! Ethan!* I cried inside, certain he had the ability to rescue me from anything – he'd done that before, hadn't he? I recalled the bloody scene at Ronan's flat. *Ethan, I need your help!* But I kept all this inside, remaining calm on the surface.

'Hey, what's your name?' I asked again, panic rising in my throat and I could taste something acidic in my mouth. *Elinor, now is not the time to vomit!* 'Hey, we need to get moving. Need to get you out of here,' I continued, although it wasn't strictly true – but if Ethan wasn't on his way to keep me from any impending danger, then maybe I should get myself and this girl to him?

She moved and slowly turned to face me, like she was coming round from a heavy sleep and I recognised her – from home, from school.

'I know you,' I said. 'You're safe now, okay?'

But *I* still didn't feel safe myself – I still felt suspicious of this find, so I continued to insist we move. I wanted to get her to Ethan, to the others – then I imagined the feelings of dread that I just couldn't shake would finally subside.

'We do need to get moving, though. I can get you out of here, but I don't know how much time we've got,' I improvised, hoping a sense of urgency would get her excited, get her moving. 'Do you understand?'

223

Guy A Johnson

But she shook her head and stared at me blankly. If anything, this made me feel a little irritated and I took a different line with her.

'Are you coming with me or what?' I asked, almost crossly. 'Look, we need to get moving. There's no one here at the moment, but they might be on their way back to get you.' Another lie that I hoped might spur some action – and it did.

'What do you mean – on their way back to get me?' she asked, a little alarmed.

I had to think quickly to keep my deception going.

'They've gone,' I told her, which was true – *someone* had definitely been and gone. 'Whoever brought you here – they've left. Gone some time, I'd guess.'

'And the others?' she asked, swallowing a lump in her throat. 'Peter and…' Her voice faded away.

*Peter?* I wondered. So she *had* been here with others – very likely whoever had been sleeping in the dormitory above us.

I shook my head, my momentary irritation dissipating – a little sympathy for the girl replacing it.

'There's no one else here, just you,' I told her and held out a hand. 'And we really need to go. Okay?'

She took a minute or so to decide if she could trust me – and then she held out hers, taking mine.

'Okay, you had better lead the way….'


We made our way up to the ground floor and she filled me in on a little of what had happened – how she'd got there and who she'd been there with.

Guy A Johnson

I had to help her walk – help *Tilly* walk. Yes, that was her name – Tilly. Tilly Harrison. She was younger than me, but slightly older than Billy. And she was acting strangely weak. She said she'd been in a room – a room that had made her dream bizarre, unreal dreams. A dream about her mother and a staircase that never ended. And she felt exhausted, drained and somehow frightened.

'But I don't know why,' she answered, almost tearful as she spoke. 'It was only a dream, right?'

*Where are you Ethan?* I kept asking myself, wishing he'd reappear and help me to help her along.

I had to struggle on my own and when we reached the laboratory floor and I called out, his voice came from just outside the main entrance.

'What is it?' I asked him, reaching him and catching something in his face – fear.

'Who is that?' he asked at the same time, and I saw the pale terror quickly harden on his face. *What was going on with him?* 'Robert! Robert! Over here!' he had cried out, before I could answer him. 'Robert! Robert!!' There was aggression and urgency in Ethan's voice – like Robert's hearing him and getting there as soon as possible was imperative.

It took several minutes before the other four came scuttling out of the shadows, with Robert reaching us first.

'What's going on? And who's this girl?' he asked, almost echoing the questions Ethan and I had asked each other.

'I found-,' I began to explain, but Ethan cut straight through me with his own version of events.

Guy A Johnson

'*He* left her behind, I'm certain,' he said, instantly confusing me. *Who was he talking about?*

Robert seemed as equally unsure.

'Elinor?' he questioned, turning to me.

'I found her below, in one of the cells. I know her from home. Her name's Tilly. Tilly Harrison, but she's not quite right. She's weak, a little disorientated. There were definitely others here. She asked about one of-.'

'*He* was here – he took them!' Ethan insisted, interrupting me again. He was angry now, his eyes bulging and red with fury. 'For God's sake Robert, *he* was here!! I'll show you!'

*Who is he?* I wondered, but I didn't ask – I just listened in and followed on, as Ethan led us all back through the laboratory area and up into the empty room in the roof.

As we made our way past all the plastic wrapped equipment and sectioned-off hospital-style beds, I asked Robert what he thought had happened.

'I'm not sure. The girl said she'd been here with others?'

'Yes. Children. And there were adults here too. She didn't say much, but she said they came here by helicopters. Taken from their school.'

Robert shared a worried look with the others.

'What is it?' I asked.

'The children were being taken to the city – our city – to a new, secret laboratory the authorities have been constructing for years. There, the children were to be sanitised and then tested.'

'Sanitised?'

226

Guy A Johnson

Robert nodded, the look in his eyes acknowledging my alarm.

'The plan was to let the authorities take things so far – we couldn't risk raising suspicions too early. Then we'd get the children out – bring them here. Nathaniel has pulled another team together to help do this. But they wouldn't have got here yet.'

'Maybe they got here early.'

'Yes. Possible. And difficult to be in touch with us. But-.'

'But what?'

'Why did they leave again?' Ethan asked, as if I'd have the answers.

I thought about what Tilly had told me so far.

'She says they thought she was a spy. That she lied about her name and-.'

'But we'd never leave a child – whatever we thought. We're not the authorities, Elinor. We're the good guys.'

'But the children aren't here, Robert. Apart from Tilly.'

'No, they're not. They're gone.'

'Maybe the authorities took them back?'

'I don't know. We weren't even expecting them to be here yet – we were here ahead of them, remember, so they *couldn't* be. And – that aside – if this is the work of the authorities and they've found out what we're doing, we wouldn't be standing here, free. There would've been a welcoming party, at the very least. No, it's something else. Something I can't explain. Something that doesn't make sense.'

'Someone else?'

'What?'

'Maybe it was someone else – someone else who took them?'

227

Guy A Johnson

'But who? Who would take hundreds and hundreds of children – and why? And how?'

A question people had asked themselves before – who would take hundreds of children? What kind of person would think that was okay?

A question no one could give a sane, rational answer to. But still it had happened – and it was happening again.

'Someone who wanted to save them.' This was from Ethan, who'd been quiet while we'd debated. '*He* took them,' he insisted again. 'And I'll show you!'

Once we reached the end of the ground floor, and it was clear where we were going next, Tilly became distressed.

'Please, not again,' she pleaded, as we stepped inside the lift that took us up – pulling away from me and slumping to the floor. Her strength seemed to be fading further. 'Please don't. Please.'

Robert intervened.

'We're not going to hurt you,' he said to her, crouching down to meet her at eye level. 'Ethan here just wants to show me something. Something that is clearly important to him. Okay?'

Tilly nodded in response, tears spilling from her eyes.

'How about you stay down here, okay? I'll leave you with Elinor.'

'But-.' I interjected. *Why did I have to miss out on whatever Ethan had found?*

'I want her to see it,' Ethan insisted, another surprise from him.

'I'll stay with you,' Michael offered, smiling softly. 'Is that alright with you, Tilly?'

She nodded, a brief, slightly reluctant nod and then the rest of us entered the lift.

228

Guy A Johnson

'Whoever was here took her up,' Robert said quietly to Ethan, pointing to the ceiling as the lift doors closed. 'Jesus, poor thing.'

*Took her up? What did this mean? Up to the empty room we were headed for?*

'It's just an empty room,' I said aloud, as the lift shuddered still and the doors parted again.

'Don't let what you see fool you, Elinor,' Robert warned, as we stepped out.

But that's all it was – like the other roof rooms I'd seen here, the space was empty. Just a blank, black empty space. No furniture. No windows. Just a single bulb in the middle of the ceiling giving us light. I went to step further into the room, but Ethan reached for my wrist and yanked me back – squeezing and pulling a little harder than necessary.

'Don't!'

'Ouch!'

'Don't!'

'He's right,' Robert offered in a softer voice. 'This place is not quite what it seems, Elinor. There's danger, torture lurking in those shadows.'

'But it's just an empty attic room.'

'That's exactly what you're supposed to think, but the Chamber of Doors is anything but an empty attic room, Elinor. It's anything but that.'

I'd gasped at the mention of the *Chamber of Doors.* It was a favourite bedtime horror story I'd heard so many times from Tristan. And here I was, right at the edge of it. How had it gone again?

*An endless opening of doors and walking over a threshold, only to be presented with another door; opening that and crossing another threshold; opening another; crossing*

229

Guy A Johnson

*another. They get into your mind, they find out what you are searching for – the whom or the what you have been looking for – and then they put it in there. In the chamber of doors. They put it just beyond the next door. And each time you think you are going to reach it, each time you open a door and step forward, it's still behind the next door. It's still just out of reach. So you go through another and another.*

Tilly had talked of being taken to a room – a room where she'd had a bizarre dream about a never-ending staircase. And she'd been frightened, hadn't she, when we'd headed for the lift – like she was terrified of where we were going?

'So, Ethan,' Robert asked my cousin, drawing me away from my thoughts, 'what is it you found here?'

'This,' Ethan answered, switching on a torch and shining it onto the back wall. Its beam was much brighter and more focussed than the dull ceiling light and created a clear circle of illumination on the far wall. Still, I had to squint to make out exactly what Ethan was trying to reveal.

It was a single letter – a large, curling capital *J* in yellow paint.

'A *J* – what does that mean?' I asked.

'It's him. He's been here. *He* took them, Robert! *He* took them!'

But I was still confused – who were they talking about?

'Who does he mean?' I asked, becoming a little anxious. 'Will someone explain what's happened?'

'Joshua,' Robert answered, heaving a sigh that worried me further. 'That's his sign, isn't it? The one he always used to leave. A single *J*. Always. So, does this mean Joshua has taken the children?'

Guy A Johnson

Joshua – Ethan's twin. Great-Aunt Penny's other son. The one Nathaniel said he'd lost track of. *That's his sign. The one he always used to leave.* What did Robert mean by that? Had he known Joshua? Maybe he had been one of the taken too – when my twin cousins had been snatched away from my great-aunt?

'And this sign from him, is it a bad thing?' I asked, wanting at least some clarity, although I was certain I knew the answer in my heart.

'It could be, Elinor,' Robert said, gravely. 'If Joshua is involved, it could be a very bad thing.'

I was about to ask why, when we heard Michael calling out below us – his voice making its way up through the lift shaft into the room.

We couldn't make out what he was saying – but the urgency in his voice was unmistakable.

So we left the mystery of Joshua for a short while, got back into the lift and descended to the floor below – to see what all the fuss was about. But by the time we got there, it seemed we were too late to help with anything.

'She just collapsed suddenly,' Michael said, looking up at us with panic in his eyes. He was kneeling on the floor, with Tilly draped limply in his arms. Her eyes were closed. 'Went out like a light.'

Robert stepped forward, checked her pulse and shook his head slowly, turning his eyes to me.

'Was she someone you knew well?' he asked, but I was too numb with shock to answer.

Tilly Harrison was dead.

231

Guy A Johnson

### *Unfold*

*The scientists Monty Harrison employed gave him just one of those twin girls – the one called Tilly. The one he claims is his niece. They kept the other one back – you've met her too, though. That time in his attic – the poorly thing, named Otterley. (Yes, he got hold of her eventually.)*

*But Monty didn't know about Otterley to start with – he just had Tilly.*

*And what a wretched thing she was – so pale, thin and poorly that she was permanently on a life-support machine, barely out of a comatose state for many years.*

*She was never a baby, either. I didn't mention that to you, did I? No, Esther – Tilly was created as a child of about seven or eight. And her growth rate is very slow – did you ever notice that? Slow for both girls. Very slow indeed.*

*The existence of Otterley wasn't kept from Monty for long.*

*He didn't hear through rumours, as you might expect – it was a very closely guarded secret. But people are strangely loyal to our gangster associate – and eventually someone told him. It was a lucrative deal, Esther – Monty paid me kindly for that information. And I told him where to find Otterley, as well.*

*I couldn't help him get her out, though – and, myself aside, he'd lost all trust in his so-called pals in the government. But he managed to get hold of Otterley all the same – used a group of rebels, from what I've heard. Convinced them he was helping them liberate a group of the taken whom the government was mistreating.*

*Once Monty had both girls, Esther, he learned the horrific truth – that they weren't created to exist independently. That while they had their own set of organs for everything, their energy – their life-force, if you like – was shared. So, only one was ever well and able*

233

*to function without medical support at any given time.  Monty employed his own set of scientists to try and resolve this, to cure them – he couldn't turn to their creators, after all. But it couldn't be done, and in the end he faced a choice – sacrifice one for the other. So, he chose the one he'd had from the beginning – the one he'd bonded with: Tilly. And the other one – Otterley – remained in his hidden attic, wired to machines, sedated.*

*Even once he had Otterley controlled, it was a long time before Tilly was well enough to be introduced to society – in fact, it took her years to gain any strength and function like a normal human.*

*You see, there's something I didn't share with him – a secret I'll tell you now. One twin is stronger than the other. One more dominant. One X and one Y, if you like.*

*So, if both were left to their own devices – if both were free of medical intervention – then the dominant one would take all the energy, would take the life-force from the other one.*

*And that one was the girl you saw in the attic – the one who was wired up and who looked deceptively weakened.*

*Otterley.*

**Fold**

Guy A Johnson

12. Agnes

As we made progress towards Monty Harrison's mansion, I couldn't help but feel Elinor slip further and further away from me again. I knew we *had* to make our way to where danger was almost certain for my nephew and his companions, but we'd originally set out to trace Ronan's steps – in the hope that it led to my lost girl. My beautiful, lost girl, who'd been through so much already and was who knows where.

'I want her back as much as you,' Xavier said, as we sped along the water.

But I shook my head at this statement. He couldn't *possibly* – it wasn't a competition, but he hardly knew her. So he claimed to have been keeping tabs on us for a long while – hidden nearby all the time? Even if this was true, it wasn't the same.

'Agnes, we *will* find her, I promise,' he added – another line I wanted to shake my head at.

'Ronan's trail has gone cold, Xavier,' I answered, turning away from him, letting the rush of air against my face dry my tears. 'That was our only, frail hope of finding her. So, how can you make that promise? What can you base it on?'

Xavier fell silent after that – he had no answer, after all – and we didn't speak again until we reached the edge of Monty's grounds.

There was a moat surrounding his property and a bridge that extended across it to let in welcome visitors and keep out unwanted creatures – installed before the floods to keep the dogs away. Xavier killed the engine as we reached it. The bridge was extended, but was designed for people on foot or in cars, and the water was significantly shallower at this end of the city. So, while the moat was flooded, the bridge was above the water.

235

Guy A Johnson

'We'll have to walk across it,' Xavier said. 'And leave the boat here.'

'What about when we get to the other side?'

'Monty's land is higher up. I've checked it out before. At worst, the water is a couple of feet deep, but when you get close to the big house, the land is just marshy. Muddy.'

Before we left the boat, Xavier lifted the lid off a box that had doubled as a passenger seat and revealed contents that surprised me.

'Need to be prepared for the worst,' he said, offering me a rifle. 'I thought Old Monty would have something like this on board. You know how to use one of these?'

'I grew up with the daily threat of the dogs,' I answered, taking it from him. 'You think my father never taught us how to protect ourselves? Is there any spare ammunition?'

Xavier took another look in the box and shook his head.

'All we've got is what's already loaded.'

A quick check revealed there were five bullets in the barrel of mine.

'Four left in mine – one's been spent already,' Xavier confirmed.

'Let's hope we don't face more than a handful of those creatures then,' I said, nodding in the direction of Monty's grand house. 'Ready to do this on foot?'

The land was as Xavier had described – the water came up to our knees once we'd crossed the bridge over the moat, but reduced in depth as we got closer to the house. Our protective suits kept the water out, but the surface became muddy and slipperier, so I had to be careful not to fall.

I'd never been near this side of the city before – let alone been invited to the gangster's mighty house – and I was a little in awe of its grandeur. It was like something from the novels Esther and I had read as teenagers – the battered Austen and Bronte books

236

Guy A Johnson

that we helped ourselves to from Mother's collection. Only, it wasn't in the best condition. The stone appeared blackened by weather and pollution, all of the windows on the top floor appeared boarded up and there was a general sense of neglect about it, enhanced by the mudslide that surrounded it where there'd doubtless once been a fine green lawn.

Reaching stone steps that led up to the main entrance, we paused – listening for signs of life, for barking and, therefore, sounds of terror. Sounds of death.

And we could hear it – the clear, angry barking of more than one creature, coming from inside.

'Ready?' Xavier asked and, as terrified as I was, I nodded. *Yes, as ready as I'd ever be.*

The violent chorus intensified once we'd entered the building, but I still managed to take in the faded glamour of Monty Harrison's house. The pink and orange marble swirl under our feet; the dust-dulled glimmer of chandeliers swinging above us; the wide staircase of red carpet that curled against the wall furthest from us; and the closed doors that led off to other rooms that were hidden in the wood paneling of the walls. Only, one of those doors was open – and beyond it was the source of the noise we were pursuing.

With my heart beating so fast I thought I might throw it up, I followed Xavier as he headed towards it – gripping my rifle tightly, hoping it wouldn't slip from my grasp. I still had the gloves on that came with my outdoor suit, and their palms had rubber pads to grip with – which was just as well as my hands were wet with perspiration inside.

Through the open panel door, we entered a short hallway that led to a large kitchen. There was glass scattered across the floor in front of two large broken windows.

237

Guy A Johnson

'Looks like something forced its way through,' Xavier commented, pointing to the shards, some of which were tinged with red.

As he continued to follow the noise of the dogs, Xavier went through another door where a set of steps immediately led down into what was a small cellar. He paused there, staring down to where the canine din intensified – and then it suddenly stopped.

They were almost silent for a minute – the raucous barking reducing to an even hum of snarls. But it was a short reprieve, as the pack we'd found took a moment to plan their attack.

They came at us slowly. I watched – numbed into almost a trance – as Xavier gradually backed up in my direction. Holding his gun out straight, but refraining from firing, he allowed what I counted as six of the creatures to paw their way up those stairs and surround us in a semi-circle.

'Xavier?' I asked, barely audible, my voice reduced by fear and the visor I still hadn't removed from my face. 'Xavier, what are you doing?'

'Just keep still,' he instructed, his volume as reduced as mine. 'Just. Keep. Still.'

As I was petrified to the spot, I had no problem following his order. And he did the same for a minute or so – kept still, not moving an inch. But then something changed – he began to slowly crouch, gradually bending his legs, his back and then his arms, lowering himself until he was on all fours.

And I knew what he was doing – I knew he was attempting one of his mind tricks. But on a pack of dogs? Was he completely mad? Were we in such deep trouble that this ridiculous, risky option was the only one we had?

Guy A Johnson

*Dear God help us,* I cried inside, feeling my limbs begin to shake, squeezing my hands tight around the rifle, for fear it would slip away from me. At that moment, I wished I'd had my sister's faith and devotion. My lack of it didn't stop me putting in a last minute plea, though. *Dear God help us all.*

Despite the insanity of Xavier's plan, it did initially have some effect – all six of the creatures watched and waited, teeth bared, deep growls still humming in their throats. One dropped its head to one side, curiously. And it might've worked – that crazy, unbelievable mind trick. Xavier just might've pulled it off and fooled the dogs into thinking he was one of them. But a blood-curdling scream below distracted us all.

In reaction, I cried out – I knew that voice! I knew that scream!

'Esther!' I hollered, dropping my rifle without thinking, and the racket it made as it clattered across the floor – coupled with the terrified cry that came from the cellar below us – broke the dogs from Xavier's trance.

But he was quick, pointing his rifle at one of them and shooting it dead before it could advance further. The confusion this caused among them bought us a couple of seconds and I grabbed mine from the floor and shot a second, as it leapt for him, freeing Xavier to shoot a third. All the time I was thinking: *I must get to her! I must get to her!* A mantra that helped pump the necessary adrenalin through my body.

Before I could take another shot, two of them were on me, their colossal weight overpowering me, pinning me to the ground. In unison, they tore back their heads and released their meaty jaws, dripping thick, foul-smelling saliva on my face, as they each prepared to take a bite from me.

239

Guy A Johnson

*I must get to her! I must get to her! I must get to her!* Round and round in my head this went, as I closed my eyes, hoping for a miracle. Two loud shots and the feeling of the animals going limp on me suggested I got one. But I couldn't move – their deaths intensified the weight upon me, as their breathless bodies relaxed.

Quickly, I counted the casualties – five dead, one dog remaining alive.

A war cry from Xavier and the sound of one more shot in the air, coupled with a yelp, told me the body count went up to six. Xavier had used my gun, as his own was spent of ammunition. He dropped it and began heaving the dead canines off me. Feeling the relief as one was pulled off, I used my free arm to help him roll away the second.

'That's Esther's crying,' were the first words I managed, wheezing a little, as my chest had been crushed. 'We need to get to her.'

Xavier nodded in agreement and helped me to my feet. But before we'd had another chance to move, a further two creatures crawled up out of that cellar. Smaller than the others, they were still upon us in seconds, knocking both of us over.

Xavier's rifle went flying across the floor, but he let it go as it was now useless to us. Mine was still close by – on the floor where he'd just let it fall. I'd taken just the one shot with it so far, Xavier also – leaving three more in the barrel.

With all the strength I had, I pushed against the front legs of the dog that was pinning me down – just keeping its teeth away from my neck and face, although I could feel its sharp claws cutting into me. And as hot meaty mucus dripped from its open jaw, I wasn't sure how long I would hold out for. All it would take was for one of my arms to lose its grip and that mouth would close in and cut out my life source.

Guy A Johnson

A sudden move from Xavier told me he'd managed to heave off the beast that was holding him down. Quicker than I could believe, he grabbed my rifle, shot it and immediately turned it on mine – shooting it in the head, a spray of red smattering across my face. Pushing yet another corpse off me, he helped me to my feet.

'Okay?' he asked, looking me up and down, seeing the tears in my outdoor suit – the claw marks below glowing scarlet as the blood began to clot.

'Esther,' was what I managed in reply, before I stumbled towards the entrance to the cellar.

But Xavier stopped me, grabbing one of my arms.

'Let me check it first,' he said, handing me the rifle – the rifle with just one bullet remaining.

And then he quickly disappeared into the room below us – before I could protest at the danger he might face.

As I waited for word of what was below – it had been Esther's cry, I was without doubt – I held the rifle firmly, finger on the trigger and turned in a slow circle, surveying the full panorama of my surroundings. It was a wreck. At my feet were the corpses of eight mighty beasts – a small mountain of bloodshot fur and warm, still muscle. Shattered glass from the smashed windows was scattered across the floor – dull diamonds rolling in dust and coloured with flecks of ruby red. Elsewhere, utensils and crockery were scattered or broken – completing the look of destruction. As I waited for Xavier's word, I kept my eyes on the entrance we'd come in by and the broken window, where the creatures had clearly entered – hoping in my heart that nothing further approached, and if it did, it came by itself.

'Just one bullet left,' I muttered, hearing Xavier finally come back up those stairs.

Guy A Johnson

'Hand me that,' he said, reaching out for the rifle. 'I'll keep guard – you go see your sister.'

'It is her?' I asked, releasing the gun to him.

He nodded, solemnly. 'She's in a very bad way, Agnes. She's a mess and very weak. I don't think she'll…'

I touched his arm, a signal he didn't need to finish his words – I didn't need to hear them. Swallowing hard, and blinking away a few tears, I quickly descended the cellar steps.

The light was dim down there, but it was light enough to see how injured she was. She was lying in a pool of blood and her neck was so badly bitten it was just a mottled mesh of blood and white flesh. There were bites elsewhere – on her arms and hands, as if she'd tried to pull the beasts' jaws from her. Her clothes were almost shredded and I could see deep, thick claw marks on her thighs and belly.

I knelt down – not a care for the blood that might stain my own torn garments – and carefully took her in my arms, cradling her limp body. She was still warm and I could feel her shallow breathing, but I was certain of Xavier's half-spoken diagnosis – my sister didn't have long.

Holding her, waiting for her to take her final breath, I took in my gloomy surroundings. The cellar was more or less empty. There was a large, bare wine rack, but little else in terms of furniture or storage. Apart from my sister's blood, the floor was covered in flood-damaged linoleum – a big square of which was torn apart where a trapdoor in the floor had been pushed open. From where I was sitting, I couldn't see where it led, but I wondered if that was how Esther got in there.

Guy A Johnson

'And did only you get this far, Esther?' I asked, suddenly thinking of the others – of Billy and Augustus. Had my fear and shock blocked them from my immediate thoughts? 'Oh my God, Esther,' I found myself whimpering, rocking slightly, as I held her tighter and felt tears streaming down my face, dripping from my chin. 'Oh my God, did they get them too? Did the beasts get to Billy? To Augustus?'

My eyes flitted around the room, searching the corners for signs of either of them – but I saw nothing but shadows.

'Esca-.'

It was barely a croak.

'Escap-.'

On her second attempt at speaking, Esther almost finished her word, but I worked it out – finished it for her.

'Did they escape, Esther?' I said, a sorrowful joy flooding my senses – she was alive, conscious even, but it couldn't last. The blood we sat in told me that. 'Billy, Augustus – they're safe?'

A blink of her eyes confirmed it: yes.

'Pock-,' she said, attempting another word. I moved my ear closer to her mouth – maybe up close her message would be clearer. It was. 'Pocket. Back.'

She had to mean her back pocket, didn't she? Of her trousers?

Carefully, I rolled her onto her side and tried on both sides. On the left, I felt something papery inside and pulled out an envelope with her name written on the front. I recognised the handwriting – Ronan's.

243

Guy A Johnson

'Read it,' her weak voice instructed and then she exhaled and was gone – and it felt like the envelope and whatever it contained was all that I had left of her.

'Xavier!' I cried out, yelling for his help – for him to use his crazy unbelievable skills to bring her back. Surely he could do that? If he could do those magic tricks with people's minds, surely he could do something as simple as bring my sister back to me? 'Xavier!'

Above, there was another commotion – the sounds of more beasts. A single gunshot and a yelp told me that Xavier had successfully spent our final bullet. But it wasn't enough. Later, I'd discover that the second dog had overpowered him – knocking him aside, knocking him unconscious, before going in search of the scream that was coming from the cellar.

I saw its eyes first – glowing in the dull light, as it reached the bottom of the stone steps. It growled fiercely, drawing back the fur around its jaw – revealing its wet pink gums and killer, yellow teeth.

*So this is where it ends,* I thought to myself, holding my dead sister closer, as if I still had to protect her. I balled my hand into a fist around that letter – oddly protecting that too, as if somehow it had to survive this ordeal. Had to see the light of day. *So these are my final moments.*

It moved towards me slowly – taking its time, as if it was taking me in, like a curiosity. Like it wasn't certain. The others had impulsively leapt at us, their bloodthirsty instincts telling them to kill without thought, but this one was different. It paced, like an animal in a cage – it paced back and forth in front of me, checking me and my sister's corpse out.

244

Guy A Johnson

*What is it you intend to do?* I thought in my head, having a silent conversation with it. *Are you just teasing me? Are you just trying to frighten me as much as you can, before you do what the others did? If you are, it's working.*

And it was. I felt sick with terror and, despite trying to stay calm and still – as if somehow that would make a difference, make me invisible – despite all of that, my body began to shake and the tears began again.

'Why don't you just get it over and done with!' I suddenly yelled at it. 'Why don't you just bloody kill me like you did my sister! Just get it over with!!' I twisted my head violently, pushing my neck out towards it, tempting its bite. 'Go on! Get it done! Do your bloody worst!'

I didn't hear the noise behind me over the din of my screaming. The click and the twist, the sound of rusty metal shifting. But the creature before me did and it stepped back, its eyes alarmed – a signal to me that something had changed. And then it retreated – stepped away from me, almost cowering its way into the shadows.

I didn't want to take my eyes off it, in case it changed its mind and came at me after all. But I knew by then that something was going on behind me. Something had entered the room – through that hole in the floor, I suspected. And I could hear it advancing.

'It's alright, you're safe,' a voice said – an unexpected voice, but one I knew. 'You've nothing to worry about.'

As the voice got closer, the dog retreated further and further into the corner.

'Just stay calm. It's alright. You're safe now, okay? No one here to hurt you.'

Guy A Johnson

It was Joe – the person who'd come out of the floor. Later, he'd tell us how he began worrying the moment we'd left and had come after us – how he'd followed Esther's scent down into the tunnels under the city and found the hatch that led into Monty's house.

'It might still hurt me, Joe,' I told him, as he carried on moving – past me and towards the cowering dog. 'And we've no ammunition left. Xavier used the last of it.' As I said this, I wondered exactly how Xavier was – he'd been silent since the final bullet was released from my rifle. 'And we need to move Esther too – we can't just leave her here.'

But Joe didn't respond to what I said – he just moved further into the room, closer to the corner, closer to the savage beast that hid in its shadow.

All the way he was saying: 'There's no need to be afraid. You're safe now. There's no one here to hurt you. Just stay calm.'

And I realised that Joe wasn't addressing me at all. It wasn't me he thought should be afraid. It wasn't me he felt he needed to comfort, to reassure of my safety.

It was the dog.

### *Unfold*

*Esther*

*You'll recall I said that I made those killer dogs my business – made a 'killing', if you like. So I guess I'd better explain myself – tell you how I did this.*

*Well, I was a trusted man in the authorities – still am, to be honest, as I've managed to keep my underhand dealings and double-crossing under the radar. I had access to those labs – the ones where the killer dogs were bred, where newer, deadlier versions were cultivated.*

*Now, to be clear – I wasn't one of those men that set the creatures free – let them loose on the land and watched their crazy experiment unfold. No, that wasn't me. I'm a business man at heart, Esther – and there was no money to be made by that particular curiosity.*

*What I did – how I earned my money – goes back to one person. It always does.*

*My old pal, Monty Harrison.*

*Yes, Esther – I supplied Monty with the animals he bred himself. And yes – gave him the means to experiment on your Joe in the most horrendous way. Inadvertently, I caused Joe's suffering – his irreversible suffering. It left me rich in one way – but you might argue that my soul is a little poorer. Assuming you believe my soul could become more impoverished.*

*So, why tell you all this?*

*Why confess the worst of my sins to you – leaving no word unconfessed, no stone unturned?*

*I figure it's only by knowing everything that you'll be in a position to forgive me.*

247

Guy A Johnson

*And why would you want to forgive me, you might ask?*

*Why would I <u>need</u> your forgiveness? Because I do, Esther.*

*Well, the answer is in the final part of my confession.*

*The answer lies in you, Esther Morton…*

**Fold**

13. Tristan

Her name was Heloise – the woman who took us through *Elysium* – the white city from my story. Not that she told us outright – we'd got beyond the point of being able to ask her without seeming awkward. But one of the men called her by it and Jessie and I both felt a sense of relief.

Heloise.

A woman whom we had both mistaken for a man in the darkness – the same darkness that we suspected kept Ronan from our detection. A woman who was about to play a significant part in one of our lives.

Heloise.

'The outer part of *Elysium* is like this for the entire circumference,' she explained, as we followed what seemed like a maze of residential homes – all in shades of white, the paths a glittering pale grey, flecks in the stones beneath us caught by the sun. 'You won't need these for this part,' she added, tapping the metal security bracelet around her wrist – a replica of the ones Nathaniel had given us.

The streets on the outskirts were narrow and short and, if I'd had to make my way back to our safe-house, I'd have failed. But Heloise moved quickly, confidently, so I had faith she'd get us back – if it were necessary.

'Everything looks so uniform,' Jessie said, once we'd traveled a good hour in near silence and Heloise nodded in agreement. It prompted an unfolding of the city's history from her.

Guy A Johnson

'That's because it was all planned and built in one go. It's not a series of organic places, like your home city. *Elysium* was built for a reason and nothing has been added, nothing structural has changed since it was first erected.'

'Nothing?' I questioned, as we turned down another street, into yet another street of tall, white buildings. I noticed three in a row were shops – a newsagent, a stationer (both open) and what looked like a food takeaway establishment (a *closed* sign across its door).

'What are you thinking?' Heloise asked, watching my curiosity.

'How unreal and normal this all seems at the same time,' I answered, after some thought. 'The ordinariness of these buildings and dry streets. And yet, it's all so bright – and that fake sky up there. Do people really go out for coffee, or take-out – live standard, everyday lives here?'

'Some do, but many work to maintain this place,' she said, giving a brief explanation of *Elysium's* working infrastructure for mine and Jessie's benefit. 'People were given a place here for only a handful of reasons. Three main reasons – you worked for the authorities already, the authorities *wanted* you to work for them, or you were rich. Everyone of good health, of working age, has to make an active contribution, whether they have money or not. And that can be anything from cleaning the streets to helping out in the great library.'

'The great library?' Jessie said in a light, mocking tone.

'Yes, but I'm afraid there won't be time for a tour on this particular visit. Or you might work in the science laboratories or the farming factories. A cook in a restaurant, a teacher in a school, a guard in the authorities. It's an endless list – and the work here is like that in any city. There's all sorts of roles that need fulfilling – to keep it working.'

250

Guy A Johnson

'To maintain law and order,' I suggested, as we turned into a new street and saw the landscape change.

The maze of white houses and grey stone paths had come to an end. And we finally faced what I learned was the core of *Elysium – Core* with a capital C. The centre of the White City. Immediately in front of us was a wide road, with what looked like four parallel railway lines running along it.

'For the trams,' Heloise said, assuming we understood this particular mode of transport. 'But that's not the way for us.'

Ahead, on the other side of the road, was a long glass-fronted building that stretched the entire length of the road and soared high, heading towards that domed roof above – curving outwards subtly, suggesting the construction was circular. The fake sun caught its panes and gave the entire building a mirrored effect. Standing in front of its entrance were six men in a dark green uniform, three of them on each side, holding what looked like black paddles in their hands. They appeared to scan people as they arrived – moving the paddles up and down them, both front and back, before they allowed them to continue into the mirrored building – glass doors parting to let them inside.

'The security is tighter in this part of the city, then?' Jessie commented, his eyes scanning all round, taking it in.

'Try not to look too much like a tourist,' Heloise warned him, lightly. 'As you can imagine, we don't get tourists here – so you'll immediately attract the wrong kind of attention. And the security guards are always on terror alert. But there's not normally as many. See – six at the main centre to the *Core*. And along the way.' She pointed with her eyes and we briefly scanned the endless glass building opposite. There were groups of

251

guards in fours at various intervals along the way. 'That's very unusual. Something's happened. Maybe something's been leaked.'

'There was something Nathaniel wasn't telling us yesterday,' I said, and Heloise gave me a stare that first appeared cold, steely – but quickly I saw her fear melt through. 'He told us he feared someone was onto him – that someone had informed on him to his colleagues. That we might have to move quickly. But there was something else. Something he wouldn't tell us.'

'What do we do?' Jessie's question – pointed at Heloise.

'We keep going,' she answered, giving each of us a quick look. 'You both okay with that?'

We were.

'Right. We need to get into that building and past those guards without any trouble.'

We heard a rumbling sound along the ground, getting closer and watched as several trams passed both ways. Like trains I'd seen from old footage, but cleaner and slimmer. Like the rest of the place, they were almost white – a pale grey – and the effect of the whole city continued to be blinding. Light reflecting off light reflecting off light. And despite the grumbling, vibrating sound as the trams sped by, they looked as if they were running on air – gliding through, powered by some invisible force. There was literally no dirt – nothing to suggest trains were creating any emissions, burning any fuel.

'They're magnificent,' I muttered, as the sight and sound of them faded away. I went to cross the empty road of rails, but Heloise stopped me.

'No, that's not the way in,' she instructed. 'The lines are live. You'll not survive the crossing.'

252

Guy A Johnson

'Then how?' I asked, wondering just how we were going to get over.

'We go under,' she answered. 'Follow me.'

Like we needed to be instructed to obey that particular command.

A hundred feet to our left was a slope that took us under the city. There, we stepped onto a travelator which guided us through an underground passage. Jessie and I stuck close to Heloise – and the other two men that were with us hung back a bit, making it less obvious we were travelling in a group.

There were two parallel travelators, moving in opposite directions and it was brightly lit – not by lighting that you could see, but the walls and the ceiling were lit up from behind, creating a warm hum of light all around us.

'It's like nothing I've seen. Like nothing I could imagine.'

'It's why we live in poverty,' Jessie returned and of course he was right.

And, while I was in awe of the spectacle this city – this *Elysium* – was showing us, I hadn't lost sight of what it truly represented: greed and power. This was the work of the selfish, manipulative few. This was where all the money, all the energy and natural resources had been spent. Why those of us living in the other cities had nothing.

But I understood why its residents had wanted to protect it and keep it to themselves. Its unnatural light was blinding, after all – and how easy it would be to simply stay here, forget what you knew was beyond it or tell yourself there was nothing you could do, no difference you could make. So, why not simply enjoy the riches on offer, like the others.

I noticed the metal band around my wrist suddenly light up – three pin-like lights, flashing in a sequence of colours: red, amber, green, red, amber, green.

253

Guy A Johnson

'What does this mean?' I asked, noticing Jessie's and Heloise's doing the same. I looked back, checking if I could see our male companions, if their bracelet lights were alternating like ours. But they were hidden behind several other people by then.

'Well, if those lights don't settle and all turn green, we're in for some unwanted fun,' Heloise answered, as we were reaching the end of the tunnel, and the travelator swerved right, taking us up a slope and into the daylight again – into a different form of the brightness we couldn't escape. 'Red lights will get you arrested, amber or flashing will get you interrogated or searched in full.' She gave us both a look that suggested neither of us would enjoy that experience. 'So you'd better pray for green by the time we reach those security guards.'

The end of the travelator took us just four metres or so from the glass doors into the *Core* – and I made a point of simply following Heloise without looking at my metal band and without looking behind. In my head, I told myself I knew what I was doing and where I was going. Jessie did the same.

And it worked – at least, it seemed to at the start.

They checked the lights on our bands – all green. And moved the black paddles around our bodies and, satisfied we weren't terrorists of any kind, waived us into the building.

But then Jessie looked back, checking out where the others had got to and he caught the eye of one of the security guards.

'You, back here a minute,' said a tall, muscly man in a black suit, who wouldn't have been out of place in old Monty Harrison's establishment. 'Just a minute, that's all.'

Guy A Johnson

'Me?' Jessie said and I feared that a slight wobble in his intonation, a flicker of doubt in his eyes or some other barely detectable reaction might just get picked up by one of the security guards.

'Yes, I just what to check your business today – what you're here for? That's all.'

*That's all.*

We weren't prepared for this. We'd not talked through a detailed cover story. Everything was on a need to know basis and Heloise was to answer any questions if we were stopped and questioned. But the guard just wanted to talk to Jessie. Why hadn't we thought through this eventuality? Heloise and the others – they knew this place well. They knew how it operated, what risks we'd face. Why hadn't they prepared us better?

'I'm visiting my parents in their lab,' Jessie replied – an answer that stunned me. Had he really said that – ventured so close to the truth? 'They're expecting me,' he added, although I could tell he had no idea how to complete this story. He had their names, of course, but we had no idea if they were still there, still alive – or, in truth, which side they supported.

But Jessie didn't have to take his story any further – and not because he'd convinced the guard. You see, Heloise and the others had been prepared for this occurrence after all. And, as soon as our two companions who'd held back saw that Jessie had stopped, they created a diversion – began an altercation, which heated up to a fight the guards were obliged to break up. A simple trick that more intelligent men should've have seen through – so I guess there was a reason these men were guarding the way into the *Core,* rather than working inside it.

Guy A Johnson

'Move on,' the three of us were told by another guard, as the one who began questioning Jessie threw himself into the fight.

Once we were inside, I turned back to see what had happened to our companions, but they'd been led away by then – and Heloise scolded me for even checking.

'We have to focus on getting through the rest of the checks – and hope Nathaniel got you the level of security you both need to get you to the centre.'

'The centre?'

'The part of the *Core* where we're heading – the part where you'll be meeting Nathaniel and helping us get those children out? Well, that has the highest security level in the city. Nathaniel is definitely the man to get you in – but whether he succeeded, that's another story. The amount of guards on the street is still worrying me. Something is definitely up. So, just stay focussed, try not to look too impressed by this place and just do everything I do. Okay?'

At first, the inside of the *Core* seemed like a huge shopping centre – like the Atrium had been in our city. Before poverty, restrictions and the floods had destroyed it.

*The floods,* I thought to myself, considering just how far I was away from my old life. Thinking how this place had never been touched by all those things – by the rationing, the pollution, the gas masks and protective suits we'd been convinced to wear. *Or the floods.* No this sparkling, pampered place had never been touched by the floods. I wondered if some of its younger residents even knew about the world beyond it.

Like the Atrium, the *Core* was constructed of steel and glass, and it reflected the outside world – the perfect sky and busy traffic of people and trams creating the landscape

256

Guy A Johnson

across its walls. And its inner walls were also glass – so everything was out in the open. You saw everything that was coming at you – but there was also nowhere to hide.

Walking through the entrance, we stepped into a huge foyer. To the left was a series of glass elevators – all the cables and mechanics visible in the transparent lift-shafts. On the right, a string of eateries – a mix of baking smells and spices hitting you instantly, despite the breezy air-conditioning that spun cool air around us and should've sucked up the cooking scents. Ahead, there was a grand escalator.

'Head for that,' Heloise instructed, and we crossed a floor of white marble towards it.

As we progressed, I couldn't help but look up at the glass ceiling above us and watch the feet moving back and forth, glimpsing just beyond them to the next floor above. Transparent layer upon layer – overhead and to the side – it was like an enormous, chilled greenhouse and the effect it created was mesmerising.

'You must stay focussed, Tristan,' Heloise said, eyes ahead, her whole being confident and in place. 'At the top,' she added, as we finally stepped onto the escalator, 'we turn right and step onto the far right travelator. It'll take us to the centre.'

So at the top, we did exactly that – stepped onto the travelator on the right and let it ferry us further into the translucent labyrinth.

Unlike the Atrium from my home town, the *Core* wasn't populated by shops or other commercial establishments. Aside from the restaurants on the ground floor, its internal rooms were set out like a series of very clinical offices. Through the glass walls, I saw desks, computers, huge television screens that stretched whole walls. Most of the people wore a uniform of white coats – like medical employees – and sometimes we went past

257

Guy A Johnson

rooms populated by people in goggles, suggesting experiments were being conducted. It was hard to see less obvious details – we were constantly on the move and both Jessie and I were doing our best not to appear too inquisitive and out of place.

We continued along the travelator for around 30 minutes, before it came to an end. When we stepped off, Heloise veered left. We followed without hesitation and reached an automated security checkpoint – our bracelets flashing red, amber, green as we approached an arch of metal, stabilizing on green just as we went through it.

'A few more checks to come until we can relax,' Heloise said in a quiet voice, once Jessie was through, but I didn't imagine we'd be relaxing at any point.

The further we travelled to the centre of the *Core,* the greater my sense of anxiety. The building's translucency added to a creeping feeling of claustrophobia – layer upon layer of glass blurring what was beyond it, obscuring the outside world and trapping us further, deeper inside.

We walked along a narrow corridor for several minutes – lab like rooms on either side, the glass frosted to just above eye-level.

'They don't want us to see in,' Jessie commented, but he got no reply from Heloise.

At the end of the corridor, we were met with a choice of three elevators and took the middle one. Inside it, we each had to touch our metal bands against a panel on the wall – another security check. I wondered what would happen if one of us didn't pass this check – and was glad I didn't have to find out.

'Where's this one taking us?' I asked our guide, but three men in black suits stepped into the lift with us at that point and she couldn't answer.

258

Guy A Johnson

To my relief, the men remained silent and stepped out seven floors later. The lift took us up another three.

We stepped out – one at a time – into what was to be our final security check, before we fulfilled Nathaniel's intentions and left this city with the children that had been taken there. When the glass doors opened, Heloise went first.

'Watch me,' she said, quietly, as she stepped into a clear box and we looked on as a thin line of light automatically scanned her body – starting from the top and working its way down. It bleeped as it covered her metal band and turned green on contact. She was through. Jessie followed and then I was last. Both of us got through without any problem – both of our light-lines turning green. I expected the light to have an impact as it scanned us – a slight buzzing sensation, perhaps, but there was nothing.

'I don't like this,' Heloise said under her breath, once I was through and we found ourselves on a platform, looking out over what I quickly learned was an aircraft hangar. Right in the very centre of the *Core*. 'It's been too easy. They appeared on such high alert outside.'

'Maybe that was their tactic?' I suggested, scanning the place, taking in the impossibility of it. *All this technology. All these riches. All in one place. And nothing for the rest of the world, as far as I knew.*

Heloise shook her head. 'It's not just that. Nobody is here. It's completely dead. Look around you.'

But Jessie and I were doing exactly that – consuming every inch of this magnificent construction. It was the first part of the building we'd been in so far that didn't appear to be constructed from glass. In fact, apart from a glass section in the roof, the entire space

259

was made from solid material. Above us, steel girders held up a roof that was covered in sheets of metal, all sprayed in white paint. Beneath us, the ground was light grey, like the streets outside – on closer inspection, it was concrete.

The platform we were stood on had a barrier around it and a small gate that opened inwards, leading to a metal staircase that would take us down to a lower level. As we descended and continued to take in the contents of the large hangar, Heloise explained what was missing.

'There should be a fleet of helicopters in here,' she said, as we stepped from the staircase onto the concrete floor.

The space was empty – a huge, empty warehouse. Against the walls, there was all nature of equipment, tidied away. Some of this was covered up and I assumed these were tools used to maintain the missing aircraft.

'How many are normally here?' Jessie asked.

'All of them…' Heloise said, absent-mindedly. 'Sorry. I don't know. 30 maybe. On the occasions I've been here before, I've had no reason to count them. But now they're gone…' She was lost in her thoughts again. 'I don't understand. If they'd been moved, wouldn't Nathaniel have known?'

'Maybe that's what he kept from us – maybe this is what he found out?' I offered.

'Surely everyone would notice if a whole fleet left this place?' Jessie asked. 'Surely it would've made one hell of a noise?'

Heloise shook her head. 'No, not necessarily – not with the soundproofing the city's glass sky-roof offers. And the sky-light in here takes you straight outside – not just out of the *Core,* but beyond the city.' Heloise thought for a minute – gathering all her thoughts and questions. 'This is a restricted area – with very restricted access. And it's not used a lot. People like Nathaniel – officials from *the Circle* – might use it to leave and enter the city. Not that often, though. But someone must know about it. Someone must have reported it. And yet we got clearance to make it this far.' She paused again, taking in a sudden sharp breath.

'What is it?' I asked, touching her arm lightly.

She flinched at this sign of affection, so I withdrew it quickly.

'Without the helicopters…' she began, but her voice faltered, suddenly overcome with emotion.

Someone else finished her sentence.

'… we cannot take the children to safety.'

The voice came from a corner of the vast space and a familiar face stepped out of the place he'd been hiding in.

'There's been a change of plan,' Nathaniel announced, addressing all three of us.

'Why is that no surprise?' Jessie said, almost spitting his bitter question. I sensed his old distrust of Nathaniel return, and I couldn't help but wonder why the man had led us this far, when there was no way for us to get out.

'You've got some explaining to do,' was my own offering.

'Yes, I have,' Nathaniel answered. His plain, honest tone was enough to placate me – enough to get me listening.

Watching my reaction, I saw Jessie begrudgingly suspend his own misgivings.

'This better be good,' he said.

261

Guy A Johnson

'I'm afraid it isn't,' Nathaniel answered, his face darkening with concern. 'I'm afraid it's the opposite – it's very bad...'

Nathaniel said he had to be quick – give us just a potted history of events, while we waited for our transport to arrive.

'Transport?' I asked.

'A helicopter, Tristan.'

'You've found them?' From Heloise.

'It's just mine. When I arrived here, I saw that the entire fleet had been taken – oddly, bar the one reserved for me. A quick investigation revealed that several of our trusted pilots are missing too. Remember we saw those helicopters flying overhead on the way here?'

Jessie and I nodded.

'Well, I'd assumed that was my *pals* in the authorities completing their plan to bring the children to the city – to test them and experiment on them in the new laboratories they'd built. Those labs are about a thirty minute journey from this part of *the Core*. But it wasn't them at all. The children were never brought here – those new labs remained empty, untouched.'

I frowned – thinking of what he'd said to us the night before about us rescuing the children from this Place. Nathaniel nodded to acknowledge my confusion, but continued his story.

'The helicopters were taken from here *before* our own plans to snatch the children could go ahead.' He said *'our'* that second time, not *'their'* – taking responsibility I noticed.

262

'So, the children never made it here. The helicopters *and* the children were taken by another group of people, it seems.'

'Why haven't we heard about this?' Heloise asked, as shocked as we were by the news. 'There's not been so much as a murmur out there.'

'This is on complete lockdown, Heloise,' Nathaniel answered. 'We couldn't afford to have a word of this leaked. Couldn't unsettle our privileged, delicate society, could we?' There was a mocking malice in his tone – as if he truly despised what this place stood for. 'And besides, the taking of the children was a closely guarded, secret operation – so not many people need to know that it hasn't gone ahead.'

'Do we know where they are?' I asked, still struggling to comprehend this latest twist in events. 'The children?'

Nathaniel shook his head.

'My pilot is out there are the moment, having a scout around – official business the rest of *the Circle* have sanctioned. But once he gets back, he'll just been working for me – following my orders. He's not found anything yet. I have heard from Robert, however,' he added in a hopeful tone.

Nathaniel looked at our blank faces, then offered an explanation.

'Robert is a trusted ally. He and a group were heading for a remote place, past the city, further east. A place where we'd hoped to take the children and care for them, till we could return them to their parents.' He paused, as if he was going to impart something else – looking at me in particular.

'What?'

263

Guy A Johnson

He paused a while and then nodded to himself, as if finally deciding what he was going to say. 'It looks like someone had already been there. Children, according to the one person they found remaining – a single child left behind.'

'*Had* been there?' I asked, corrugating my forehead.

'All vanished by the time Robert arrived. But we know these children arrived by helicopter. And I suspect the fleet we saw in the sky a few days ago was taking those children away again.'

'But they left one behind?' I questioned.

'Yes,' Nathaniel answered. 'I've not got to the bottom of that particular oddity yet. Robert's transmission was brief and his speech broken up. Ah.' The tone in his voice was suddenly lighter and he looked up. 'Looks like my pilot and our lift is here. I'll explain the rest on the way.'

Looking up, I noticed something darken the skylight in the roof – like the effect of a dark cloud moving over.

'You might want to put these on,' Heloise suggested, passing Jessie and I a set of ear defenders she'd taken from an equipment store to our right.

We put them on and watched as the roof opened up and a thunderous noise – accompanied by a small hurricane – suddenly tore through the quiet. Minutes later, a helicopter landed, its twin set of blades eventually churning to a stop.

'We really haven't got long,' Nathaniel explained, as we all made steps towards the lone aircraft. 'When I first got back to the city, I was called to *the Circle* chambers and quizzed by some of my colleagues. That's when they informed me of the missing helicopters, of the fact their plans had been intercepted. I knew this last night, but I daren't

264

Guy A Johnson

tell you earlier – I had to make sure you ventured this far, as this is the only safe way I can get you back out of the city now. I feared you'd refuse, if you knew our plans were changing again – feared you'd think the whole thing was another deception on my part. And I appreciate, there have been many so far. So, I just stuck to my original story.'

He paused, gathering his thoughts – allowing us time to react, should we need to. But our silence gave him permission to continue.

'When I arrived back here, it was clear my fellow members of *the Circle* suspected I'd had a hand in this disruption. It's why I thought Ronan might have betrayed me. But the very fact I had returned to *Elysium* seemed to calm their suspicions and they backed off. This regain of trust bought me a little time – it also allowed me to get your security clearance with little question and no detection, as far as I know.'

He nodded at my metal bracelet.

'But I don't doubt for a minute that I'm still being watched. So, it's not safe for us to stay longer than we need to. Ready?'

It wasn't a question as far as I was concerned and I followed Nathaniel up the short ladder into the helicopter. But I noticed my friend holding back.

'Jessie?' I questioned and he threw me a sheepish look. 'Jessie? What is it?'

'Are they really here – in this city?'

The question was for Nathaniel.

'It's not safe here, Jessie,' the man answered. 'You know that? You're not an official resident.'

'I am at the moment,' he answered, tapping his metal band. 'And you didn't answer my question: are they still here?'

Guy A Johnson

'Yes. Yes they are.'

His parents.

'Alive?'

'Yes, definitely alive.'

'I still want answers from them, Nathaniel. It's why I came this far.'

'I understand, Jessie.'

I felt my heart retract in my chest as I realised my friend's intentions – I couldn't quite believe it.

'And it's not like there isn't work to do here. We could do with another man like you on the inside.'

Jessie wasn't leaving.

Jessie was staying behind to find his parents – to get the answers Nathaniel had failed to give him.

'Of course, you'll need a companion,' Nathaniel added and Heloise nodded back at him, understanding his statement as an instruction. 'Okay. It's decided. But we've not another minute to waste. You men must say your goodbyes and we must be on our way.'

There was only time for a brief, tight hug – no words, and all tears swallowed back – and then Jessie and I parted. Heart heavy, it was all I could do not to sob, once the helicopter was airborne and I watched my pal rapidly shrink away.

Nathaniel patted my knee in a fatherly manner.

'Okay, time for the truth,' he shouted above the noise of helicopter blades, in a voice that tried to sound comforting – but his very words had me on alert.

266

'The truth?' I asked, wondering if events were about to take another unexpected turn. How much more could I take?

'Don't look so worried. It's the truth I hinted about a while back, before I put you off its trail. First, you need to know where we're going.'

He pointed ahead, as if I could see *anything* on our skyline path. 'We're heading to the camp where we'd intended to take the children. We're going to meet my friend Robert and his companions – and the child they found left behind there. *And* there's someone else you'll be pleased to see.'

'Someone I know?' I asked, hopeful.

'Yes. Young Elinor. Safe and well.'

Relief flooded through me and those restrained tears were finally unleashed.

'I'm afraid what I'm going to tell you next isn't going to help settle your emotions, Tristan,' he added, as we were taken higher and higher.

I took a good, long look below: the landscape we had covered, and the uncharted areas we hadn't, appeared like a textured map – all hills, rocks, greenery and water. In the centre of this picture, I saw the glass roofed city – safeguarded by the mighty wall around it. And, as we flew higher still and *Elysium* began to shrink away, the vastness of the surrounding area grew and grew – a sight both breathtaking and terrifying at the same time.

'I owe you some answers, Tristan,' Nathaniel continued. 'I questioned you about what you knew about your twin – challenging your certainty that you didn't have one. Remember?'

This drew all my attention from the outside world and I looked just at him, my eyes suddenly hard. So, we were back to this subject again.

Guy A Johnson

'I remember,' I answered, wondering where it was going to take us this time.

'I was pushing to see how much you already knew – how much you might give away to me. But I realised by your complete refusal to believe that you knew nothing. Then I foolishly slipped up about your father – when I said I thought you'd found him, it's because I *knew* you had. And when it was clear you were in the dark about this too, I felt I had to put you off the scent quickly. I needed you to stay focused, Tristan – and I'm sorry for how I've handled this. For how you might feel right now. But I will tell you everything – and it'll be the truth this time. About your twin and your father.'

I was about to protest at these claims again – and about how I doubted he understood what it meant to tell the truth – but he held a hand out to silence me.

'Just hear me out. Things aren't what you think they are. I'll get straight to it, no more side-stepping the facts: Albert wasn't your father, Tristan. He was just the man who took care of you. Your real father wasn't fit to do so. And so Albert took you in. And your twin-.'

'But I don't have a twin-.' I interrupted, shaking my head at him, unable to simply accept this. 'I *can't* have a twin. I'd know. I'd-.'

'You do, Tristan,' Nathaniel countered, firm but calm. 'I'm sorry. It's time you knew about this. It'll make you stronger. It'll make you more determined to help me win this war.'

'This war?'

Nathaniel nodded solemnly.

Guy A Johnson

'There's no avoiding a war with the authorities now, Tristan. They have to be beaten, destroyed. They won't hand over all they've achieved just because the people ask. Just because they deserve some of the comforts that have been hoarded by so very few.'

He paused for a second.

'Would you like me to continue?'

I nodded my agreement. Yes, I was prepared to listen, maybe even prepared to believe him.

'When I said I thought you'd already found your father, I had good reason, Tristan. I genuinely I thought you'd been reunited with him.'

'Why would you think that?'

'Because you know him, Tristan. Because you've spent time with him.'

My head began spinning faster than the blades that propelled us into the sky.

'Who is he, Nathaniel? Who is my father? And this twin you claim I have – who is he or she?'

'He,' Nathaniel confirmed, but it was all he managed before an almighty boom cracked through the clouds and we felt the whole sky shudder. 'Oh my God!'

'What was that?' I asked, reading terror in Nathaniel's voice.

He cried out to our pilot to dip down a little lower and seek out the source of the noise.

'An explosion, Tristan,' he managed, gravely, and we both watched in silence as we fell back through the atmosphere and the detail of *Elysium* was in our sights again.

269

Guy A Johnson

We saw huge flames roaring up out of the west side of the city, but it was hard to tell if the protection the wall gave had been violated. A second boom saw smoke and fire erupt on the eastern side – and our pilot automatically took us heavenward again.

'This was *never* the plan,' Nathaniel said, as if he feared I'd assumed it was. '*These are not my plans* – not my doing! I don't understand! This wasn't how we planned to destroy the city! This wasn't the plan!!'

As we were spun away, heading east, he continued to rant, almost like a mad man.

'These aren't my plans! We should destroy the authorities, the power they have, not the city! This is not the answer!'

And, as we sped towards our intended destination, I had opposing thoughts, tearing me apart inside – an accountable joy that Elinor would be waiting for me there, and indescribable grief as I imagined the friend I'd left behind, facing danger, as *Elysium* was attacked.

'Oh, Jessie, why did you not just get on board?' I lamented, as Nathaniel continued to rant. 'What am I going to say to Billy, to Esther – and to Elinor and Agnes?'

Eventually, a numbness flooded my senses – my extreme emotions finally tiring out. Nathaniel calmed likewise. And there was nothing we could do at that moment – we couldn't go back, our pilot wouldn't have taken us even if we'd insisted.

We were silent for a long while, lost in our thoughts. But once we'd travelled further away, it finally seemed a good time to get our talking done – before we landed and it was too late.

'Tell me about my father, then,' I instructed the man. 'And my twin. Tell me everything you know...'

270

Guy A Johnson

Guy A Johnson

### Unfold

*Esther, there was so much I could've shown you, you know?*

*If we'd just got that bit closer.*

*If you'd just let me in – rather than cutting me off like you did, and turning our union into the reluctant relationship it became.*

*The city you've lived in all your life isn't quite what it appears – like so many things, you'll soon discover. It isn't a 'city' as such, which is why it doesn't have a name – more like an enclosure. One of many. An area cordoned off by the authorities and monitored. A living laboratory, you might say. Yes – the experiments that went on during the days of the dogs and the takings still continue. The floods didn't bring an end to all that evil – they were merely a means to keep you hemmed in. Invisible bars that kept you all caged.*

*That shouldn't surprise you, Esther – not after everything that I've revealed.*

*And while I say your home didn't have a name, it was labelled by the authorities. Section 71 – that's what we call it in our reports.*

*Section 71 – my own favourite experiment, and the only place you've ever known.*

*But Esther, it could've been so very different.*

*If you'd just let me in. If things hadn't turned out the way they did.*

*I could've shown you the world – I could've shown you Elysium, and more.*

*Elysium – the authority's headquarters. A city beyond your imagination. The very pinnacle of existence for those who live there – a place for the elite of this world.*

*But there's much more out there, Esther – much more out there we could have discovered. If only…*

*I digress.*

Guy A Johnson

*I promised you answers, didn't I?*

*I promised to tell you the truth.*

*The truth about you, Esther.*

*The reason your forgiveness is so very important to me…*

**Fold**

Guy A Johnson

14 – Elinor

After Tilly Harrison collapsed, everything happened very quickly.

Her revival.

The message from Nathaniel.

Then our escape.

It all happened in such a rush of time that it's hard to remember in full detail.

As Tilly faded in Michael's arms, I became numb with shock – unable to move or think clearly, or focus on what was being said or what was happening around me.

One minute she'd been alive, the next she was gone. Her decline had been so very rapid – and she was only a year or so younger than me.

But she'd gone in seconds.

*Check the girl's pulse – feel anything?*

*Let's get her up. You've seen this place – full of beds, of equipment.*

*Any of you check this out, last time we were here? Know how it works?*

*Michael – isn't this your area of expertise?*

Michael – the lock cutter.

Hearing his name broke me from my dull trance.

'Michael – we need to move her,' Robert said, gently, and I watched as he took Tilly from Michael's arms, lifting her up – allowing Michael to stand again.

And just as quickly, she was back – Tilly Harrison was alive once more.

I watched as Robert carried her into the laboratory area – while two of our other companions rushed ahead, ripping away at the transparent sheeting that covered one of the

274

Guy A Johnson

beds and its accompanying equipment. Robert rushed with them, calling out instructions and they obeyed. Within a matter of minutes, Tilly was hooked up to a machine – a tube in her mouth, helping her breath, wires taped to her body, monitoring her activity.

'Michael is a doctor and a surgeon,' Robert explained, as I watched Tilly's chest artificially inflate and deflate. 'One of his many talents.'

This last comment was delivered lightheartedly, but it didn't break my solemnity.

'Will she be alright?' I asked, still stunned by her rapid resurrection.

'She's alive, Elinor – but it's mainly that machine keeping her going. We daren't take her off it, in case she relapses. And we don't want to move her – not if we can help it.'

This prompted another question.

'Does that mean we can't leave?'

'It means we shouldn't move her – not until we understand what is causing this. Michael is going to see if he has the right equipment to take some tests. While he does that, all you can do is wait and hope.'

More questions.

'What about the children she told us about? And the sign we found in that room – the letter *J* you all think my cousin Joshua left?'

'These are things I'm going to ask you not to worry about,' Robert said, his voice somehow reassuring. It made me realise how different he seemed from when I'd first met him – how different from the man who'd recorded my message and tried to be mysterious. 'There's some radio equipment we brought with us. I'm going to try and get hold of Nathaniel – seek his advice. You okay to stay here and watch, while I do that?'

Guy A Johnson

I nodded and kept my eyes on the girl who was now half-machine – alive but *not* alive – while Robert disappeared and made contact with his leader.

'We're to move,' Robert announced with a sense of urgency, when he returned twenty or so minutes later. He seemed a little out of breath, as if he had sped back to share this news – and there was concern in his eyes that the others quickly picked up on.

'What is it?' I asked, but it went unanswered.

'Can we move her?' Robert asked Michael a question of his own, referring to Tilly. 'Get her into a chair? Is any of that machinery portable?'

'I'm sure we can sort something – if we need to?' Michael confirmed.

'We do. And thank you, Michael.'

'Are we going through the trees again – back to the boat and the others?' I questioned, thinking about the river road – not keen to return to the water, surprised at how quickly I'd got used to dry ground.

'No, we're not,' Robert answered. 'I radioed the boat and they're leaving without us.'

'Leaving us?'

'Don't worry, Elinor, we're taking another way out of here. For a good reason, you'll see. Michael – is the girl stable for now?'

'Yes, she is.'

'Good. I need you to come with me – we've some things to sort out before we leave. Ethan – you stay here with the sick girl and Elinor.'

Guy A Johnson

Ethan nodded and I felt a small comfort in the fact he didn't protest – although I wondered if we were really the right people to sort Tilly out, should something go wrong.

'Look, she's breathing very peacefully, very rhythmically,' Michael commented, as if reading my mind. He pointed at her chest and I watched it steadily rise and fall. 'I'm sure we won't be long. Maybe you could talk to her while we're gone. And if anything happens, you can send Ethan here after us. Okay?'

I looked up at my cousin, who smiled very softly and somehow I felt reassured.

'Okay,' I answered and pulled up a stool that had been pushed into a corner. Sitting down, I took one of Tilly's hands – careful not to loosen the wire that had been attached to it – and gave it a gentle squeeze.

As I wondered what exactly I should say to an unconscious person, Ethan began a conversation of his own.

'It was something I did as a child,' he started, looking at me directly for a moment, then flitting his eyes away.

'Something you did?' I questioned; it was as if he'd started in the middle of things – the first part of this exchange going on inside his head.

'The *J,* ' Ethan offered, still looking away. 'When we were younger. It was a sign I left – to get him into trouble.'

'Joshua?' I asked and he nodded, finally looking up and catching my eyes again. There was a look of shame in them. 'Can you tell me more?' I prompted, after he'd fallen silent for a while.

He was quiet for a little longer, then nodded – reluctantly at first, then nodding with increased assurance. He took in a long breath, sniffed back tears and began.

277

'It was a trick I played – when it looked like I was going to get into trouble. I'd blame him. If there was a breakage in the house, or if a fight started out between us, I'd point the finger at him. We were twins but from an early age we were also enemies – fighting for our mother's love. And it was easy to blame Joshua – he was clumsy and he was stronger than me. Much, much stronger – so Mother always took my side if there were cuts and bruises, as if someone with his strength should've known better.'

*Mother* – he meant Great-Aunt Penny. It was so odd to hear her referred to as *Mother* – she was one of the least motherly people I knew. Cold and strict – that's how I saw her. When I thought of that concept – *motherly* – I imagined mine. Agnes – kind, loving, cooking me hot food, protecting me with blankets and hugs.

'I got the idea one day when I stole from Mother,' Ethan continued, drawing me away from thoughts of Agnes – thoughts that were making me long for her arms around me, to make things better, to make everything feel safe. 'Took from the shop. Stole money from the till to buy alcohol from a much older boy. I was only eleven. You know about the shop?'

I shook my head – *you know about the shop* suggested something specific, not just one we might have bought from before the floods.

'Well, your great-aunt and –uncle own a shop. It doesn't make money any more, of course. The floods saw to that. But they still look after it, like one day they'll be able to open it again.' He paused, letting me take this in. 'I lived there for a while, you know. Locked up in the attic. Caged like an animal. Until recently.'

'Locked up?' I questioned and Ethan tapped the side of his head with a finger.

Guy A Johnson

'To keep me away from other people. Didn't think it was safe to let me out in public,' he explained, a sudden, manic grin springing onto his face.

'Why?' I asked, feeling nervous. Was it right they'd left me and Tilly alone with him? I'd begun to trust Ethan, but news that my great-aunt and –uncle had reason to keep him imprisoned was unsettling. 'How come I didn't know about you?'

Ethan shrugged, dropped his grin and then answered my first question:

'I attacked someone,' he said. 'I attacked Ronan.' He paused, then added: 'I did him some serious damage, Elinor.' Another pause, as he waited for my reaction.

'I'm glad,' I eventually answered, with firmness. And I was – wherever Ronan was now, it was good to hear that something bad had happened to him at some point. It evened things out a bit. 'Can you continue your story – about stealing from the shop?'

'Oh, yes,' Ethan said, remembering the explanation he'd offered. 'I took money from the till – but I wanted to make it look like Joshua had done it. The shop was beautifully furnished – ruined now by the water – but it was fitted out with luxurious furnishings, including a polished wooden counter. I took Joshua's pen knife and curved a *J* in its surface. A deep, clear cut that couldn't be mistaken. Then I put the knife back in his room. It worked a treat – Mother found the damage and then the knife in his bedside drawer. She was so furious with him, so preoccupied with her anger, she didn't notice the smell of alcohol on the breath of her other twin.

'As it worked that first time, I continued to leave the *J* sign in the wake of anything I did. I stole jewelry from Mother and drew his initial in lipstick on her dresser mirror. Broke windows at the school one evening – encouraged by older boys – and sprayed his signature in yellow paint.'

Guy A Johnson

Yellow – like the *J* on the wall of that strange, empty attic room. The *J* that had got everyone worried.

'Mother worked it out eventually. I left his signature at some vandalism I did at a grocery, not far from the family shop. But Joshua was with Father – your Great-Uncle Jimmy,' he added, as if this needed confirming. 'And finally she listened to his innocent pleadings. Not long after that, we were taken.'

Ethan fell suddenly solemn. The storytelling had somehow animated him, but that single word – *taken* – had the effect of plummeting the vibrancy down from his face, draining it of energy.

'Ethan?'

'I wish I could say the rivalry finished at that point,' he continued, slowly, pain evident in each word he spoke. 'I wish I could say we were united by that terrible experience. But that isn't what happened at all, Elinor. It's like they knew.'

'Who?'

'The people who took us. The government.' He shrugged, as if he wasn't entirely sure of the answer to my question. 'But it's like they knew we were rivals. One smart, one strong. Tested us for different things. I was sat in a big, white exam room for days – sat with a hundred other children, completing test after written test. We ate our meals in there and were only taken out for trips to the bathroom or to sleep. They took Joshua somewhere else. Kept him away from me – at first.'

He paused, drew in deeply and, on exhale, tears fell easily from his eyes.

'They gave me a choice,' he continued and again it felt like he'd left some of the story out – either he'd played it out in his head, or he had skipped ahead, to avoid dragging

Guy A Johnson

out his pain. As he spoke, his tears continued to fall, dripping from his lips as he mouthed them, falling further to his chin. 'It was me or him. But I was to choose who was saved. Me or him. I chose me, Elinor – I chose to save myself. I let Joshua suffer so that I could save myself.'

That was all he could manage, before the sobbing kicked in. I wanted to ask him what he meant, what had happened – what had he done that was so bad? What were the details of this choice he'd had to make? But his grief at this memory took over his whole physical being – his face was wretched with pain, the whites of his eyes red and his frame shaking violently as he howled like he was in the most terrifying of nightmares. I wondered if it was enough to wake Tilly from her coma. And worse, I wondered if my cousin might just erupt – and his grief lead him to lash out in violence. *I attacked Ronan. I did him some serious damage, Elinor.* And Great-Aunt Penny and Great-Uncle Jimmy had kept him contained. *Locked up in the attic. To keep me away from other people. Didn't think it was safe to let me out in public.* If this state of wild anguish continued, would Ethan lash out at me?

As he began to settle, I tried moving him onto safer territory – by asking questions about Nathaniel and how he knew the others in our small group.

'At the home,' he answered, calmer. 'They put us in a home. After the authorities had finished with us. I was so damaged from the experience, Elinor, that I could hardly remember who I was; neither Joshua nor I could tell anyone where we'd come from – where our family home was. That place they took me and Joshua to, Elinor? Where they tested and experimented on us? They destroyed all records – didn't leave a trace of paper to show what went on there. Went on *here*.'

281

Guy A Johnson

That single word sent a shiver down my spine: *here*. We'd come back to the place of Ethan's nightmare. To the place he'd been forced to make that *choice*. As I took this in, Ethan continued.

'It was a terrible place – the home we ended up in, after they shut this down. We were fed and had somewhere warm, but we weren't looked after. And we were all damaged, so all sorts of things happened. All sorts of cruelties, Elinor. You see, it's all we knew. And that's where I met Michael and some of the others – we were inmates in that new prison.'

'Was Joshua there?'

'Briefly.'

I creased my forehead to show I needed an explanation.

'When I said all sorts of things happened? Well, there were guards – guardians, we were told, but they were guards, like prison guards. Adults in charge who were supposed to look after us. But they were no better than the scientists we'd encountered here.'

That word again: *here*. Only three different letters making it up – but it was connected to a history with so many elements.

'They beat us, Elinor. Sometimes they let us starve. Sometimes their cruelty was much worse. But the experiments continued in much the same way – social experiments, you might say. There were no scientists in the home, but the guards still observed as the crueller boys picked on the weaker ones. But Joshua – nobody picked on him, because they all knew his strength. That didn't mean he wasn't affected by it all. Quite the opposite – he was strong, very strong – but sensitive too. Sensitive to others' suffering. And one morning, I woke to find out just how affected he was.'

Guy A Johnson

Ethan paused and I read his face – like a map of pain, the landmarks created from long buried anguish lining his skin, creasing in folds of aching. My plan to take him away from this subject had failed.

'Joshua had stored away a piece of broken glass and been biding his time – been planning to end some of the misery at that place.'

He faltered again and was silent for so long I thought that might be it – that his story wouldn't continue. But suddenly he started up again – as if he had to get the whole thing out, as if that would somehow make a difference to him. And I imagined that he'd not had many chances to tell anyone, if he'd been locked up by his parents for years.

'One day, I woke to find three of our guards and three of our most sadistic inmates with their throats slit. And Joshua was missing. But he left a sign behind, so we knew it was him. So *I* knew it was him.'

Another pause followed and this time I filled the silence.

'He left your symbol – he left a *J*?'

Ethan nodded, numb, solemn.

'On my chest,' he managed, his voice thin, not looking up at me. 'In blood, Elinor.'

He looked up then – straight into my eyes – and I saw the Ethan who'd rescued me from Ronan's flat. I saw danger in those eyes – a damage beyond repair.

I went to speak, opened my mouth in the hope that something of comfort would come out – something would bring back the Ethan I'd got to know over the last day. But no words came out – just a quiet breath.

283

Guy A Johnson

If it hadn't been for the explosion, I suspect we might have stayed like that – silent and staring. But a loud bang interrupted our stillness – alarming our senses into animation. Minutes later, we heard feet running in our direction and one of our group returned.

'We need to move,' we were told by a member of the crew I didn't know that well – Dominic. 'Our explosives made a huge noise and we don't know if the enemy is watching this place or not. We need to stay out of sight and together – so you must all come with me.'

'What about Tilly?' I asked, as another part of my mind was thinking about the blast we'd heard – the blast we'd caused, it seemed. *Our explosives,* he'd said.

'There's got to be a chair we can push her in,' Dominic suggested and Ethan moved quickly, finding a wheelchair folded up not far from her bed.

Ethan lifted her gently, removing the electrodes that had been attached to her body. But he kept the breathing equipment in place – detaching it from the main machine that was motoring it and plugging it into a smaller, portable machine.

'Let's hope this one's got enough power to last,' he said, balancing a small box on the back of the chair, before he started pushing Tilly in the direction we'd heard the big bang.

If it hadn't been for the sense of urgency in Dominic's voice, as he encouraged us to move quickly, I might have questioned the ease with which Ethan had moved Tilly – the expertise he'd exhibited when he swapped her monitor. Later, when I'd had time to think, it would come back to me – and when I found out the rest of Ethan and Joshua's story, it would make sense.

Guy A Johnson

But as we hurried after Dominic – Ethan pushing Tilly as fast as he could across the dry, yet stony ground, doing his utmost to keep her steady – none of that mattered. I just wanted to know what had happened. And what we had blown apart.

The site of the explosion was at the furthest point from where we started – just beyond the buildings. What we saw on arrival was a lip of rubble surrounding a gaping mouth in the ground. Michael shone a torch into it – grinning so proudly that it was obvious he was the creator of this crude opening. And the beam of the torch revealed steps – crooked, grey teeth – that led down into a tunnel under the earth.

'This is the way out of here?' I asked, immediately wondering if heading back to the river road was a safer option. It would be flooded underground, surely? Not to mention dark and dangerous. 'Are we really heading into there?'

'It's quite safe Elinor!' a voice shouted back up at me. It was Robert's – he'd already descended deep into the tunnel. He took a number of steps back up, stepping into the torchlight so I could see him. 'Quite safe. Nathaniel's explained it all. He wouldn't put you in any danger.'

I thought to argue that point, but Ethan pushed past me and, with the help of Michael, gingerly took himself and Tilly down those stone steps. They went slowly at first, as the treads were shattered at the top – fractured and loosened by the blast. Not wanting to be left behind, I followed quickly, hoping my instincts were wrong, careful at every step on those obliterated stone stairs.

Hoping that Nathaniel really wouldn't put us in unnecessary danger.

285

Guy A Johnson

And hoping – as I went further and further underground – that the endless succession of steps would eventually come to an end.

'How did you know where to set the charges?' Ethan asked Michael, once we were at the bottom of the steps.

I took out the torch Robert had given me earlier, switched it on and twirled its beam around what appeared to be an underground cave. I thought one of the group might chide me for wasting its battery, but they left me to explore without comment.

'Nathaniel gave us coordinates. This place was buried long ago. Says the track is about a mile in.'

'The track?' I asked, taking in the details around me.

Once I'd finished descending the crumbling stairs, I found myself in a large open space. The ground was dirty, but there was something underneath the dirt. I brushed my foot over it and felt something smooth against the sole of my shoe. I shone the torch – there were tiles beneath me, grey and cracked. Opposite the steps I'd come down, there was an opening – it was tiled as well, in dirty white, with a blue line of tiles in the middle. Shining the light in there, I could see the passageway turn a corner.

'What is this place?' I asked, watching as Robert headed towards that tunnel, the others following.

'A train station,' Ethan called back, his eyes urging me to keep up with the group. 'An underground train station.'

*The track is about a mile in,* Robert had said.

'Where are we heading?' I asked, equally perplexed and excited. *Were we getting on a train? Was that our route home?*

286

'We're heading home,' Michael answered and I felt my heart swell with sudden love for this lock-cutter, emergency surgeon and explosives expert.

But Robert threw him a sharp, cross look – as if Michael had said something he shouldn't have, made a promise he couldn't keep – and annexed this answer with a word that immediately deflated that surge.

'Eventually,' he said, holding Michael with his glare. Then he looked away again, as we reached and turned the corner in that tiled passageway. 'There's somewhere else we need to stop off on the way. Something Nathaniel wants us to find before we leave.'

At the end of the tunnel, we came into an open space again. We stopped a moment – Michael wanted to check Tilly over before we ventured any further.

'Seems fine, breathing steadily,' he said, as I flicked the torchlight around the space.

Ahead of us were three sets of metal stairs that would take us further under the earth.

'Escalators,' Ethan explained. 'We'll need to walk down them, as they're out of service. You okay, Elinor?'

I nodded – I had to be brave, but I also had to ask a question that had been preying on my mind.

'What if the water gets in? What if we're trapped under here?'

Ethan looked into my eyes, softening and went to say something, but Robert barked orders that we needed to start up again and Ethan moved to assist Michael with carrying Tilly down those steel stairs.

'It won't get in,' Dominic reassured me. 'Look about you. There's no water. No damp. And this place has been hidden away for decades. I think we're safe.'

287

Guy A Johnson

Reassured, I took my first steps on the still escalators and descended further underground.

At the bottom, there was a series of tunnels to follow and they were marked with a series of codes: NE1a, NE1b, NE1c. As we approached, Robert shone his torch over them and I took the opportunity to catch up with him, to find out more about where we were headed.

'Why aren't we going straight home?' I asked, as he lit up a sign with NE1d on it and then shook his head.

'Nathaniel gave me specific coordinates,' Robert muttered, more to himself than me. 'But these tunnels aren't marked with it. He said NE1e,' he continued, as if I'd asked him.

'And where will that take us?'

'To the right train – and to some answers. Can't just head home empty handed, not after coming all this way. Not after losing those children.'

*The children.* I'd almost forgotten my original task – to gain the trust of those children who'd been taken. To win them over, to smooth the way for Nathaniel, Robert and the others to take them back to safety. But they were gone – disappearing before we'd arrived and now my adventure had taken a completely different turn.

'Could you have misheard him?' I questioned, as we stalled at the mouths of the four tunnels. 'Could the *e* have been a *b* or a *c*? How clear was the radio transmission?'

Robert nodded, as if I had a point.

'Maybe I just heard the end sound. Maybe it is one of these. You think we should take a punt with one of them?'

288

Guy A Johnson

I nodded quickly, encouraged by his including me in the decision making.

'Which one then, Elinor?'

I tried to consider if either was weighted with significance, but neither the *b* nor the *c* held any special meaning for me. Hearing Tilly coughing herself awake alarmed me, but also made the decision feel more urgent – we had to keep moving.

'Let's take the *c* route,' I suggested quickly and Robert nodded in agreement, shining his torch down that particular tiled tunnel.

'*C* it is then – *c* for courage,' he said, striding ahead, with me following closely, looking back over my shoulder, as Ethan and Michael carried Tilly and her equipment. Her eyes sparkled in the dark, the light of our torches reflecting in them – so she was awake again.

At the end of tunnel marked NE1c, we came into another open space, with a concrete platform. And I knew from books that this was a train platform. Looking over its edge, I could see tracks.

'Where do we go from here?' I asked.

'We follow the tracks until we find our train,' Robert said, stepping down onto the line. 'And when we find it, we hope we can get it working.'

'Isn't it dangerous?' I asked, as he reached out a hand.

'Yes, everything is dangerous. Every step of this journey we've taken is dangerous. It's just about knowing where to put your feet. See there and there?'

He flashed his torched at two sections of the metal tracks.

'They might be live – so careful when you get down here. Yes Elinor, we are going to follow this route, dangers and all. So just make sure you avoid them. Okay?'

He kept that hand held out, while I remained – undecided – on the platform. The others were still behind me – and waited for me to make my move. I wondered if I had power there – if I could refuse to go further. And if I refused to step on those tracks and take my chances with the danger they posed, would they follow me back up to the surface? Back up to where there was dry land, food supplies, blankets to keep us warm and medical supplies to keep Tilly alive?

'You don't want to turn back, Elinor.'

Ethan – up close, speaking softly in my ear.

'There's nothing but darkness back there.'

'But there's darkness up ahead,' I answered, thinking of the tunnel the tracks led into.

Ethan shone a torch into it – lighting it slightly, making a point.

'I'll do whatever you choose, cousin,' he told me, giving me the power to pick his path as well as mine.

'Let's do it,' I told Robert, finally taking his hand.

Finally stepping down onto the tracks.

Stepping down into darkness and danger.


Eventually, we found a train.

A three carriage train that, to everyone's surprise, started without any problems.

And eventually, we did get home – back to our drowned city.

But not until we'd completed the next part of our adventure – the next unforeseen detour in our journey.

Guy A Johnson

'What is it?' I asked after a while, as the train came to a stop again.

I was upfront in the driver's compartment – allowed to sit next to Michael, whose latest uncovered talent was that of a vehicle expert. *'Never driven one of these before, though,'* he'd warned just me, as I'd climbed in after him – the others in our group staying back in the carriage just behind us.

'It's the track,' he answered, pointing through the window into the grey shadows ahead. 'See? It runs out. And there's something blocking the way.'

Behind, a door slid open and Robert joined us.

'We're here,' he answered, making it clear he wasn't surprised we'd stopped.

'And what's *here*?' Michael asked, a slight irritation in his voice – suggesting he'd not been fully consulted about our travel plans.

Robert shrugged. 'Answers, I think,' he said, almost casually, heading back through to the carriage, where he pressed a button on the wall and a door to the outside opened automatically. 'Come on,' he called back and we watched the others follow him – including Tilly, who was now walking slowly, hardly assisted, at her own stubborn insistence. This had annoyed those helping her, but I admired her strength. 'Nathaniel couldn't be certain,' Robert continued, talking loudly, making sure none of us missed what he was saying, 'but he suspected there was something down here we might want to see. Something we might want to take back.'

There was little alternative but to join in. And, switching off the train's controls, Michael followed, cupping my elbow to encourage me along.

Where the train tracks ended, the ground was loose, gravelly under our feet.

*'But dry,'* I reassured myself.

291

Guy A Johnson

Ten or so metres ahead, the tunnel narrowed and the walls closed in on us from the sides and above. Robert continued to lead, flicking his torch around, but I couldn't see what was in front of us, as we were too crowded in.

'There's a door,' one of the others shouted back.

'We're going in,' Robert announced and I heard him try its handle – it opened.

Tilly was ahead of me and through the door and inside whatever we had found before me, but I heard her reaction and her words left a chill on skin.

'I've been here before,' she said, stepping into what turned out to be a huge storage space.

Dimly lit by round lights sunk into the ceiling, it was claustrophobically packed with row after row of high shelves. Like a library, only not of books, but of vials of yellow liquid, held upright, each labelled with a strange code – XY123AB1, XY123AB2, XY123AB3 and so on.

'I've been here before,' Tilly repeated, looking back at me with a stare that made the goosepimples on my skin freeze further. 'And it was with you, Elinor.'

Then the weirdest thing happened – Tilly put thoughts into my head. It was like she entered my mind and I was seeing a vision of hers, or a dream.

*We're running – you're ahead, leading, looking for something specific. Each shelf is labelled with a code – a numerical and alphabetical combination. You read these aloud as you go.*

*'XY123HE1, XY124HE2, XY125HE3.'*

*'What are you looking for?' I ask eventually.*

*You don't answer – instead, you stop. You've found it.*

292

Guy A Johnson

*'XY136HF1,'* *you announce, pulling a tray out from one of the shelves, tipping it towards me so that I can see the contents – a selection of upright vials holding a light yellow liquid. Each one is labelled – XY136HF1.*

*'This one's yours,'* *you say, holding a glass tube out to me.*

And she was as shocked as me – as if she couldn't believe it and didn't know how she was doing it. And I realised it wasn't a dream she was sharing, but a premonition.

Tilly had seen this future – Tilly had somehow known this was where we'd end up.

'We were here,' she said, sounding animated for the first time since she'd collapsed. The machine attached to her began to work harder in reaction – the gentle hum of its motor whirring faster with excitement. Michael stepped towards her, concerned it might malfunction. 'And we found it, Elinor – we found it!'

'Found what?' Robert asked, as I remained frozen to the spot.

But something stopped her answering.

Something stopped everyone in their tracks – a single sound.

A sound I never expected to hear in my entire life.

The sound of terror.

The sound of death.

A bark.

Guy A Johnson

*Unfold*

*The truth, Esther, was never going to be easy – not for you. And if I weren't such a selfish man, I'd keep it from you. But I am selfish – and I do want you to know it.*

*You see, there comes a time in every man's life that he envies another. And me – I envied Monty Harrison. At least, I envied what was created for him – fatherhood.*

*So I decided to have some of that for myself.*

*Unlike Monty, I had the scientists completely on my side and they did everything the right way – no tricks, no surprises, no unnecessary experiments.*

*We chose a suitable mother in a stable family and intervened at the first given opportunity.*

*Sent your mother a letter from the local hospital, advising her that she needed a review of her health – following a recent scare among young mothers. And while she was there, the scientists' work began.*

*Nine months later, you were born.*

*But I hadn't really thought my plans through, Esther. While I knew you were mine – early tests of your DNA proved a perfect match, there could be no doubts – I hadn't considered exactly how I'd play a part in your life.*

*Years went by with me watching your progress from the shadows.*

*Then I saw my chance – the death of your father. And what followed was a gentle, well-judged pursuit of your mother's affections.*

*It all looked to be going so well until that evening at Monty Harrison's house. You remember Esther – I got us champagne. I was so close that my eagerness blinded my judgement – and what I'd intended as a fatherly kiss, you mistook as something else.*

294

Guy A Johnson

*Something you didn't altogether reject. I hadn't expected that. But then, days later, we met on that second occasion and I knew the gravity of my error – the hate in your eyes when your mother introduced me as her new partner.*

*The unshakable assumption in your cold, angry eyes that I'd knowingly invited you into a deception against her.*

*And I had Esther – it just wasn't the one you thought it was.*

*I'd never wanted to be your lover, Esther, far from it – just your father...*

**Fold**

Guy A Johnson

15. Billy

After we'd left the train – Marcie stayed behind, refusing to change her mind – Augustus, Otterley and I headed further along the tunnel, our furry friend venturing ahead and then rejoining us, as if he were reassuring us that it was safe to proceed. There were no more train tracks, as they had come to a sudden end. Instead, we walked on dry, loose gravel and the tunnel seemed to close in around us at every step. And then, as Otterley had predicted, we found a door.

*It's open,* she said in our heads – continuing to use her strange telepathy to communicate with us. Neither of us protested – our outward silence felt safer, as we kept our noise levels to a minimum. We individually asked her questions in our own heads, and she put the answers in both our minds.

*Should we go in?* I asked and she answered:

*Yes, Billy, we should go in* – her reply leaving Augustus with no doubt about the question I'd posed.

So in we went – but what and who we found beyond that door? We could never have predicted that.

Inside was a vast storage area – the space lined with shelf after shelf after shelf, housing a strange liquid in tiny vials.

*I know this place,* Otterley told us. *She dreamt it. We dreamt it.*

*Who?* I asked, but then I realised instantly. 'Tilly? Your kind of twin?' I said, out loud for Augustus' benefit.

Augustus looked alarmed.

296

Guy A Johnson

'There's two of you?' he said, like it was partly a question – but mainly a revelation. 'Are you the one I rescued all those years ago?'

'Yes,' Otterley answered, no longer in our heads. 'But I'm connected to another one. A friend of Billy's would you believe? But I've never met her.'

'She lives with you though,' I said, realising that I'd neglected to tell her something very important. 'At that house we found you in. Tilly lives there with her uncle.'

Before Otterley could react to this revelation, something else distracted us – the dog began barking insistently and then ran ahead of us, further into the room, so far that his bark faded a little.

And then something else occurred.

Otterley went back inside our heads. But it wasn't just her. There were two voices.

*Tilly?* she asked.

*Otterley?* came an answer.

*Are you here?*

*Yes, I'm here. Not far from you.*

*You really exist then? You're not just a dream?*

*No I'm real.*

'She's here,' Otterley told us, as if we hadn't heard it all. '*Here!*' she stressed, pointing at the ground we stood on, as if there was any doubt what she meant.

We heard the dog's barking return to us – and following gingerly behind it, another party of people like ours. Several men, flashing torches in our faces, as they cautiously approached us.

Guy A Johnson

*There's nothing to be afraid of,* a voice told us all – Tilly's voice, although it didn't quite sound like Tilly. It was weaker. And then I saw her – in the middle of the group, held in someone's arms, with something covering her face. A mask that was helping her breath.

I knew the man too – the man who was carrying her. I'd seen his mad face and crazy eyes before. At my great-aunt and –uncle's old shop. Hidden in the attic. It was Ethan – my crazy cousin Ethan. And I felt my senses flood with fear.

*You're safe, Billy,* Otterley said in our heads. In all our heads, it turned out – both groups.

'Billy?' a voice questioned and then someone stepped forward from the rear of the group, shining their torch in my eyes. Someone even more unexpected than Ethan.

'Stop it,' I said, squinting as I was blinded by the beam.

'Sorry,' the voice apologised, before killing the light.

Then, when I opened my eyes, I saw her for the first time in months.

Saw the face I thought I'd lost forever.

'Elinor. My dearest Elinor.' These weren't my words, though.

From behind me, before I had a chance to talk to my cousin, Augustus stepped forward and threw his arms around her.

'Oh, Elinor – we thought we'd lost you forever! We thought we'd lost you forever!'

And he wept – held her and wept, as if she'd died and come back to life.

Wept as if she'd meant more to him than life itself.

And then Elinor asked him the oddest question – a question that prompted many other questions in its wake:

'You're my grandfather, aren't you?' she said.

298

Guy A Johnson

Guy A Johnson

16. Tristan

The journey home – back to the drowned city I'd been away from for so long, the city where I'd left Agnes, where I'd left my father too, it turned out. That journey was the longest I ever encountered. Longer than the outbound journey – despite the fact we flew back with great speed.

But there were diversions on the way to lengthen it – and reunions that I'd never expected.

First, we flew to the camp where Nathaniel had intended to take the children. The camp where just one child had been left. A friend of Billy's, it turned out.

'We're going to pick up a small party from there,' Nathaniel instructed the pilot, not explaining to either of us who or what this small party consisted of.

As we descended, what looked like a concentration camp from years long gone came into focus. Around ten similar buildings – huge, like warehouses – were enclosed by high, chain link fencing. I shuddered, suppressing memories I had of an almost identical place.

'This is where you were going to bring the children?' I questioned, wondering what minds younger than mine would have made of these prison conditions.

'Yes,' was all Nathaniel answered with, unprepared to explore my opinions or the history that informed them.

Suddenly, the helicopter dipped down from the sky and we landed on a dry area of ground. Minutes later, the blades had relaxed to a standstill and it was safe to leave. As I stepped out and scuffed the soles of my shoes across the dry ground, I wondered just how far I was from home.

*Not a puddle in sight,* I thought to myself, as Nathaniel stepped down behind me.

'Stay here – with the pilot,' he instructed, and I wondered for a moment if he feared we might be abandoned, that this lone loyal pilot might flee and finally join the others – wherever they had gone to. 'They are in building 9,' Nathaniel continued, pointing ahead to one of the large buildings, where I could just make out a light. 'Some old friends to greet us,' he said, to explain whom he meant by *they.* I didn't think for a moment he meant friends of mine. 'I won't be long, okay?'

'Okay,' I agreed and watched him rush ahead, towards that dimly lit building, while I stretched my feet.

He returned quickly, accompanied by a mixed group of children and men. Some strangers, some well-known to me.

'Tristan!' a female called out and moments later Elinor – our lost girl – was in my arms, holding me so tight I thought I'd break, both of us sobbing without shame.

'I can't believe it's you! I can't believe it's you!' I told her, over and over – a more eloquent or intelligent response beyond me at that moment.

Billy quickly joined our little reunion – Elinor opening her arms a little begrudgingly, but letting him join our embrace all the same. As we held each other, I scanned the rest of the party.

There were five men I didn't know at all. Their names were thrown my way – *Michael, Robert, Dominic, Finn, Ethan* – but I didn't remember them and didn't need to then. Once we were home, I'd see them time and again and I'd learn their names for good. There were three girls as well – two of them sisters, twins, possibly, one of whom was sick and attached to a mobile life-support machine.

301

Guy A Johnson

And at the back, trailing behind was Augustus – a tame canine keeping in with his pace. We shared a brief nod of acknowledgement and then I helped the children into the helicopter, before clambering back in myself.

And then, when we were all settled and strapped in safely, the helicopter took off again.

'No more diversions,' Nathaniel promised me, reaching over and tapping my knee as a reassurance. 'No more delays in getting you what you need.'

'Thank you,' I answered and – despite all that had happened, all I'd been through with Jessie, leaving him behind in *Elysium* while it was under attack, all the secrets that Nathaniel had unveiled to me… Despite all that, I was thankful.

I had Elinor back – tucked up tight to my left, unbelievably safe and healthy, well looked after, by all accounts. And we were heading back to Agnes, who would be overwhelmed with happiness – as stricken with it as she was her grief, when we thought we'd lost our girl.

As we flew, Elinor babbled on like we'd never been parted, like she would at the end of a normal day – me coming home from a day with Jessie, she back from school. And in her babbling, she explained how she'd been underground, travelling on a train, of all things.

'Then we ran out of track – and then we ran into Billy, Augustus and the others. They had a train too – but Augustus didn't think it was safe to travel back on their train, not with Tilly so weak. Said it was too dark, too unknown. But Robert said we had to head back out, in any case – that Nathaniel was on his way in a helicopter! And then you came to get us – I didn't know that bit! It was a surprise!'

302

'Yes, we did,' I answered, thinking about that reunion, thinking about where we were heading – home.

Warmed by that comfort, I put aside the pain I might also endure when I got there – the confrontation with the man I now knew was my father, and a reunion with a twin brother I never thought I had. As all these thoughts exhausted my brain, I let sleep come over me, suffocating me with its heavy covers until a gentle nudge from Elinor woke me from its dense cocoon.

'We're here, Tristan,' she hummed gently in my ear. 'We're home…'

Guy A Johnson

17. Agnes

'It's alright, you're safe,' Joe had reassured the dog, as it retreated into a corner. 'Just stay calm. It's alright. You're safe now, okay? No one here to hurt you.'

'It might still hurt me, Joe,' I'd said, still thinking he was addressing Xavier and I – even when he advanced beyond me and towards the cowering animal. 'And we've no ammunition left. Xavier used the last of it. And we need to move Esther too – we can't just leave her here,' I pleaded, her body in my arms, her blood pooling around us both.

But Joe didn't answer, didn't acknowledge any of what I said or what he must've seen. Didn't check on Xavier, either, who remained silent and unmoving. Joe just moved further into the room, closer to the corner, closer to the creature that had retreated to the shadows.

And all the way, he kept up with his reassuring words and tone: 'There's no need to be afraid. You're safe now. There's no one here to hurt you. Just stay calm.'

'Joe, what is going on?' I pleaded, trying not to raise my voice, yet struggling to stay calm.

It was Xavier – finally coming to and breaking his silence – who explained his actions.

'Joe's connecting with him, Agnes,' he managed, his voice groggy, his words a struggle. 'It's not what it seems, is it Joe? It's no ordinary creature – is it?'

'Just let me get it calm, so we're all safe,' Joe said, addressing us for the first time since he'd climbed out from a hatch in the floor. 'Then I'll explain.'

Guy A Johnson

And so I waited, biting back my impatience, somehow managing to keep the immeasurable grief for my sister at bay, while Joe disappeared into the darkness with the dog who'd been inches from my throat.

I listened and heard soft voices and then Joe reappeared, the creature at his side. Only, when I looked at it this time, I saw it differently. Next to Joe, I saw features that my terror had instinctively told me to ignore. Features that weren't strictly canine.

'It's like you,' I gasped, and the creature tilted its head to one side, its eyes heavy with sorrow.

'Yes,' Joe answered.

'Why didn't I see? And why did he still attack me?' I asked, so confused, as I tried to comprehend too many incomprehensible things. 'Why would you do that?' I asked the creature – once a woman or a man? – directly.

But Joe answered for it.

'He's been subjected to more than me – his transformation more advanced. And it's saved his life – it's why the pack accepted him.' *Him* – so this pitiful creature had once been a man? A son, a brother, a husband and even a father? 'One of just a few of us that Monty experimented on and kept alive. There may be others. He won't hurt you now, Agnes. You can trust him.'

'Trust him?' I exclaimed, louder than I intended and the creature beside Joe flinched – and then spoke for the first time.

'I was with the pack,' he said, his voice gravely – as if the vocal chords had been strained or severed. 'I couldn't appear weak, but you were stronger. You've fought them all and now the pack is gone.'

Guy A Johnson

'Did you do this? Did you?' I asked, lifting my arms, holding Esther a little closer to him. 'Did you do this to show you weren't weak?'

He shook his head, solemnly.

'No, but I didn't stop it.'

And then he did something that surprised me – something that shouldn't have, but it was such a human thing and he looked so far from human that it seemed out of place: he stood up and held out his arms.

'Let me help you. Let me help you take her somewhere safer. Somewhere to rest.'

Joe nodded, encouraging me to accept the help of this poor, savage abomination of two species. And so I reluctantly let the beast before me take Esther from my arms, trusting Joe's judgement, and then we all followed him – Joe, Xavier and I – as he carried my sister through the once grand, now tired house. Across the dulled marbled flooring, up the stairs, along a lengthy hallway, where her blood stained a thick white carpet red. And then up another staircase – spiral, hidden behind a panel in the wall.

Up into the attic of the house – a strange space filled with medical equipment.

'How did you know this was here?' I asked him, taking in these new surroundings.

'Because I used to work for Monty,' he answered, laying my sister's body to rest on a hospital-style bed. 'And then one day I said the wrong thing and then…'

He didn't need to finish his sentence – the consequences were clear for us all to see.

*'He,'* I reminded myself of the human inside the creature before me. *'He – not it.'*

And the more time I spent in his presence, the more his human features surfaced, his canine ones fading a little. His eyes, the shape in his face, especially the mouth. The

306

Guy A Johnson

digits on his hands and feet became fingers and toes – and where I'd seen claws before, I could now see dirty, painfully overgrown nails.

Unlike Joe, he wasn't just covered in patches of thick, coarse hair – every inch of his skin was smothered in it. But the thick, arterial skin that throbbed from his pelvis to his neck was almost identical in its appearance to the one Joe had around his neck.

As he attended to my long-gone sister – shifting her gently and putting covers over her, as if she was a patient needing comfort, not a corpse needing a final resting place – I wondered if there was anything I could do for this wretched creature, this person. To somehow return the kindness and unexpected care he was showing Esther. Then it came to me – the simplest gesture, a show of acceptance to his humanity.

'What's your name?' I asked and he turned to face me – his mouth curving to create a smile of sorts, his eyes soft and slightly wet.

'Ely,' he answered with his throaty voice. 'They used to call me Ely.' Then he turned away and began fiddling about with a monitor not far from Esther's bed – switching it on and off, pushing buttons until its lights came out and it released a *beep*. Then he took some wires in his hands and attempted to place electrodes on different parts of Esther's body – her neck, chest, waist, arms, legs. Only, his damaged hands made him clumsy and Joe, realising what he was doing, stepped in to assist.

'She's been out too long. Lost too much blood,' Joe said to Ely, his voice quiet and sympathetic – as if he understood why our new companion was clinging onto such a tiny hope. Why he couldn't simply stand by and not fight for every last second of Esther's life. He had to wire her up to the life-support machine; had to place a mask over her face, in the hope it would balloon her deflated lungs and bring back her breathing; had to see to her

307

wounds with dampened lint, clearing away the drying blood; had to instruct Joe on how best to hold together the tears in her skin and apply the surgical strips that just must help seal them up.

I simply watched, astonished, not allowing myself to believe in that hope – fearing if I did I might curse it. A childish notion that ignored the matter of how unlikely it already was.

And then it happened.

A beep on the machine.

The flat line on its monitor suddenly leaping to a regular pulse.

A gentle, rhythmic rise and fall in her chest.

'You brought her back,' I gasped, still not really believing what I saw – still finding it hard to reconcile the creature I'd bared my neck to with this hirsute man who'd just breathed life back into my sister.

'Yes,' he answered, smiling that awkward, damaged smile again. 'But it's early days,' he added, to keep my joy measured.

I wanted to stay, to keep vigil by her bed until the moment she woke up, but Xavier insisted it wasn't safe for us to stay.

'Not on dry land, not for long,' he said and Ely backed him up.

'There could be others,' he added, meaning the dogs who'd attacked us – the ones he'd run with. 'You managed to kill the whole of that pack, but that doesn't mean Monty Harrison didn't release more.'

Guy A Johnson

'Who'll look after her, though?' I pleaded, knowing we couldn't leave her by herself. She needed constant care. And even if she hadn't, the shock of waking up here, without someone to explain what had happened, might be enough to finish her for good.

'I will,' Joe said, and I heard his heartache, his sorrowfulness in every syllable.

I thought of how much he'd not wanted Esther to see him like this.

*I look like a beast, Agnes. I look like a beast from the worst of nightmares,* he'd said to me. And then I'd kept Esther and Billy from entering the bedroom, when they'd arrived at short notice that day we cleared up Ronan's blood-soaked flat. *Mother's* flat.

And I recalled the promise I'd made him – once we'd brought the likes of Monty Harrison to justice, I'd help him bring his own suffering to an end. I'd have done it too – I'd have ended the sorry life he'd been left with.

But if Joe stayed with Esther – if he was there when she woke and she knew that he was still living, albeit his appearance was a physical wreck – I could never fulfill that promise. And Joe couldn't sanction it either.

'I'll stay,' Joe insisted, making it clear he knew all the consequences of that gesture. 'It'll be fine, Agnes. It'll all be fine. Get back to the safety of the floods. And check that monster hasn't escaped from Augustus' house.'

'We'll come back and check when it's safe,' Xavier added, to stress that Joe and Esther weren't simply being abandoned. 'And I'll make provisions to move Esther. Get her back home.' A promise I wasn't certain Xavier could keep – but it provided enough reassurance that I felt I could leave.

Before we left, Ely checked the cellar to be certain none of the dogs had survived.

309

'All clear,' he reported and then we set about a search of the rest of the property.

We checked for food – to feed all of us – before we set off back to Cedar Street and I sought out something for Ely to wear amongst Monty's finely tailored items. And Xavier went in search of something else – *Something to keep us safe,* he'd said, eventually returning with three rifles and a box of bullets he found stored away in one of the many bedrooms.

I took one, but Ely refused his.

'I've a better way of keeping you safe,' he said.

When we were finally ready to leave – pulling our tattered and bloodied protective clothing back on before we stepped outside and crossed the marshy land back towards of the speedboat – Ely went down on all fours and the kind, damaged man took on the guise of a cruel, deadly creature again.

There were no further signs of dogs or any other life-forms and we quickly reached the boat. Once on board, Ely stood up to become a man again and I handed him the clothes I'd found to allow him a little more dignity – transforming him back to his natural species just that little bit more.

'There might be a cure, a way to reverse all this,' I found myself saying.

If the hallowed wonders of science could create all this damage, all this evil – then surely it could do the reverse?

'There might,' Ely answered, taking comfort in my intentions, but not clinging to the hope they implied. 'They might.'

And then Xavier revved the engine of Monty's boat and we began our journey back to Cedar Street – hearts heavy with the dread at what might await us there.

We stopped at Augustus' house first – Ely and I staying in the boat and Xavier rushing in, to check on Monty.

*I knocked him unconscious and tied him to a chair, upright,* Xavier had told me earlier. *The old man helped me. Used some electric cable he had lying around. We tied him up tight. He'll live, but he won't be able to escape when he comes around.*

But he'd misjudged Monty Harrison's resolve, and he found the chair on its side and the cut lengths of the cable on the floor.

'Looks like he had a knife,' Xavier reported, his face pale with concern. 'No sign of Augustus and the others being back yet, either. We must be cautious now. He could have gone anywhere. He'll know we took his boat and he'll very quickly work out that we went to *Breakers* – and that we know about what he kept there. He might assume the mess we left at his house was us too.'

'Oh god – Esther!' I gasped, thinking of her fragile existence in that secret attic.

'I'll go back, as soon as you and Ely are somewhere safe,' Xavier promised me, trying to quash my anxieties. 'And I left Joe with one of these,' he added, holding up the rifle slung over his shoulder, 'so they'll not be totally defenseless. But right now, let's get you back home. You and Ely both have wounds we've not yet addressed.'

'You too,' I answered, instinctively reaching out and feeling one of the many claw marks that throbbed on his face.

Xavier put a hand over mine and it rested there a while – and I felt that old intimacy returning as he lingered there for just a second too long.

Guy A Johnson

'Time to move on,' I said, quietly, and Xavier started the engine on the boat, understanding the many meanings in that single line.

Then he turned Monty Harrison's speedboat around and took Ely and I back to the safety of my flooded house.

As I took the first of those sodden steps up to the first floor, it felt like I'd been away for weeks. Yet, it had only been a matter of days, but so much had happened and I'd learned of so many new horrors that it felt so much longer.

I felt older too – my bones aching from a lack of sleep, my skin scraped with cuts and marks, wrinkling me beyond my years. After I'd settled Ely in Xavier's bed – slipping him under the same covers I'd tucked around Joe only days before – I ran myself a bath, using a bottle of blossom-scented bubbles that Jessie gave me months ago. A treat that I'd used sparingly.

Thinking of Jessie made me wonder just where he and Tristan had got to. Had they found whatever answers they'd gone in search of? Had they found any trace of my lost Elinor? And when would they be back to answer these questions of mine? When would Tristan be back to hold me again, to kiss me with his firm but gentle lips? Imagining the smell of him about me, I turned off the taps as my bath was now full and turned to close the door.

And he was there, behind me – as if from nowhere, my Tristan returned.

My Tristan returned.

Then his arms were around me, embracing my dirty, hurting body, kissing my bloodied lips, kissing me passionately, not caring that I wasn't at my best.

312

Guy A Johnson

But something wasn't right. Something wasn't quite *him*. Something that made me pull away. A doubt. And it was enough to break the spell he'd cast.

'You shouldn't have…' was all I could manage to say to Xavier, turning away from him in shame.

I knew he wasn't solely to blame.

What had he said about his deceptive ability and what others saw in him?

*It's down to the recipient. I can only suggest something that might already be there. A need. A want. You saw what you wanted to see, to an extent.*

So I was partly to blame for this – but had I wanted Tristan so badly that I'd imagined Xavier in his place? Or was Tristan just an excuse to get closer to the man who'd once – briefly – been the love of my life? In that moment, I wasn't sure any more.

Xavier was such an important part of my life – albeit we'd spent a limited amount of time together. But each time had been intense and the last few days had brought me closer to him. And Tristan's lengthy absence – the sense I had that he was never coming back – that didn't help.

'You want me to go?' Xavier asked, as I kept my gaze averted from his – I couldn't trust what I might see in those eyes. How I might deceive myself into another kiss.

'Esther and Joe need you,' I answered and he nodded and immediately disappeared.

More tricks from the master – but again, was I seeing what I wanted or had Xavier instigated this particular vanishing?

Hearing the door below close seconds later, I locked myself in the bathroom – I was getting used to having Ely around, but he was still a stranger and Xavier's absence left me a little vulnerable. Then I removed my clothes and immersed myself in the hot, perfumed

313

bath water, kidding myself that – if I stayed below the surface long enough – I'd soak off some of the horror from the last few days...


For days, it was just Ely and me.

He spent most of those days sleeping – I spent most of them anticipating the return of my friends and family. Having found Esther in the state we did, I couldn't help but fret about the fate of the others – young Billy, Augustus and the girl who Xavier had reported to be with them.

*Oh, Augustus – where did you take them?*

I was so caught up with my thoughts and fears that I'd completely forgotten about the letter Esther had in her possession. *Read it,* her weak voice had pleaded, before she'd fallen unconscious. It was only when I checked through the pockets of my protective outdoor suit that I found it – wrinkled and torn in places, from where I'd initially crushed it up in my fist.

Upon finding it, I was apprehensive about its contents – my sister had used the last of her energy to insist I take a look, and I found its potential importance daunting. I feared what I'd find – it was written in Ronan's hand after all. But scanning it quickly, I realised it might give me some answers about his history, his motives – and more.

So, I took a chair at my kitchen table, took the crinkled pages from their envelope and began to read:

*Dear Esther*

Guy A Johnson

*I'm not sure whether you'll ever see this letter. I'm not entirely sure you should – not with what I've got to say. But I need to tell someone, and that someone really should be you.*

*See, I'm going to write down all that I know, in the hope it might reach you one day. If it does – maybe you'll be able to do something to change the course of things, before it's all too late.*

*And if my words don't make their way to you in time, it might just be too late – for all of us.*

*You see, he's had a plan all along – a dark, deadly plan – and it's all finally coming together.*

*Unless we stop him.*

*Unless _you_ stop him.*

It was a hand on my shoulder that jolted me awake.

His hand.

Opening my heavy eyelids and focussing, I saw he was back.

Xavier – Xavier as Tristan again, my wishful thinking betraying me.

'I thought I'd asked you to leave?' I asked, still fuzzy with unexpected sleep, but awake enough to feel guilty that I'd allowed this deception to occur a second time.

'I think I remember you asking me not to,' he answered.

*Tristan* answered.

Not Tristan as Xavier – no, not this time.

It was just Tristan.

315

Guy A Johnson

18. Tristan

The helicopter dropped us at *St Peter's* – in the very spot, according to Tilly Harrison, that the helicopters took the children in the first place.

*'We thought we were being rescued,'* she told me during our flight home. *'From the floods.'*

There, we found the school abandoned and we guessed it hadn't been occupied since the children had been taken.

'Best get that one back to her family,' I said to Robert, who was the leader of band I'd found Elinor and Tilly with – nodding at Marcie Coleman, a girl who'd swapped names and places with Tilly and ended up on dangerous journey of her own.

To my surprise Nathaniel and his party stayed with us – and the pilot alone ascended back up into the clouds in the helicopter.

'You're staying?' I asked, a little concerned. 'Not heading back? What about Jessie – and Heloise?'

'I've other allies in that city – they'll do the work that's necessary there,' he answered. 'But I need to set up a new base – with my new allies. The authorities will be in no doubt by now that it was I that betrayed them. So, I need to find somewhere to lay low and think about everything that's happened and what we do next.'

'You think the authorities were behind those explosions?' I suggested, hoping to get behind his thinking a little more.

Nathaniel shook his head.

Guy A Johnson

'Would the government destroy its own safe-hold – to spite me and my friends who wish to bring their downfall? I very much doubt it. That city – *Elysium* – is a lifetime's achievement to the rest of *the Circle*. They would protect it at the cost of their own lives – of their families' lives, even. No, some other group is behind this, I'm certain – with an agenda that I don't understand and that worries me.'

'Joshua's?'

This was the name of Ethan's twin. Ethan and Joshua – the long-lost children of Penny and Jimmy. Ethan was also the face I'd seen at that locked up shop when Jessie and I had first gone looking for Elinor. Penny and Jimmy's old shop – another fact that had passed me by. *You'd never have had reason to know about it or visit it,* Agnes would later say. *It's easy to hide secrets in a city that's mainly out of sight.*

Joshua was considered a dangerous man – a once good child who'd been damaged and twisted by the cruelties inflicted upon him. It also looked as if he was involved in intercepting the authorities' attempt at taking all our children.

'I don't know, Tristan. Joshua could be behind all this. But I've not seen nor heard of him in years. But if it is him, I certainly don't understand his motives – at least, not for taking the children and leaving that one child behind, defenseless. But all *that* we can deal with later. Right now-.'

'We need to get these children back to their homes,' I said, finishing his sentence, glancing at Elinor, Tilly and Billy, who were explaining all about *St Peter's* to the new girl in their group – Otterley. The child who Augustus claimed was Tilly's twin, and both as old as me – a fact I found incredulous. 'People are waiting for them.'

317

Guy A Johnson

We located the wooden boats the school used in emergencies and piled in, preparing to row those final streets back to our homes. We took four boats and split our party in two. Elinor and Billy stepped into a boat with me, while Nathaniel, Augustus, Tilly, Otterley and the tame dog they'd adopted squeezed into another – they followed me as I headed for Cedar Street. Robert and Michael took the rest of our group in the other two boats, promising to get back in touch once they'd returned Marcie to her parents.

'You have your radio safe, yes?' Nathaniel called out as we parted company, padding his own pocket to indicate he had his.

Robert tapped his pocket in reply and nodded in our direction as a confirmation that we'd see him soon.


At Cedar Street, Nathaniel carried on in the direction of the Cadley House – returning Augustus home, taking the telekinetic twins with him, along with the dog.

*Should we not destroy that thing?'* I'd questioned before, but Billy had been insistent that it was domesticated. *'He's our pet,'* he'd argued, like he understood that archaic notion.

'I'll want to talk to you later,' I said to Augustus, a warning that he had answers to some of my remaining questions. 'Once I've returned this one to her mother,' I added, looking to Elinor, who was excited and nervous in equal measure.

Elinor – who was the old man's granddaughter.

And this *old man* had also brought up Xavier Riley as his son.

Xavier, who I'd been led to believe was my arch-enemy – my father's murderer. But my father wasn't who I thought he was – or even dead, for that matter. And my relationship with Xavier was also of a different nature than that I'd believed.

Inside, I shook my brain about – an attempt to organise the jumble of information that was unsettling my grey-matter. So many connections; so many new versions of old histories to understand.

'Shall we meet at Papa Harold's,' Augustus cried back. 'I could do with popping in to see my old friend. That sound alright to you?'

I nodded in reply – yes, it was an appropriate place to hear my story completed.


We found Agnes asleep at the kitchen table and, when I woke her, she seemed a little confused to start with and said the oddest thing:

'I thought I'd asked you to leave?'

'I think I remember you asking me not to,' I answered, kissing the top of her head, waiting to kiss her more and be the receiver of all her affection and attention. But I knew I had to be restrained – I knew I had to put someone else first.

'Agnes,' I said, watching her eyes become more alert and I'd moved to one side, so she could see the girl who was standing in my shadow – trembling with anticipation. 'Agnes, she's here…'

They both cried so hard and howled so loudly that I feared for mother and daughter in the initial minutes of their reunion. Feared a madness had infected them both and would leave their minds silly and their bodies defenseless against anything.

319

Guy A Johnson

*Calm down,* I wanted to say. *You'll kill yourselves with this craziness.* But I simply watched their joy explode again and again – with tears, shrieks and laughter – until I found myself joining in and becoming giddy and sick with happiness myself.


Later, I had different business to deal with.

With Agnes and Elinor eventually calm – and both Billy and Elinor fed and ready for bed – I made a quick call on Agnes' telephone to arrange the meeting I didn't want to put off another day.

'You can come now,' the recipient answered. 'Everyone is here who you'll need to see.'

And so I left Agnes' house and went next door – to Papa Harold's as I'd agreed with Augustus earlier.

I knocked and entered without waiting for permission and took heavy steps through his flooded ground floor and up those squeaking, damp stairs. When I reached the top, I found those I expected to see – old Harold himself and Augustus, sat around the kitchen table, mugs of something or other in front of them, hunched together like old cronies.

In the corner of the room, head hanging low, as if he was ashamed or shy, was a man I didn't recognise. An awkward, hairy man who later introduced himself, when put on the spot, as *Ely*.

As I stepped further into the room, *he* came into my view – the man I'd come looking for all those years ago.

The man the authorities had led me to believe had killed Albert.

Sat in a comfortable chair in the corner opposite Ely.

Guy A Johnson

*'Albert wasn't your father, Tristan,'* Nathaniel had explained as the helicopter had whisked us away from a burning *Elysium*. *'And neither is he dead. Albert was a man who agreed to take you in, when your real father wasn't capable. And he is missing – he went missing around the time you remember Xavier Riley turning up at Albert's film shop. The other men you remember from that time – they probably helped Albert disappear. If you still want to find him, I suggest you find them first.'*

And the irony was I knew where one of those men was – Father Neil, the holy man at the church Jessie and I had completed repairs for, before we'd set out on our journey.

*'But I'm afraid to say the authorities manipulated you, Tristan. They sent you after the wrong man for their own purposes. You see, Xavier Riley had been trouble over the years. Not working for anyone in particular, he caused the government no end of problems and their plan was to use you to get rid of him. Only, you didn't find him. I had a bit of a hand in that – made sure word got to him about the assignment you'd been given. And there's something else you should know about Xavier Riley...'*

'So, turns out we're brothers,' I said to the man himself – a man I hadn't seen since we'd been taken and put through horrors together in those government laboratories. 'I take it they bothered to tell you?'

'They did,' Xavier offered, remaining where he was, his face almost expressionless.

I nodded at him, as if to suggest I wasn't going to angle my questioning at him.

Then I turned my eyes on my father – the man who'd been under my nose since I'd arrived in the city over five years back and never said a word of the truth.

Guy A Johnson

'So, are you going to explain it to me, to us both?' I asked him, feeling my fury rise, but managing to restrain it. 'Are you going to explain why I was given away and brought up by a stranger?'

He left it a minute or so, taking a long sip from the mug of whatever – later I learned it was from a bottle of contraband whiskey – before he commenced with the story of mine and Xavier's beginnings.

'You know the tale of my mother? That when I was a boy, the dogs took her and dragged her from this very house – took her into the forest and ripped her apart?' Papa Harold opened, his eyes earnest and full of pain, as he flicked them from me to Xavier and back again. I nodded, not checking to see how my brother – my twin brother – responded. 'You know where I'm going with this?' he checked and I nodded again, but I wanted him to continue.

'Just tell me,' I told him and Papa Harold nodded several times to confirm he would.

'That wasn't the tale of my mother – but of yours. They got in and they attacked us both. We did our best to keep you both safe, and we managed that part, but they were evil creatures. And they were determined to take her, and overpowered every effort I made to intervene. They could've taken me, but it was somehow like they knew – that taking your mother would leave the most damage behind. And it did. I couldn't cope – couldn't face a single thing, including looking after you boys. You were so young – barely weeks old at that point. I didn't trust myself, either – how could I protect either of you if I couldn't save your mother? So, I thought you'd be better off with someone else.

Guy A Johnson

'I had no family left, and neither had your mother. But I had my good friends Albert and Augustus – whom I met at various anti-authority groups I'd attended over the years. They're brothers – did you know that?'

I shook my head – no, that wasn't a detail Nathaniel had shared with me.

'Yes, brothers – and both troublemakers in their own ways. But neither had children, so handing you both over had seemed such a good idea. Twins are hard to look after, but I thought you'd be fine if we split you. You were hardly likely to remember. If it hadn't been for the takings, I think you'd have had good lives.'

'My mother – Albert's wife – left us both when I was only six,' I countered, the bitterness in my voice unmistakable.

Before I continued, or Papa Harold could answer this, a question came from the armchair in the corner.

'What was her name?' From Xavier.

'Marie,' our father answer, an enduring sense of loss clear in every syllable.

It was enough to calm my fires.

'And do you have any photographs we can see?' Xavier continued, pulling himself up out of the comfortable chair and heading toward the table where the old men were sat.

I'd remained standing since I'd entered the room. When Xavier drew out a chair and sat at the table with them, he indicated a fourth chair – suggesting I might occupy it. With reluctance, I did. And, as I sat down, Papa Harold got up, shuffled to a battered old dresser in the corner and rummaged through its drawers for pictures of our mother.

Thereon, the evening took a different, unexpected turn, as we sat with our father and found ourselves coming together over tales of a mother neither of us had ever met. We

323

Guy A Johnson

stayed like that until the early hours, drinking the last of his whiskey with him – hardly noticing when Ely and Augustus crept away.

'We'll catch up tomorrow, son,' the latter told Xavier, not afraid to stake his claim as father – he had, after all, brought my brother up.

My brother. My twin. Xavier Riley was my twin. It felt wrong and right at the same time, but eventually I would get used to it. We were not natural or identical twins, though – we were, like many of our generation, an experiment in our mother's womb. Twins of a very unnatural origin.

It was about 3am when we decided to leave Papa Harold for the night – despite his best efforts, he was barely awake.

'We can talk another day,' Xavier reassured him, when we saw him off to bed. 'There'll be plenty of other nights to catch up on each other's lives.'

That left just Xavier and me.

'Fancy some fresh air?' he suggested, indicating we went outside.

'Do you know where we can find some?' I answered – the first joke we ever shared, I realised later.

'The night air might clear our heads a little. Feels a little enclosed in here – a bit stuffy.'

I agreed and we took ourselves down Papa Harold's stairs, out to the front of his house, and stood on his front steps – looking down the road and up at the sky, as the river road gently swished around our legs, protected as always by the clumsy rubber gear we wore outside.

Guy A Johnson

'There's still a lot to do, isn't there?' Xavier began, taking our conversation in a different direction. 'You've seen what's out there now, haven't you? You've seen the truth about the authorities. So you know we need to do something about it. We can't just leave things.'

I shook my head, taking in a deep breath of cold air.

'No, we can't. Not now. A war has begun, Xavier. When we left that other city, it was on fire. I left a friend behind too. And then there's the children who have been taken who-knows-where, not forgetting Monty Harrison and whatever his masterplan is.'

'Yes, I heard all that from Nathaniel. There's a certain amount of chaos out there – let's hope that will work to our advantage. Do you want to know something you haven't been told yet?'

'What?'

'That the authorities told me the same thing about you – approached me, told me you were a dangerous man. Said you were a threat to Augustus and they paid me to come looking for you. But I also heard you that were on a similar mission – paid to assassinate me. So I watched you from the shadows, brother. Watched and waited, thinking you were the enemy too.'

*Brother* – that title, that connection again, which seemed to roll off Xavier's tongue with an ease I couldn't quite find.

'So they told you the same lies,' I said, thinking what a thick web the authorities had spun around us.

'Not quite, Tristan – not quite. You see, you might not be a danger – at least not then, but I was. Those experiments left me with a unique skill and when I escaped from those laboratories, I used it against them. It got me into places and I did a lot of damage. Blew up a number of authority buildings. Sabotaged their plans from the inside. And killed a few of the men who were responsible for what happened to us.'

He paused, taking in more cold night air, looking up into the starry night – contemplating his own revelations.

'So what happens now?' I asked, breaking his gazing.

'We fight the good fight, Tristan. As brothers, not enemies,' he answered, turning and looking straight into my eyes. 'If there's a war raging, let's make sure we're on the same side.'

'Fighting the good fight?

'Yes.'

'And we rescue those children from wherever they've been taken?'

'We do, if we can, brother,' – not quite the full commitment I wanted; not what I'd have got from Jessie.

'I intend to go back for Jessie too.'

To this, Xavier simply nodded – committing to nothing, but acknowledging my own promise.

'But all of this can wait another day, right? You've a woman to get back to after all.'

A woman with whom my twin shared a child – another bullet that had blasted through my skull, leaving mental shrapnel to work its way through my mind.

'Where will you go?' I asked him.

'Tonight?'

I nodded.

Guy A Johnson

'I'll go to Augustus' house. He's still my father, after all. Nothing has changed there. So, until tomorrow,' he said holding out his hand and when I shook it, the strangest thing happened – Xavier disappeared, though I could still feel his grip.

Then I watched as one of our small wooden boats appeared to row itself in the direction of the Cadley House.

*So that's your trick,* I thought to myself, amused, watching until the little boat and my brother disappeared into the darkness...

Guy A Johnson

**Asleep**

*I'm in a house.*

*In a room.*

*In a corner.*

*I'm near a window and can see out onto the street. And I realise I'm several storeys up.*

*The road is flooded. A river road, they call it round here.*

*There are people out there in boats, worried people with worried voices. Shouting, crying out. I can't hear what they're saying, but I feel their panic. I know that disaster has struck. That tragedy is nearby.*

*I turn away, back into the room and that's when I see him. It.*

*Him.*

*It.*

*He goes from one to the other in my head – a man and then a beast, a beast and then a man.*

*Unafraid, I ask him a question.*

*'What's my name?'*

*He answers as I hear the shot ring out.*

**Awake.**

Guy A Johnson

19. Tilly/Otterley


It's not quite like we saw in our dreams.

Not everything is as we foresaw.

'Do you remember that the road here was dry – the floods were gone from this street?' we ask ourselves.

'Yes, and the mask we had on our face – we couldn't get it off and we suffocated?'

'And we saw something coming over the horizon – like a flood, only it wasn't a flood, was it?'

'No, it was an army – an army of *them.*'

Of dogs – but we don't want to say it and do our very best not to think it, either.

And this is how we are. This is how we communicate, think and feel – as one. Fused together from the moment we met in that underground store – where all those vials were catalogued. Including the vial that belonged to us – the one marked XY136HF1. We breeze in and out of our separate heads like others walk in and out of rooms in a house.

One part of us is weaker than the other – the part of us they've been calling Tilly. Weakened because the other one of us is stronger – and weakened further by the trauma she felt when she was tortured in that strange room of doors. The *Tilly* part of us stays in the bed in the room that is full of books, in the old man's house with the never-ending, curling staircase. Hooked up to all sorts of fancy machinery to keep her going. While the other is free to move around, come and go – and is our eyes and ears for the rest of the world.

'But our other dreams came true, didn't they?'

329

Guy A Johnson

'Yes they did – and we dreamed about him, didn't we?'

Our eyes turned to the doorway.

'Yes, we dreamed about him.'

He stood there for a minute – the quiet man, who was half beast.

'Hello Ely,' we said.

He pulled something that we assumed was a smile and then continued his way to the next floor.

'So, what of our dreams – have they let us down?'

We thought for a moment.

'They never let us down.'

'Never.'

'So it's still to come then? *Them* – their army? And the war.'

We paused, thought again – searching through the dreams we could remember and then nodded.

'Yes, the war is still to come...'

Guy A Johnson

20. Agnes

Those early days feel like a dream now.

The feelings that burned my body and soul with their brightness seem unreal – like something I couldn't have felt. Like something I could never have imagined.

And every morning for weeks, I'd wake up and run to her room – have to check it wasn't a dream. That my beautiful Elinor was really back.

Although it would never be the same.

She would never be the same either.

Not after what she'd been through.

'There's going to be a war,' she'd tell me, her adult eyes betraying her teenage years. 'I'm going to help us find the children and Jessie. I'm going to help us win.'

There was too much of her father in her.

*Her father. That kiss.*

The smallest thing – and yet such a big betrayal. I wanted to tell Tristan – to release it and watch it flutter away like the trapped moth it was. But I knew I couldn't. Unknowingly, I'd betrayed him with his own brother. Another fact that seemed like a dream in the early days.

No, I would have to keep that a secret.

But our family was used to secrets and we needed some new ones to replace the ones that had escaped from our vaults.

Like Esther's secret – or Ronan's, depending on how you looked at it.

Guy A Johnson

And, as I waited for my sister to recover – visiting her whenever I could at the mansion that was once Monty Harrison's house and was now Nathaniel's headquarters, as he planned his crusade against the authorities – as I waited for Esther to come round, I kept that secret to myself, telling no one.

Wondering if she'd read that letter before she'd been attacked.

Wondering whether this was the one secret I could bury for good – the one secret that could remain true to its name.

Yet there was a part of it that worried me the most – a part that Ronan hadn't explained in full: *And if my words don't make their way to you in time, it might just be too late – for all of us. You see, he's had a plan all along – a dark, deadly plan – and it's all finally coming together. Unless we stop him. Unless you stop him.*

Ronan meant Monty Harrison, but this was one part of his story he didn't fully explain. And his confession ended after he'd revealed the vile truth about his and Esther's connection – as if he hadn't had the chance to complete it.

Both men were missing.

Ronan was believed to have fled to the authorities' headquarters – a city its inhabitants referred to as *Elysium.* But Monty could have been anywhere, although there'd been no trace of him locally.

*'So we're safe for now,'* I consoled myself – comforted by the return of my daughter whenever I thought about the unknown dangers that lay ahead for us all. *'We're safe for now…'*

Guy A Johnson

*Awake*

*I see her – the woman. Her throat bloody, torn ragged by the teeth of some beast, drowning in a pool of red.*

*But suddenly there's a man and a woman with her and the woman cradles her, weeping. It seems she's dead – gone for good.*

*Then the scene changes and there's a fourth being in the room – a beast that stands up and transforms into a man. And he reaches out for the dead woman and carries her from the room.*

*And we follow him – out into a hallway with a marble floor and chandeliers. Up a grand staircase, along a hallway of white carpet. Then up and up a spiral staircase into an attic room. A room like a hospital.*

*And he puts her on a bed and he saves her. This dog-man. He sets about mending the savaged woman and he brings her back to life.*

*And he says his name.*

*Ely, he says.*

*The scene changes again. The woman is still in the bed – kept alive by a machine. Another man is there – another dog-man. And he turns his head – towards the back of the room. His face lights up and cries for joy, as a young boy slowly walks forward and falls into his embrace.*

*Awake*

Guy A Johnson

21. Billy

When I returned to that house – where the rabid beasts had chased us back down into those tunnels underground – I did it with a mix of fear and excitement.

He took me – Augustus. He and I travelled in a speedboat, driven by one of Nathaniel's men. The boat was moored just outside the grounds of the grand mansion and we had to walk across marshy land before we reached it. I held tightly to Augustus' hand the whole way, but he reassured me we had nothing to fear.

'They're all gone,' he said, gripping back with certainty. 'Tristan, Xavier and Nathaniel's men went to Monty Harrison's club – to the basement where he was breeding the beasts. Defeated his men – and put all those poor creatures to sleep, as you know. There's been not one single sighting since – not one body in the river roads, young Billy. And even if there was…' He stopped and made me look back at the boat – where our driver was watching, a rifle in his hands, ready to shoot if necessary. 'And up ahead too,' Augustus added, as we approached the steps up to the house – where two men stood sentry, rifles on their shoulders.

Each day since we'd returned, Nathaniel had used his helicopter to bring his men to our city and Monty Harrison's old house had become the headquarters for his planning. I commented to Augustus that they weren't wearing protective suits or masks.

'You only need the suits to keep the water off your clothes,' he answered. 'And the masks…. Well, you know that they're not needed. Just another rule the authorities imposed to see what we'd do. Another part of the experiment we were all a part of.'

'And are we still a part of it – are we still living in their big laboratory?'

334

Guy A Johnson

Tristan had explained to Elinor and me one evening how our city was really just a huge enclosure – one of many – that the authorities kept an eye on and did things to watch our reactions.

*'Like the floods?'* I'd asked.

*'Like the floods.'*

*'And the dogs – did they set the dogs upon us?'*

*'Yes, yes, they did,'* he'd answered, solemnly.

'I'm not sure how things stand now, young Billy,' Augustus answered, as we entered the reception hall, where dusty chandeliers hung from the ceiling and swirling orange marble flooring lay beneath us. 'Things have changed. And we've found and destroyed some of the means they had to watch us. So it's difficult to know who is in the enclosure anymore – where it starts, where it ends. And are they watching us still – or are we watching them now?'

'But you're not here to discuss strategy, are you?' Nathaniel said, coming out of a huge hall to our left, where dances and parties must have flourished in the past. He held out his hand to Augustus and they shook heartily. 'You're here for a very different reason, Billy, aren't you?'

I nodded. I was. And that mix of excitement and fear curdled in my guts again, leaving me a little sick with anticipation.

It was a day of reunions in our family.

My cousin Ethan was meeting with Great-Aunt Penny and Great-Uncle Jimmy for the first time since I'd let him out of their old shop. And I had a reunion of my very own.

Guy A Johnson

'I think you know the way,' Nathaniel said, and Augustus and I made our way up the grand staircase – towards the attic room full of medical equipment, where I'd get to see mother. Mother who was still alive – but also asleep.

And father too. I'd get to see him again. Although, I'd been warned about him.

*He's altered, Billy. On the outside. He won't look like the man you remember. But he's the same on the inside,* Tristan had said.

*Is he like Ely?* I'd asked.

*Yes – like Ely. His bark is worse than his bite.*

This was apparently a joke, but I took it as a kind of reassurance – everything I saw would not be as bad as it looked.

Augustus and I were halfway up the stairs, when our furry friend scarpered out from nowhere and joined us. Nathaniel had kept him at the big house, for fear our neighbours would destroy him on sight. We stopped for a minute at the turn in the stairs and made a fuss of him – stroking his back and playing with his ears in a way that made his tail wag. Sometimes he'd try to lick me, but I didn't quite like that.

'You've not given him a name yet,' Augustus said, once one of Nathaniel's men had called him away.

'Yes I have,' I answered, 'it's the name he's always had. The name you gave him.'

Augustus looked at me quizzically.

'Hope,' I answered. 'His name is Hope.'

And then we continued up the stairs, along the white carpet that was stained with tear-shaped blood, and up a spiral staircase behind a hidden door, until we reached my mother and father…

336

*To be continued – Guy A Johnson is currently writing the final books in the Submersion series…*

CPSIA information can be obtained
at www.ICGtesting.com
Printed in the USA
LVHW051236050520
654998LV00016B/2934